The Long Ride

Mary T. Bell

Books authored by Mary T. Bell
Dehydration Made Simple
Mary Bell's Complete Dehydrator Cookbook
Just Jerky
Food Drying with an Attitude
Jerky People
Jerky - The Complete Guide to Making It
Cutting Across Time

The Dry Store
28097 Goodview Drive
Lanesboro, MN 55949

marytbell@drystore.com

The Long Ride / Mary Bell
ISBN 978-0-578-85600-1

Cover Design and Layout by Hilma Bonhiver
Copy Editing by Jo Anne Agrimson
Map by Judy Smithson
Cover Consultation by Ira Newman

Dedicated to the horse
for its gifts of
transportation and
transformation

Especially
Rosy's Catch
Sal's buddy Thief
Elle's Bond
Kitty's Rio
Maia's pal Justice
Lydia's gal Liberty
And our dear, sweet Romeo

"The emancipation of women may have begun
not with the vote, nor in the cities
where women marched and carried signs and protested
but rather when they mounted a good cow horse
and realized how different and fine the view. . .
From the back of a horse, the world looked wider."

Joyce Gibson
Cowgirls

Chapter 1

Parting is Such Sweet Sorrow

Black jack, now alone in the pasture, loped back-and-forth along the green electric-ribbon fence protesting the loss of his pals, Liberty and Justice. His long thick black tail whipped the air. Nostrils flaring. Stopping suddenly, he dug his hooves into the dry soil just short of the ribbon, snorted and screamed intensely, like a stallion catching a whiff of a fine mare. Acting like his heart was broken, he pleaded, "Don't go! Don't leave me. Please don't go!"

Liberty is our red chestnut, 15 hand Quarter Horse mare with "a-to-die-for" thick, multi-colored mane and tail. She, the object of Jack's deepest affection, answered his cry with a rippling bleat that sounded more like a sheep than a horse's whinny. In the horse trailer, Justice, my twenty-year old, 14.2 hand, deep chocolate, Morab gelding stood alongside Liberty and added a string of long, slow whinnies to communicate his displeasure.

Chapter 2

Westward Ho

Rosy's silver chevy pickup with its Triple-R logo painted on her driver's side door rumbled down our driveway just before dawn, headlights blinking between oaks and maples like strobe lights. Catch and Thief, Rosy's two Quarter Horses were secured inside her trailer. Our trail boss rolled to a stop under the yard light perched atop a telephone pole. Rosy's younger sister, Sal, was hunkered down in the passenger seat, looking like she hadn't gotten enough sleep.

Elle and her sidekick, Kitty, followed behind in Elle's black super deluxe F250, hauling their two horses, Bond and Rio. As Elle pulled in behind Rosy, Kitty waved from the passenger window. Barely waiting for Elle to come to a complete stop, Kitty bounded cat-like out of the cab with a throaty holler, "Top o' the morning."

Smiling, Elle calmly pushed her truck door open, got out and delivered her usual firm handshake to everyone. Sal climbed out of the truck, gave a sullen nod to all of us, then looked toward the road, watching another set of headlights bounce up our driveway.

Lydia, the newest member of this group, swung open the door of her shiny red Mercedes and stepped out, wearing ridiculous high-heeled cowboy boots made of intricately tooled red leather. She placed a red leather cowboy hat over her dyed red-ink, shoulder-length hair and squealed, "I am so excited!"

Sal yanked her sweatshirt hood down over her forehead and slipped her hands into the pockets of her faded gray sweatpants before complaining loud enough for everyone to hear, "She's way too much."

"I could use some help moving my stuff," Lydia said sweetly.

As we schlepped Lydia's stuff from her Mercedes to my trailer tack room, Sal grumbled, "She's got more crap than the rest of us put together."

Rosy pressed two fingers to her lips. "Shh. Give Lydia a break. This is her first long ride."

Sal snapped back. "Effin' princess."

Rosy narrowed her eyes and pressed her lips together, "You give her a break. I mean it, Sal."

Lydia raised her eyebrows when she entered my tack room. "Wow! This is the – ah, um – the most unique trailer I've ever seen." Twirling like a ballerina perched on a music box, she sang, "Totally marvelous, Maia. Purple is my second favorite color. Bet you didn't know that."

Sal feigned a choke. "Gee, who'd ever guess you like bright colors?"

Rosy checked her watch. "Time to roll, ladies. We must get to camp before sundown."

My husband Mark wrapped me in his arms, kissed me and whispered, "Have fun, Maia," then patted my butt. "I miss you already."

Lydia tossed her yellow rhinestone satchel onto my passenger seat, climbed aboard and placed a frilly pink satin pillow on her lap. "Sweet guy you got."

"I'm lucky," I said, looking in my mirror and watching Mark disappear as I pulled in behind Elle.

Turning onto the road to leave my home, I wondered if I'd made the right decision to venture on such a long trip for the next ten days with five very different women.

Sal and Rosy remind me of those painted Russian dolls that fit one inside of the other. In more ways than one, Rosy is the larger doll. Her strength and leadership have earned everyone's respect. Maybe it was her skill at training horses that gave Rosy the ability to sense people's needs. She is a good leader and a really good trail boss.

Rosy's sister Sal, on the other hand, always looks out for herself. Without a doubt Sal has been the most challenging woman to get along with on any previous ride. She walks and talks like a true cowgirl. In reality, she's about as tough as freshly baked angel food cake minus the sugar.

Elle gets high marks in confidence and athleticism. Nothing ever seems to stress her out, but she probably wouldn't let on if it did. She'll do more than her share of hard work to make this trail ride memorable.

Memorable. That's Kitty. She is as willful as her high-stepping horse, Rio. Kitty's spark of energy and can-do attitude will liven up the trip. If we come across any men—no matter who they are or what their married

4

status—well, watch out, 'cause Kitty's always on the prowl.

Just then, Lydia tapped my arm. I put my thoughts aside, wondering if she was already regretting her choice to come with us. Instead, she held up her cell phone and asked, "Where should I put this?"

"In the glove compartment with mine."

In planning this ride, we unanimously agreed that a real adventure, a long ride, should be free of distractions, especially electronic gadgets. We vowed not to use our cell phones and instructed our families, friends, business contacts, everyone, to respect our decision to go silent. The only exception would be if we got into trouble or experienced an emergency.

I wondered about Lydia, the newest member of our group. How will she, our princess, handle the long days of riding and the nights with no comforts of home? Time will tell, I thought, and concentrated on the early morning beauty.

Fog clung to the valley floor and obscured our drive through the bluffs and valleys. Morning light struck the deep green and burgundy sumac seed-heads. Slivers of orange and yellow leaves sharply contrasted with still green leaves in the run-up to fall. A grove of walnut trees crowned the hilltop. Their lime green nuts dangled among leaves beginning to yellow and brown.

As we sped past our Amish neighbors, they momentarily stopped and waved as they loaded their buggy with fresh produce for the Farmer's Market. When Rosy made a sharp left turn off our gravel road onto a paved two-lane highway, a black-brown woolly bear caterpillar was crossing pavement as expansive and dangerous as a great desert. I watched as Rosy's tires squished and ended its transformation into an Isabella Tiger moth.

I was mesmerized looking out my truck window at the patchworked landscape of gold and green crops edged with trees and the white limestone outcroppings. Lazily grazing the hillsides were black and red Angus, white Charolais, brown and white Hereford and black and white Holstein cattle.

Our homeland is a place where small-scale agriculture is still practiced. Where farmers sculpt any flat land with contoured crops and create artful fields. Southeastern Minnesota is known as the Driftless area and referred to as Bluff Country. Thousands of years ago glaciers stopped at an arbitrary border leaving behind land crushed flat and chewed. But the glaciers left untouched this land, that's textured with tall bluffs and broad valleys.

An aerial picture of this landscape with its varied colors and textures would make a great puzzle. Green grassy waterways that look like pathways separate corn, soybean and alfalfa fields. These green veins follow the sloping land and help prevent cascading rain from eroding the soil and keep brown, soil-filled water from entering the rivers and ending up in the ocean.

Half an hour later, my hands gripped the steering wheel, and I held the speedometer at seventy as our convoy merged onto Interstate 90, heading west. This was the first time I'd trailered our horses alone, without Mark. My insecurities flared. Since Lydia does not yet own her own horse, I loaned her Liberty. On this trip I'd have two horses to care of, plus mentor Lydia. So many things could be difficult. Will I be able to pull my own weight with this group and not hold the others back? What if we had nothing but bad weather? What if someone got hurt? Will my good old Justice be up to the challenge? What if my family needs me? Will Mark keep up with the harvest? I shook my head, trying to rid myself of my fears.

Lydia's red nails flashed as she twisted open her thermos and refilled our coffee cups. She took a sip and smiled broadly. "This trip is a dream come true, Maia. It's a once-in-a-lifetime opportunity. I told my husband I was doing it." She rolled her shoulders back, lifted her head, raised her cup and toasted the road ahead. "I made up my mind. I said I was going on this ride no matter what he did or said."

"I admire your courage," I replied, attempting to relax my grip, wishing I could capture more of Lydia's excitement and let go of my nerves.

Chapter 3

"You'll Have a Great Time"

It was a bitter cold night when eight of us gathered at Ray and Rosy's home place at the Triple-R-Ranch they've run for forty plus years. During that time, they've earned a stellar reputation for raising and training Quarter horses, fantastic animals that perform splendidly in the show ring and run a fast quarter mile. The scads of blue, red and white award ribbons decorating their walls attested to their talent. To combine their passion for horses and people, Ray and Rosy also board horses and offer riding lessons.

Winter had not loosened its hold on our corner of the state, but that night, no place could be cozier than Ray and Rosy's. Surrounded by photos of riders proudly perched on horses, some in meadows, others lined up on mountaintops, riders posed next to their trusty steeds and smiling kids piled on ponies, our conversation just naturally flowed to talk of horses and trail rides.

Maybe it was Ray's desk that conjured the talk of adventure. On one end sat a bronze statue of a horse reared up on its hind legs, forever frozen, with a decked-out cowboy on a fancy saddle waving his ten-gallon hat. On the other side of his desk sat a gunmetal sculpture of Native Americans sitting around a campfire passing a long pipe.

Once each year Ray and Rosy invite a few of their clients to join them on a week-long trail ride. Some years back, my husband Mark and I joined this group on a five-day pack trip in British Columbia where we rented horses. Another year, Ray hauled our horses, Black Jack and Justice, to the Teddy Roosevelt National Park outside Medora, North Dakota, for a weeklong ride. Though we never became the masterful cowboy in that bronze statue, we did have our share of moments where we felt like true cowboys, sitting around campfires after a day's ride.

Kitty reminisced about that adventure. "Oh my God," she raved. "Riding alongside those wild horses was beyond breathtaking." She locked eyes with Ray. "Where to next, boss?"

Ray got everyone's attention with a deep groan, unsnapped his brown Carhart vest, leaned back in his brown leather La-Z-Boy and raised his arms toward the ceiling before slowly dropping his hands down and rubbing his bald head. He glanced at Rosy for a second, then sighed, "I can't commit to a ride right now. With all the colts coming this spring we have to focus on getting some horses sold."

Rosy winced.

We all knew that Ray and Rosy owned too many horses, had stacks of unpaid bills and suffered a continuously short supply of cash.

Ray shrugged. "This is a make-or-break year." He took a deep breath. "I just can't see clear to do another trip." He tapped his fingers on his tattered armchair, and a hand towel covering a worn spot fell to the floor. He reached down to pick it up and tenderly flattened it back in place. He caressed that towel the way my grandma adjusted her doilies, moving from one piece of furniture to the next, making sure each meticulously crocheted cover was perfectly positioned.

Ray forced a smile and turned to look at each one of us, searching for some sign of solidarity. But when no one responded, he turned to Rosy. "Well, that's the way it's gotta be."

Earl Norquist the III, sister Sal's husband, lifted his empty wine glass, tipped it toward his wife and said with a detectable slur. "Sal dragged me along on that one ride and I swore then that it would be the last time my butt would ever touch a saddle." Earl's a short, skinny guy with a big belly, thinning white hair and an enormous self-importance that rarely went unnoticed. He belched, "Horses are not only expensive, they're primitive."

Kitty twirled a lock of hair around her pointer finger as her blue eyes circled the room, checking everyone out. Everyone except Earl. A wily smile crept across her face. "Just because the men don't want to go—or can't—doesn't mean we ladies shouldn't." She rubbed her hands together then assertively clenched her waist.

Elle lit up. "You are so right! More than once we've talked about doing an all-woman trail ride. This just might be the time to stop talking and saddle up."

Kitty thrust her chest out and shimmied her shoulders back. "This is our time, ladies." She winked at Mark. "Who needs men when we've got horses?"

Mark bent over and grabbed his gut like he'd been punched. "Low blow, girl," he grunted. This wasn't the first time I witnessed the two of them banter. Flirt is another word. I knew full well that if I ever needed replacing, Kitty'd be first to sign Mark's dance card. Her backstory included indiscriminate dalliances with married and unmarried men. Kitty was the floor manager of The Esquire, a businessman's club, and her workplace provided her ample hunting ground. After learning about her proclivity for men, Mark and I sat down and clarified our marital boundaries.

Kitty paraded around the room, then plopped down next to Rosy, pushing into her like a long-lost cat, rubbing Rosy's arm and purring. "Let's do the Black Hills without the boys!"

Immediately, Ray brightened. "That's a great idea, Kitty. I'll stay home and take care of business."

Rosy looked at Ray, her eyes inquisitive. "You sure?" she asked.

Ray nodded with certainty.

Rosy scooched over to give Kitty more space, and, for a moment, pondered the proposition. "South Dakota's about six hundred miles due west. If we'd go in early September after school starts, there'd be fewer people. We'd have warm days and cool nights. If we hit the road by dawn, we could make it to the horse camp at French Creek before sundown."

Kitty settled back into the sofa. "I'm in."

Elle nodded, "Me, too."

Earl refilled his wine glass, tipping it again in Sal's direction. "Go if you must, my dear, just count me out."

"No problem," Sal said, mirroring his gesture with her goblet. "Count me in, ladies."

Then Rosy asked, "Maia, what about you?"

Insecurity flushed through me. I'd never been on a long ride without Mark. Going alone meant I'd have to take complete responsibility for everything. In that instant I worried that I wasn't up to the challenge. Horses pull me like a magnet, and yet, strangely, they scare me. Trail riding had strengthened my bond with Justice and given me unparalleled opportunity to experience nature, something I absolutely love. I sucked in a deep breath, let it out slowly. "Well, that sounds like quite the adventure. I'll have to think about it."

"Do it," Mark urged. "You'll have a great time."

I flashed him my *don't-tell-me-what-to-do,* look. But before I could say anything, Kitty shot two thumbs up. Rosy, who knew me and my insecuritics, smiled, her eyes communicating understanding.

I shocked myself when I blurted, "Okay, I'll go." Right then and there the hook was set for an all-women's ride early next September.

Delighted, Rosy offered to reserve campsites and arrange corral space at the French Creek Horse Campground in Custer State Park.

Ray cleared his throat. "What about Lydia?"

Sal crossed her eyes. "What about Princess Lydia? Going with us?" She chugged her wine. "The first time that woman came into the barn dressed like a damn high fashion queen she turned me off." Sal shook her head. "Remember her diamond chandelier earrings?"

"True," Rosy chuckled. "Lydia can be a bit over the top."

Ray raised his voice, "Lydia's worked hard toward her goal of becoming a good enough equestrian to tackle a long ride."

Sal placed the empty wine bottle on the coffee table with a deliberate clunk. "We'd be crazy to let her tag along. She's a royal pain in the ass. We all know that Lydia's not part of our herd."

It's true that humans, like horses, are herd animals, and when someone new comes into a group it can take some time for them to establish their fit.

Ray shook a finger at Sal. "Stop that now. Everyone is entitled to a chance." He retracted his finger. "We've all got our shortcomings."

To be clear, Sal has been a consistent and dominant pain-in-our-saddle-hugging-asses, second only to Earl. Nobody said much more, knowing that if Ray said Lydia should go, she'd be invited.

Our evening ended with Kitty telling the story about a gift she got from a judge she'd been dating. "I opened this fancy wrapped box and it contained this enormous black cowboy hat that had a helmet embedded inside of it."

Rosy laughed and pointed at Kitty. "When she put that hat on, she looked like Yosemite Sam. The brim practically covered her shoulders."

Everyone, including Earl, joined the wine-inspired laughter.

As we left the party, winter hung like frozen laundry in the cold night air. Mark asked, "So will you go?" He knew how I loved horses and ached to ride, but he was also aware of my fear of getting hurt. At seventy, I'm the oldest member of this group. So far, I'd been lucky to avoid getting seriously injured, although I'd been tossed off more than once and had my share of sore muscles and impressive bruises. It was lack of confidence and fear of damage to my ego that were my monster demons.

Driving home, I stared out our truck passenger window and watched for deer as moonlight illuminated glistening snow like diamonds, and I wondered if an all-female ride was right for me.

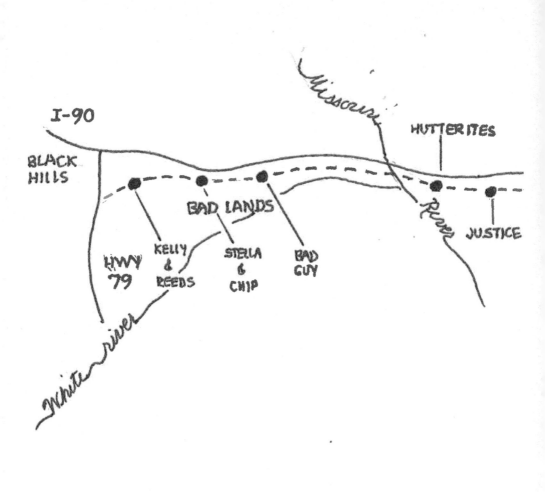

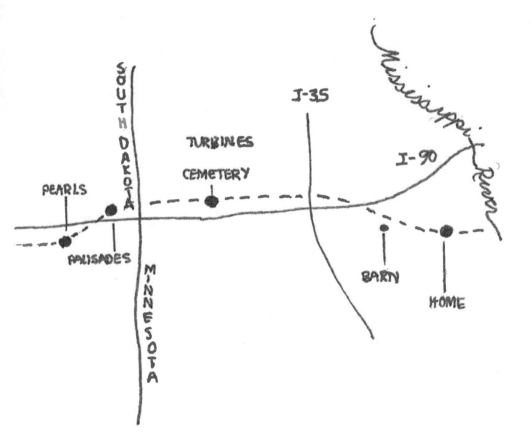

Chapter 4

Getting Buffaloed

Hundreds of giant wind turbines stood like soldiers all along Interstate 90. Their enormous white blades busily captured the wind, turning the gears of green power, surrounded by blue stem prairie grasses swaying back and forth, undulating, tossing seeds to the wind. Not so long ago this land was blanketed with majestic native grasses stretching farther than eyes could see.

Riding shotgun, Lydia pulled down the visor, flipped open the mirror, freshened her lipstick and pressed her lips together.

I asked, "Ever wonder why older women are drawn to horses? I mean really, why are we so attracted to these beautiful creatures?" Lydia narrowed her eyes and clicked her nails.

I chuckled. "Right after we bought Liberty, a good friend accused me of self-medicating by being around a mare. She said that hormone replacement therapy is made from the urine of pregnant mares." I raised my right arm and touched the ceiling liner. "Well I'm way past that, dear, but I've always thought hormone replacement was an interesting concept and horse urine might explain it. I do wonder if a woman can get an estrogen fix simply by being around a mare?"

Lydia lifted an eyebrow. "I'm riding your mare Liberty." She cocked her head coquettishly. "I'm almost through menopause," tapping a professionally manicured nail on her cheek. "I wonder?"

"I don't know if it's true, but it sure would be more appealing than swallowing a pill," I said.

She combed through her shoulder-length red hair with her long nails and ended her performance by tucking a strand of hair behind her ear. "That sure is something to think about."

Fields and forests flew past. Gone were the light greens of spring and summer to be replaced with the dark, almost foreboding greens and browns of an impending fall.

"Wanna hear about my breakthrough with Justice?" I asked. Lydia looked puzzled. "We'd been on the trail for a couple hours when Justice started acting funny. Inside my head I asked, 'What is it?' Then somehow, though not in words, I heard, 'I gotta pee!' I pulled his reins back and stood in the stirrups to lift my weight off his kidneys and within seconds he peed. It was amazing!"

Lydia looked at me suspiciously. "Telepathy with your horse?"

"Scout's honor," I said, placing three fingers on my forehead. "That is exactly what happened. Somehow, I understood his need; and ever since, when he fidgets, I stop and lift my body off the saddle. It is surprising how many times he does his business. Our relationship has continued to grow deeper and become even more respectful. When I use the horse pick to clean his hooves, I then set each hoof down gently. When I put on his bridle, I'm careful the bit doesn't bang against his teeth. Justice has elevated my sensitivity, not only to him, but to the world around me. My hearing has become more acute. When I see him twist and turn his ears, I hear more. Sometimes, it's like I can see through his eyes. I know that sounds wacky, but Justice is remarkably aware of the world around him. Horses are herd animals and they are always on the alert for something that might want to eat them. Fear of predators is the biggest reason any horse, and that includes your Liberty, can be dangerous. A frightened horse can dump its rider in a heartbeat. With the weight off its back, it can run faster and escape any imagined monster. You know what I mean?"

Lydia's mouth was open, and she was about to respond when a swarm of motorcycles roared past, violating our calm. She wagged a finger at the bikers and yelled, "Slow down! Get a horse!"

I enjoyed her outburst. A queue of disheveled men hunched forward into a headwind holding onto their crotch rockets then evaporated into the road ahead. "Motorcyclists," I said. "Just another type of herd, sister."

Miles flew by and the rolling plains gave way to flatter land. My gas gauge was leaning close to empty when Rosy's right blinker flashed. I had to push hard against the strong prairie gusts to force my truck door open at the Pot of Gold Gas Station and Trading Post.

Lydia looked around and spotted a sign for a Pawn Shop. Unable to resist the lure, she bolted out the passenger door. "Be quick," I yelled. "This is not the time for you to shop."

I opened our horses' windows and they poked their heads out and sucked in fresh air. I stroked the large white star between Justices eyes and planted a kiss on the small white snip decorating his nose. I offered first Justice then Liberty a bucket of water, but they were occupied sensing being in a new place. A couple fuel pumps away, Kitty was talking and laughing with guys fussing over their motorcycles.

Sal scampered back balancing an armful of junk food. "Take your pick," she said, using her teeth to rip open a bag of chips.

Rosy cringed. "You always buy crap."

"It's my body and I'll eat and drink whatever I please, thank you. I hate kale. And carrots. Carrots are for horses." Sal popped open a can of Coke and took a sip, unzipped her fanny pack, opened an airplane bottle of Johnny Walker and refilled the can.

Kitty sauntered back slowly, turning several times to wave at a motorcyclist dressed head to toe in jet black. His matching helmet balanced on the seat of his sleek black Harley. "Those are the bikers that just passed us," she said. "Maybe at some point I could share some quality time with that rough rider."

"You sure know how to round men up like cattle," Elle said, pushing her truck door open.

Returning from the shop, Lydia drew our attention as she tried to run in her ridiculous high-heeled boots while trying to keep her hat from blowing away. "Oh, my God, that pawn shop had stuff stacked to the ceiling." She shouted. "There were televisions, microwaves, stacks of kitchen stuff, antiques, saddles, jewelry and even bicycles." Sliding onto the passenger seat, she demanded, "Promise me we will stop here on our way home." It struck me that Sal had it right about Lydia. Maybe on our way back home Lydia could ride with Elle or Rosy.

We hit the road and watched a matrix of white contrails tear apart the blue sky. Vestiges of airplanes whisked busy, busy people from one place to another. Clusters of wind turbines and massive pylons propped up lazy high-tension lines crossing the landscape. Around us, daisy-like flowers with dinner-plate size leaves infiltrated massive clumps of purple asters.

Lydia propped her fancy satin pillow up against her window, yawned and proceeded to catch up on her beauty sleep. I had to chuckle hearing our Princess snore. Two hours later a gigantic cement teepee and billboard welcomed us to South Dakota, informing us we'd entered a place of great places and great faces. I remembered as a kid traveling with my folks. I always expected an actual black line on the ground demarcating the exact spot where we'd leave one state and enter another. When my daughter Molly was little, she expected to hear a beep when we crossed a state line. Sometimes I wished that life was so straightforward and simple with clear boundaries and everything inside lines.

"Notice anything different?" I asked as Lydia woke up. She turned her head from side to side as if I posed a trick question. "No windmill turbines. We've got turbines all over the place in Minnesota," I said. "I've not seen a single one in South Dakota. With this relentless wind, you'd think there'd be turbines everywhere." I shook my head. "What a missed opportunity."

Suddenly a motorcycle pack clogged the passing lane and hovered a few feet away from Elle's rig where Kitty was riding shotgun. One of the bikers looked like the guy Kitty had hustled back at the fuel stop. Elle opened her driver's window and pointed her slender middle finger, signaling her displeasure. The biker returned her gesture by raising his black-gloved finger, then drifted ahead, pipes throbbing. I almost heard Elle mutter, "Asshole." I imagined that Kitty would vigorously defend men. "Don't flip them the bird, Elle," she'd scold. "They have such great potential."

Comforted by the hum of my truck tires, I dismissed the bikers and enjoyed the changing landscape. Eastern South Dakota is flat with endless crops, factory farms and ponds. For the most part, small neatly squared farms are history. We witnessed remnants of the past, relics of yesterday, abandoned buildings, dilapidated barns, rusted sheds lying amongst weed-infested farm equipment and discarded vehicles scattered willy-nilly. Skinny metal granaries, some short and fat, some optimistically tall that shared space with conifer windbreaks. Giant feedlots had hundreds of animals clustered around wooden troughs. Cattle were housed in huge sprawling containment corrals. We saw huge air-conditioned tractors that can cultivate a city block in three swaths. A blue Harvestore silo with an enormous dent in its base hosted a sign, "Jesus is Lord."

Focusing on an unfolding road can present a perfect opportunity to spill the beans. Lydia prattled on about being an empty nester. How disappointed she was when her daughters moved to Dallas to be near their paternal grandfather and live the high life in Texas. She rattled on about her husband's love of golf. "Richard needs to be the boss. Making money is his passion. He thinks horses are too expensive," she said. "I've tried to talk with him about getting a horse, but he simply refuses and brushes me off, saying, "You'll get over it, just like you do with everything else." To me, Richard sounded more like a Dick.

Passing an RV caravan, I recalled a time I witnessed one of Ray's clients complaining about horses being expensive. Ray looked that man square in the face and said, "Cheaper than a kid. They grow faster. Are pretty well trained by the age of five. If you treat a horse right, it will become your best friend." Ray glared at the guy. "What price would you put on that? Hmm?"

I was grateful that from the get-go Mark welcomed horses into our lives. He would agree with Richard about horses being expensive. Many times, Mark would say that horse scent was very expensive perfume. He was taking into account building a barn, buying a truck and trailer, paying a farrier, having enough hay and always needing more tack.

"The truth is, we live in the same house, Richard and I," said Lydia, "but we live in separate worlds."

One at a time a finger shot up from her smooth hand. "My jobs," she said, "First, manage the house. Second, raise the girls. Third, entertain." As she talked, she squeezed her hand into a tight fist. "After the girls left, I took English riding lessons with the black coat, breeches, knee length paddock boots and black helmet."

It crossed my mind that this could have explained why Dick thought horse-riding was expensive.

Slowly she unclenched her fist. "Never, not once, did I ride outside the safety of an arena. Then one day it dawned on me that a Western saddle might be a better fit. That's when I found Ray and Rosy." She sighed, like the weight of the world lifted

For a long time, she stared out her passenger window, then finally asked, "How'd you ever find two horses named Liberty and Justice?"

I smiled. "When we bought Justice, his was name was Scout, but I wanted to call him Justice. Well, you know Ray. He knows everything. He told me to call him Scout Justice, then gradually drop the Scout. Same with Liberty, who was Petunia in her previous life. Her owners called her Pet, they said, because she so loved human touch."

Lydia grinned like a little kid that had just found an Easter egg. "So when I finally get my horse I can give it any name no matter what it was called before?" She thought and then true to her glitzy character announced, "I'll call him Prince." Her eyes welled with tears. "Maia, this trip is a dream come true." She dabbed her eyes with a tissue. "I'm so grateful that everyone agreed to let me come along. Especially you, for letting me ride your Liberty."

"She is a sweet lady," I said, looking in my side mirror, checking the trailer. "She's the only horse I've ever known to pull her head out of a grain bucket just to be touched by a human hand." I pushed my left signal and moved into the fast lane to pass a string of semis.

Outside of Sioux Falls, Rosy led us into a 1950s style filling station to gas up and grab some food. At the counter, directly across from us, a grizzly old cowboy twisted plastic tabs off little cream containers, knocked back each one like a shot of whiskey then gulped coffee as a chaser. "My kind of guy," Sal said loud enough for him to hear. He cocked his head and blew her a kiss.

After a lunch of roast beef, potatoes, carrots and gravy, I stood in line to pay my bill. Lydia was flipping through a magazine when a good-looking cowboy sauntered up next to her and said something. Abruptly she shoved the magazine back into the rack and shot him a nasty, sour look, acting like somehow she'd been violated. Walking back to the truck, she complained, "I hate getting hit on!"

I couldn't help but wonder if she was the kind of woman who grooms herself to get attention, but then when she gets it, responds like she's been done wrong.

Popping up out of a grassy side ditch, a rooster pheasant showed off his flashy iridescent, green and black head, red eye wattle and white ringed neck. Another male strutted along the access road with his head held high like a wrestler entering the ring. A dowdy brown female, sensibly dressed, sprang out of the ditch, utterly indifferent to their cocky presence. Transfixed, Lydia asked, "How could anyone ever kill such a beautiful bird?"

"I don't particularly mind hunting," I said, "Not my sport, though, as long as I can go to the grocery store. But I do have a problem with hunters that don't eat what they kill."

Lydia sighed, "I can't imagine killing anything."

"Me, either," I said. "Although I do get tremendous satisfaction squishing ticks."

The highway dipped down at the grand Overlook and revealed the spectacular Missouri River Valley Gorge and the man-made reservoir at Chamberlain. We cruised down the long hill toward the turquoise-blue Missouri, sometimes called "smoky water." Lydia leaned forward as if that action would bring her closer to the magnificent waterway. She reminded me of riding in the car with my family after church on Sunday. Whenever I'd spot a horse, I'd roll down my window, somehow believing that would get me closer to it.

The moment my truck tires hit the concrete bridge, I tightened my grip and lifted my foot off the gas and sensed the power of the river. Lydia leaned back and pointed at a fisherman who'd just landed a catfish that twisted and turned in its futile struggle for freedom.

My truck engine strained as we climbed the western slope and it felt like the weight of the trailer was pulling us backward, towards home. I kept the pedal to the floor until we leveled off on the high plateau. The sky widened and the open range undulated with rolling hills. Gigantic stacks of round hay bales reminded me of pyramids. Cattle wandered along the hillsides. Rust red sorghum fields knifed through miles of yellow sunflowers that dutifully followed the sun. We watched an antelope, sprint across the road.

No longer feeling like a horse eager to get to the barn, my energy shifted. I wanted to savor the romantic yet somewhat untamed West. Native people had lived here for thousands of years, before white Europeans imposed themselves, their beliefs and culture, upon this land, writing history as seen through their eyes. What did pioneer women think when they arrived on this great plateau to live in a sod house with none of our modern conveniences? No running water, electricity, or heat on demand. It was hard to imagine the utter loneliness of living with a man you may or may not love, who may or may not love you and yet fighting to survive.

Deep in thought I jerked when Lydia asked, "Maia, how'd you get into horses?"

"It was my Dad," I said as my heart sank. "Dad lived to be ninety-two. Until his dying day, he talked horse every chance he got." Born and raised on a farm in southwestern Wisconsin, he farmed with work horses when they were absolutely essential. He was in his thirties when WWII stopped the clock. As the oldest son, he left the farm, the lifestyle he loved, his horses, the dirt beneath his fingernails and joined the war effort to make flamethrowers for the military.

So much of who I am was shaped by my parents, who were uncomplicated, hard-working descendants of a long line of farmers. Like their chickens, they barely scratched out a living. Their ways were simple: finish what you start; and you're only as good as your word. Dad's response to getting tossed around by life was to get back in the saddle. When I asked him how to build a house, he replied without hesitation. "Start by digging the basement." In other words, begin with a solid foundation because too often words and plans stifle creativity.

I recalled when Mom and Dad bought their first black and white television. We watched every episode of *Bonanza, Paladin, Roy Rogers, Davy Crockett, Gunsmoke* and *Hopalong Cassidy*. We had no horses while I was growing up, but I rode ponies at my Uncle Charlie's farm. As soon as all of us kids were out of the house, Dad got back into the horse world. Before they left their farm, Dad gave me his saddle, which remained perched upon a chair in my office while I contemplated riding again. Then, one summer, horses came galloping back into my life. "We were on a fly-fishing trip in Montana and went on several trail rides. I'd just finished a very challenging project and vowed if it turned out successfully, I'd get a horse and name it Justice. When we returned from that trip, I bumped into an old friend, who, in the course of conversation, mentioned that her sister was looking for a good home for one of her horses. Winona was a five-year-old Arab that Ray had trained for the show ring. The deal was that I could have Winona for free, but only if I took riding lessons with Ray."

Lydia squeezed her pillow. "Your dream came true."

I smiled. "Yours can come true, too."

"Thanks to you," she said, laying her pillow down.

As we passed Belvidere and Kadoka and were approaching Cactus Flat, dozens of turkey vultures soared overhead, tilting their slotted, finger-like wing tips, gradually increasing their lift as they took advantage of thermal updrafts. A clump of tumbleweed bounced like a ball across the desert floor. Cradled in red and purple stripes, the sun had begun its downward descent. To our south, jagged tower-like pinnacles and tapering spires reminded me of medieval castles. The Lakota call this place, *Mako Sica*. *Mako* is land. *Sica* is bad. Badland.

Today, this silent land still projects a strong and powerful voice. Millions of years ago this barren, arid terrain was a jungle, roamed by dinosaurs, hippos, camels, rhinos and three-toed horses. Indigenous people lived in the Badlands, followed its streams, stalked wild game and survived the extremes of summers and winters. The violence of the U.S. Army and the white settlers, the sturdy men and women who claimed this land as their own, was a nightmare. The horror of the Wounded Knee massacre. Despair. Mothers, fathers, children herded onto reservations.

An abandoned semi-trailer container parked along the Interstate emblazoned with a Wall Drug advertisement on its broadside promised cold drinks and the best chocolate malts ever. Making a sharp left turn we got our first glimpse of *Pah Sapa*, the hills of black. The hills were dark islands that rose out of a hundred shades of tan. "Those hills look more like mountains," said Lydia. "I wonder if people coming from the east would say they look like mountains and western traveler would call them hills?"

"Good point," I said.

We stopped at a gas station in Hermosa, where Elle, Kitty and I bought fishing licenses. A sign behind the checkout clerk read, "If we don't have it, you don't need it."

"This is my kind of store," said Sal, balancing more bags of fast food in her arms. Rosy shook her head.

As we left the main highway we immediately began to ooh and aah at the spectacular rockfalls and towering trees that bordered the narrow highway leading into Custer State Park. We opened our windows and practically drank the pungent conifer air. Dense Ponderosa pine forests absorb sunlight and create consistent shadows, making the Black Hills a stark comparison to the rest of the land where everything craves protection from the sun and wind. It felt like we entered a sacred place that oozed strengthening, healing energy. Lydia pointed at an old covered wagon which reminded us that not too long ago these hills of gold attracted a mad rush of men who'd caught that fever.

Our little caravan made a right turn just before the livery stable and we slowed to a crawl as we descended down a steep washboard gravel road, and crossed an old-fashioned, single lane wooden bridge. At the bottom, not twenty feet from the truck, a freaking giant bison stood statue-like against a backdrop of granite and ponderosa pines.

A nearby sign articulated the irony. "Buffalo are Dangerous. Do Not Approach."

With a straight face Lydia asked, "Think that buffalo knew to sit next to that sign?"

I had to hold back my laugh.

"Custer Park's reported to have the smartest and largest land mammal. Now, that guy over there is short-sighted and has a keen sense of smell. They've been clocked at forty miles an hour and can outrun a horse and turn on a dime. Never forget, there are 1,500 buffalo free ranging throughout this park's 73,000 acres. They can be unpredictable, so remember: always give them the right of way."

Lydia gasped, "I've never been this close to a buffalo. Is he even real?"

"Technically," I said, "they're not really buffalo."

She shrugged.

"True buffalo roam in Asia and Africa. In North and South America, bison roam the prairies and plains, not buffalos."

She objected. "But *Home on the Range*, where buffalo roam and the deer and the antelope play?"

I laughed, "The songwriter needed three syllables, not two. Trust me, buffalos are really bison. But it's okay if we call them buffalos, everyone does."

Lydia's smile returned.

We looped around the campground and spotted horse trailers, trucks, RVs, folks sitting around fires, horses tied to hitching posts and tie lines, with lots of horses corralled under metal roofs.

Lydia spotted a lone blue tent and her eyes widened. "Who in their right mind would sleep in a tent with those unpredictable beasts roaming everywhere?"

"Not us," I said, pulling into our campsite.

When I unloaded Justice, he stepped down, spun around like a colt, flicked his ears and swished his black tail, checking out his new home. At first refusing to leave the trailer, Liberty finally mustered the courage to back out and step down. Rosy led her two Quarter Horses to the side of her trailer. Catch and Thief, like Rosy and Sal are siblings. Rosy rides Catch and loans Thief to Sal. Catch and Thief are almost identical 14.3 hand sorrels with wavy flaxen manes and lush long tails. Their reddish-brown bodies shimmer and glisten in the sun light. These rock-solid trail horses have nice round, muscular hind ends. Sometimes their soft eyes seem to look right into our souls. The only difference is the size of the lightning blaze between their eyes. Thief's is longer. Sal and Rosy, however, have more differences than similarities.

Rio, Kitty's high-energy, dark liver chestnut, 14 hand Morgan gelding put on quite the show as he danced around with his impressive head held high. His mane, as lush as a lion's. His long thick black tail flowed gracefully. Rio is confident in himself. He knows his own power. If there was any horse you would want to take to war with you, it would be Rio. If it's true that animals and humans have similar personalities, both Rio and Kitty are always on the lookout for taking advantage of an opportunity.

As Elle led Bond, her majestic 14.2 hand, black bay Arab gelding to the corral, he kept his muzzle touching her back. Bond needs to feel secure. He is a follower, not a leader. He is aloof and yet loving. He has a small white star centered between his big wide eyes. His small ears are best described as perky. He has an elegant coat that looks and feels like a combination of a seal and mink. He sports a luxurious mane and tail. With a compact body and short back, he is built for speed and distance.

A thin, white-haired man sporting a handlebar mustache approached us holding hands with a woman decked out in a turquoise-fringed blouse and an eye-catching gold and silver buckle the size of a football. Smiling, he reached his hand out to Rosy. "I'm Alex Lucas. Everyone calls me Ace. This is Lucille, my wife."

Lucille leaned into him and said, "I'm the better half." They smiled at each other, signaling they'd used that line before. "We're your Camp Hosts. Our job is to help you gals have a fantastic time." She pointed at a cement building. "We've got hot showers and flush toilets and a horse shower out back."

"Where's the hot tub?" Lydia asked.

Lucille responded with a dull glare, then said, "No hot tub here, sorry."

Ace looked at Rosy. "We got a call from Lance the livery stable guy and he'll be arriving soon with your weed-free hay."

"We know the rules," Rosy said defensively. "Been feeding our horses weed-free hay pellets for the last two days." When a pickup truck pulled in, Kitty stared at a drop-dead rugged cowboy who looked like he came straight out of Central Casting as he climbed down from the cab of a truck loaded with bales of hay.

As we all turned our heads to take a long look, Kitty shoved Rio's reins into Elle's hand. "I'll help haul hay," she said dashing off to help the irresistible cowboy. When Lance left, Kitty-the-cougar fanned herself with her hand. "Did I just die and go to heaven?"

"You? In Heaven?" Sal snickered. "That's not a connection I'd make." Rosy held back a laugh, coughed and took control. "We'll need to get up early and ride over to the Blue Bell Lodge for a good breakfast, then we'll head north to the fire tower."

Totally exhausted, we all said goodnight. Lydia crawled onto her cot under my sturdy truck topper. We were safe inside our covered truck bed on our side-by-side cots. I curled up in my sleeping bag and listened to campers talk, fires crackle, and generators hum.

We were sound asleep when we felt our truck rock back and forth. "Earthquake!" I yelled, bolting up.

Lydia peered out her side window and whispered, "It's a freakin' buffalo, Maia." Just inches away, a buffalo was pushing its head against our bumper. I didn't breathe until the creature ambled off, heading straight toward that lone blue tent. Lucky for those inside, the buffalo turned before dramatically changing the camper's destiny.

Lydia snuggled back into her sleeping bag. "That was close," she said. "Now we can brag about the time we got buffaloed."

Chapter 5

Mother Nature Speaks

As far as I'm concerned, it's nothing short of heaven to wake to the smell of wood smoke and the clip-clop of horses. While I dressed, I watched as Elle knelt down and nurtured our first fire. Never married, no children, Elle has two dogs she loves like kids. She's talked about her grandpa, mother and brother, but never once has she mentioned any–not one–romantic relationship. Elle always maintains her distance. We all know she studied to be a nurse, but after her dad died, she took over her family's banking business.

Once, Ray winked when he told me, "Elle's got money. . . Old money." Ray and Rosy's Triple-R Ranch is a great boarding and training facility, as well as a terrific gossip hub. The first thing I learned about Elle at the Triple-R was that she wrote out a check for ten grand after watching Ray ride Bond for less than thirty minutes. Bond's previous owners had paid Ray to train him for the ring but seldom let him out of his ten by ten-foot stall except for training and performing.

After she purchased Bond, Elle sold her car and bought a matching truck and horse trailer. She put her city house on the market and bought a farm, built an elegant horse barn and established riding trails throughout her wooded property. Now, Bond had a splendid pasture, miles of trails and an immaculate stall, complete with piped-in classical music.

At the corral, I unlatched the gate and slipped leads on Liberty and Justice to take them to the creek. Other horses nickered their enthusiastic greetings as we made our way through the campground. At the creek, Liberty swung her head side to side, grazing the water's surface. Justice, a no-fooling around practical guy, dipped his muzzle into the stream and sucked up the cold water.

With our horses watered and fed, I joined my companions at the fire for a cup of steaming hot coffee. Lydia strutted over wearing a red satin blouse, skintight black jeans and shiny black ostrich boots. Her hair was perfectly coiffed, her eyes masterfully accented, looking like she just stepped out of a New York salon.

Donned in a wrinkled plaid shirt, hair askew, Sal rubbed her eyes. "How in the hell do you do that?"

Lydia batted her eyelashes, and deliberately lifted one pinky, holding it daintily aloft. "Practice," she replied, placing her red cowboy hat snugly over her shiny hair. She giggled, "You won't believe what happened to us last night."

Kitty lifted an eyebrow and cocked her head. "I'll bite. What?"

Lydia dangled the strand of coarse buffalo hair she found hanging off my truck bumper like a necklace. Then spread her arms wide. "A ginormous buffalo used Maia's bumper as a scratching post."

Rosy laughed. "That's a good one."

Lydia carefully placed the mat of buffalo hair on top of our picnic table. "That beast was big and scary."

"Oh, that's so terrible. Did our little princess get scared?" Sal pretended to sniffle.

"Ladies, stop," Rosy commanded. "It's time to saddle up. I want breakfast."

All Triple-R Ranch riders are taught Ray and Rosy's saddling process. It is mandatory that we do it their way. No shortcuts. No alternatives or excuses. Being a well-trained Triple-R Ranch rider, I first check Justice's back for sores or any debris. Then after brushing him I made sure the saddle pad was clean before setting it on his back. After placing the saddle on his back I stepped back to make sure it was centered. I flip the right stirrup up over the saddle. Unwrap the leather latigo, grab the cinch and thread the latigo through. I attach the back cinch, wrap the breast collar around his chest and hook it to the saddle. I hold Justice's bridle in front of his face and untie his halter. Immediately he responds by doing what Ray taught him and drops his head to make it easier for me to install his bridle. I slip my left thumb into his mouth and that triggers him to take the bit. With the chinstrap secure, I tighten the cinch and wait for any reaction. Justice has a habit of sucking in a deep breath just before the cinch is pulled to give him more breathing room. I thread my leather reins through my fingers and make the left rein shorter as my insurance policy. With one rein shorter all Justice could do was move in a circle, and not bolt or buck. With my left foot in the stirrup and my hand on the saddle horn, I swing my right leg up over, gently sit down, make my reins equal length and then lovingly stroke his mane.

Even after perfecting this ritual, ever since I got back into riding, I fret about something going wrong every time I head out on a trail ride, no matter how prepared I am. Perched on top of a half-ton animal that naturally fears predators is why being a little nervous makes good sense. I've learned that survival, that protecting themselves, is any horse's number one priority. No matter how steady, even the most reliable horse can spook. A sudden movement or a high-pitched noise can produce a shy or a buck. When an equine freaks out it can quickly and efficiently toss a rider off like a piece of laundry blown from a clothesline.

One time, Elle got bucked off when a flock of geese rose up off a pond. That impact with Mother Earth resulted in a compound fracture, her tibia piercing her skin. Winona, my Arabian, launched me when a flock of turkey vultures perched in treetops flapped their wings, creating frightening sounds and casting scary shadows on the forest floor. I landed on my butt. Lucky for me I didn't get seriously hurt, although my confidence suffered considerable damage. Learning to ride Winona, I might as well have been learning how to drive a Lamborghini.

Right after I was thrown, I asked Ray to find me a horse that wasn't so skittish. That horse was Justice, a veteran mount who'd been around the block a few times and had carried rookies like me before. He'd seen it all, done it all and did not waste any energy when something out of the ordinary happened.

I thought about how Ray constantly reminded us to ride with our whole body. He'd say, "Imagine your horse's hooves are your feet. Breathe in unison with your horse." Over and over again he'd tell us that when our horse blows, we should blow, too. That blowing releases tension. He'd talk about how when the energy blend of horse and rider is just right, that there's seldom a need for a kick, or the tap of a spur, the sting of a whip or a sharp jerk of the reins.

As Kitty and Rio led us out of camp, I felt Justice's energy build. Rio held his head high and proud, his ears erect, registering every sound. Bond followed immediately behind Rio. Splashing across the creek we watched a great Blue Heron lift off the bank, squawk and disappear downstream. Elle pointed at a huge boulder that split the current, making a vee, and remarked, "That could be a great fishing spot."

Two buffalos stood at a clearing, tails pointing up, wallowing, pawing the ground, creating little dust clouds. Our horses were on high alert but didn't spook as we patiently waited for the beasts to move on. I could feel Justice pull and stretch as he climbed a steep rocky hill. As we trotted past the livery stable, Kitty kept twisting around, searching for Lance, the young stud who'd delivered hay. Then straight ahead, nestled in gigantic ponderosa pines, stood the impressive Blue Bell Lodge.

Every time I step down out of the saddle, as soon as my boots hit the ground, somehow I feel shorter. As we tied our horses to a hitching post, we saw a horse with a red ribbon tied on its tail standing alone at another hitching post. "Be careful around that horse, ladies. A red ribbon is a signal that that horse is a kicker," Rosy said. "It's trail etiquette to warn other riders to steer clear of its backside." She held the door open to the Blue Bell. The interior of the lodge was decorated with wagon wheel chandeliers, saddle-covered stools and dead animal heads mounted on heavy wooden plaques.

Lydia gushed, "It's so perfect. So Western."

Our waiter pulled a black pen burdened with cowboy fringe from a red holster strapped around his waist. Rosy, Sal and Elle ordered the Western Omelet. Lydia and I chose Buffalo Benedict. Kitty seductively caressed her neck and said to the young man, "I'll take your Cowboy Up."

Sal groaned, "Of course you will."

After breakfast, we left the lodge and the red-ribbon-tagged kicker issued high-pitched screams as we walked away. I remembered the good-looking cowboy who'd approached Lydia in the truck stop restaurant and how she rejected him. Was she like that horse? Was her red hat a red ribbon? Was she really signaling, come over here cowpoke so I can kick you? In the process of getting to know another person, it can be like putting a puzzle together without a box-top picture to serve as a guide.

Our trail led to a grassy meadow where Rosy raised her left hand, giving the "yes" signal to gallop. Everyone raised their hands. I shifted my hips forward, issued a kissing sound and felt Justice's muscles stretch. His legs like steam pistons shot forward fast as a greyhound chasing a rabbit. Wind slapped my face. Ground raced past. I felt like Pegasus. When Justice's breath became labored, I gently pulled his reins back and he slowed. Justice was spent. Not me. I was exhilarated. I looked at Lydia who wore an ear-to-ear smile.

The trail turned into a steep rock pile and several times we had to turn our horses perpendicular to the hill to give them needed breaks. Moving up, Sal held Thief's reins too tight and he kept thrusting his head as we zig-zagged around switchbacks.

"Loosen your reins," Rosy yelled. "Trust him, Sal, let him do the work. Forget about yourself."

"This is a hill from Hell," Sal yelled back. "I hate this shit."

As we broke over the ridge at about 6,000 feet, the Mount Coolidge red granite fire tower looked like a medieval castle. The green and brown lichen covering the rocky ledge reminded me of a Jackson Pollack I'd seen on a trip to Chicago many years earlier.

Our thirsty horses drank from an old stone trough as we stood in silence at the overlook taking in the vast panorama. Rosy broke the silence, "This is why I love riding."

To our east, dramatic Badland sandstone spires sprouted against the horizon. Southward, the wind created wave after wave as it blew over the expansive grasslands. To our north stood Mount Rushmore with eroded granite pillars, towers and spires known collectively as the Needles that were formed millions of years ago when the earth's crust shrugged and the wind chiseled stone into turrets and pinnacles.

With our senses filled to the brim, we began our return to camp. At the stable, Lance the hay-guy, leaned against the corral railing and tipped his hat in Kitty's direction.

Kitty returned the gesture and said loud enough for Lance to have been deaf not to hear, "Now that's my kind of cowboy."

"Looks like trouble to me," Sal groused.

Kitty winked, "Sometimes trouble can be a lot of fun."

"Grow up," Sal grumbled.

Long, late-day shadows lined the road as we entered the campground. A gang of men trotted past us and Kitty squealed, "Am I dreaming?"

"You are incorrigible!" Sal barked, turning Thief toward Rosy's trailer.

Kitty retaliated, "I know who I am and I make no apology for it."

Rosy smiled at Kitty. "That is the truth."

At the end of a long ride, a good rider's habit was to loosen the horse's front cinch to give him time to cool down before removing the saddle. Ray claimed this helped prevent saddle sores from developing. Then it was time for us to take care of ourselves.

Together we made a supper of sliced potatoes, onions, fresh chopped basil, slivers of dried beef and pats of butter wrapped in aluminum foil. We grilled them alongside six pork chops and rehydrate a package of dried applesauce. In preparation for this ride, we had decided to experiment with various dried foods. The six of us split all food cost and, of course, everyone brought treats and their favorite liquids.

Settled back in our chairs around the fire, we were just getting comfortable when, suddenly, Lydia stood up and ordered us to cover our eyes. She dashed away and returned shouting, "Keep your eyes closed!" Then feigned a choke. "Ok. Open." The princess held a horse-head shaped cake.

Wide-eyed, Sal asked, "Did you make it?"

"Are you kidding?" Lydia, said, "I ordered it." Vigorously shaking a can of whipped cream, adding the crowning glory. "Who wants cake?" Sal smiled at Lydia and was first to raise her hand.

Our camp hosts, Ace and Lucille, were making their nightly patrol and stopped by. We asked them about our intention of riding the east French Creek trail loop. Our plan was to have lunch in an old grove of ponderosa pines and then find the reflecting rock wall.

"If you poke around, you should find the side wall that's got the carved rock art," Lucille said. "It's supposed to tell a migration story."

Ace brushed his hands over the fire and assumed The Thinker's statue pose. "Good day's ride you've got planned. Give yourself enough time. That trail is not real popular anymore. It don't take long for a trail to get overgrown if it's not ridden. So, be careful. It's easier than you might think to get lost going up 'n down these hills."

Lydia was perched on top of our picnic table, touching up her fingernail polish. The fire glowed. Flames rose hypnotically. It was like watching waves or a waterfall. Rosy jumped as if struck by lightning, pointing at the sky. "Check that out." Faint green flashes popped against a dark backdrop. Wisps of colored lights appeared, blues, oranges and various shades of green.

"Oh, my God, it's an aurora," I said, breathless, springing to my feet. Witnessing the Northern Lights had been on my bucket list a long, long time. Luminous green and red curtains twisted and turned, tossing about in an invisible wind. It was a magical cosmic dance of light and color that quickly spread across the entire sky. Intense greens flowed into reds which then splashed orange then pink. Sheets of light arched and waved, as if responding to some wonderful and mysterious choreographer's commands. It was like watching music.

Elle asked if anyone else had heard that the Northern Lights are considered to be a special form of energy. "When I was a nurse, I heard a couple say they were going to fly to Alaska during an aurora to conceive a gifted child."

Light shifted, flitted up, then down. It was cosmic fireworks. All around camp, horses whinnied. "The animals are picking up on the energy," said Rosy, leaving to check our horses.

Lydia held her hands up, careful not to damage her polish. Her voice quivered. "Why exactly is this happening?"

"Nothing to fret your pretty little head about," Sal replied. "Just pretend you're on the red carpet at the Oscars and the lights are camera strobes."

Lydia spastically shook her fingers dry.

Elle shared her knowledge of the cosmos. "Auroras happen when solar flares and solar winds interact with our atmosphere. Flares can be larger than the earth." Awestruck, she said softly, "We are witnessing a beautiful expression of universal energy. There's nothing to fear Lydia."

Rosy returned, knelt down, picked up a stick, jabbed the fire and assured us that although our horses were somewhat animated, and that they were fine. Sparks jumped out of the glowing red fire pit. In the distance a coyote howled, and within seconds, its call was echoed by other coyotes invisible in the night.

Lydia stood perfectly still for a second fixated on looking at the northern lights, then bolted to my truck. Rosy shouted after her, "Remember, Suzie-Q, we need to be on the trail before sunrise if we're going to make it back here before dark."

"What a wuss," said Sal, hoisting her wine glass to her lips.

Kitty fanned herself with her hand. "I'm feeling a charge. I think I'll saddle up Rio and ride to the livery stable."

Rosy slammed her foot down. "No one goes off alone. I'm talking to you, Miss Kitty."

Defiantly Kitty replied, "Alone? I won't be alone long."

Rosy glared. "Don't even think about it. I'll get a damn pail of water and throw it on you."

Sal rolled her eyes. "Does your libido ever turn off?"

Kitty fired back, "Yours ever turn on?"

"Enough!" yelled Rosy. "Bedtime."

Lydia was cocooned in her sleeping bag when I crawled onto my cot. She whined, "Maia, those lights really scared me. I'm not kidding. I want it to stop."

Feeling exactly the opposite, I stared at the night sky, not wanting to miss one moment of the spectacular Aurora Borealis.

Chapter 6

Rise and Shine

I woke out of a deep sleep into a world of near-dead darkness, dreaming that a black and white paint pony with a head on both ends of its body ran straight through our campground. I tossed and turned, wondering what it could mean. The next thing I knew, Kitty was pounding on my truck window. "Rise and shine!"

Hustling to get out of camp early, we tried our best not to disturb our fellow campers. While I saddled Justice, he fidgeted and twitched like something was bothering him. I pressed my face into his neck, inhaled his smell and asked. "What's with you?"

I searched his big brown eyes, but they gave me no clue.

Rosy stood next to Catch and read her list. "Cook stove, fuel canister, matches, nesting pots, utensils, dried spaghetti, treats, water bottles, purifier, first aid kit, bug spray, sunscreen, blanket, binoculars and wire cutter." She looked up and reminded everyone. "Take your horses' hobbles." With everything under control, she then ordered, "Cowgirl up!"

In the half-light of dawn, Rio led us out of camp through great pockets of otherworldly mist. The chorus of the robins blended with the chatter of Western bluebirds.

Justice kept flinging his head back in the direction of camp again and again, he stopped and extended his front hooves into the ground, refusing to budge. I bent over his neck and stroked his ears and waited for him to soften under my touch. I thought about what Ray would say. "When you relax, your horse will, too." I breathed in the crisp, moist fresh air and got lost in the glistening droplets of dew decorating the vegetation. In a few minutes Justice relaxed and responded to my calf and leg pressure and the shifting of my weight.

Rio stopped abruptly. His eyes and ears focused intently on the underbrush. Two mule deer stood motionless. Without any warning, they sprung up, then landed straight down on all fours, their black-tipped tails flashing as they sped away.

The trail widened and Lydia brought Liberty alongside us. I asked, "Did you know that every horse carries its own rose?"

She wrinkled her brow, "Get out of here."

"You'll see." Bond was directly in front of us. "Watch his butt," I said. It didn't take long for Bond to lift his tail, shift it to one side and poop. "Wait!" I said, "When he finishes his business, his anus will fold in like an origami rose."

Bond obliged and Lydia squinted. She chuckled, "It's true! It's a rose. Maia, I think you've been paying too much attention to horses' asses."

"No doubt I've run into my share," I replied, falling back in line.

Stopping at the creek to filter water, Kitty squatted down. Rio was directly behind her, standing still as a statue; then, in one swift motion, he thrust his head forward and pushed her into the cold stream. "You are such a rascal," she scolded, climbing up the bank, half-pissed, half-thrilled. "That's enough of your antics."

Rosy shook her head. "Should've named him Trouble."

"Trouble's for cowboys. Besides, I like challenges," Kitty replied, sitting down and removing her boots. "That was just horseplay."

Lydia snickered, "Did you say foreplay?"

"Not you, too," snarled Sal at Lydia.

Kitty laughed.

"Rio's the busiest and most challenging horse I've ever known," said Rosy.

Kitty let the water drain out of her boots. "I really like that about him," wringing her socks. "He's something big to love that fits between my legs."

Rosy, perched on Catch, shook her head. "Miss Kitty you are so bad."

We'd ridden about an hour when an intoxicatingly heavy pine fragrance overwhelmed our senses as we entered a magnificent old-growth ponderosa forest. Wind, like soft voices, whispered through the tall conifers. Lydia hopped off Liberty and immediately began to gather pinecones decorating the forest floor. Arms overflowing, she announced her intention of making a keepsake wreath to memorialize her first totally amazing trail ride.

Sal staggered, stiff-legged like an old, over-rode cowpoke, stopped and complained. "Gol-darn knees don't work."

"You've gotta remember to keep your weight balanced," Rosy said, offering her a hand. "Sit straight in your saddle, then every few minutes take one foot out of the stirrup and stretch out your leg."

Sal leaned against Thief, lifted her flask of alcohol and gulped. "Words to live by. Thanks, Sis."

I took Justice's hobbles out of my saddle bags. He paid attention as I buckled a leather bracelet-like hobble on his front left pastern; then I straightened the connecting chain and secured the other end to his right leg.

We spread out a blanket and laid down and watched as each trusty steed reacted differently to how hobbles restricted their wanderings. Justice made little bunny-hops. Liberty barely moved and kept her head down. Bond refused to step forward and drifted backwards. Catch made clean meticulous sweeps one way then turned 180 degrees in the other direction. Thief kept turning in circles. Rio, the cerebral trickster, figured the hobbles out and his roaming range was completely unrestricted.

Elle lit the pack stove and within a few minutes we dished up a hot spaghetti lunch. For dessert, Rosy passed around a bag of scratch-made chocolate chip cookies. Lying stretched out on a blanket on the forest floor, we gazed up at the canopy. The thick pine tree bark reminded me of something reptilian, something with a salmon gray underbelly. These trees, these majestic living ancestors, wore signs of fire and limb loss.

Gradually, one by one our horses gathered around us, as if eavesdropping Rio bobbed his head up and down, clearly becoming part of our conversations. Liberty kept inching her way a little closer, seeming curious to know if we were talking about her.

I shared my two-headed pony dream.

Rosy chuckled. "A two-headed horse? Sounds like twice the feed."

I puzzled. Why would I imagine a horse having two heads, one on each end? Perhaps the dream was my questioning this adventure. Perhaps it was just a crazy dream.

Lydia lifted a pinecone to her nose and inhaled the sap and pine esters, then rolled over to face Rosy. "How will I ever be able to choose the right horse?"

Rosy sat up. "First, you have to honestly evaluate your riding ability. Then ask yourself what you want to accomplish. Then, be truthful about committing to a long-term relationship."

"I can do that," said Lydia.

Rosy patted Lydia's knee. "We've seen it happen so many times that it's not funny." She rested her hand on the blanket. "A woman will come to us saying she wants a horse. We ask what she has in mind and nine times out of ten she wants a big, black prancing stallion with a long flowing tail and lush mane. It always reminds us of a guy that wants a pretty woman hanging off his arm."

Straight-faced, Lydia said, "I'd like a black one."

Sal choked.

Rosy rolled her eyes. "Let's put it this way, getting a horse is like choosing a mate: you want to make damn sure you pick the right one." Lydia flinched. "When checking out a horse, look into its eyes and you can see kindness, intelligence, stubbornness, aloofness and even fear."

Elle smiled, "I felt Bond's kindness the very first time I saw him."

"There are lots of things to take into consideration when horse shopping," said Rosy. "A gelding will eliminate the hormone problem. A mare in heat can be a challenge if there's a stallion in the neighborhood." She appeared lost in thought for a moment, then told about a trail ride they took with a hundred other riders. "There was this guy riding a stallion right behind a young gal on a mare. The stallion got a whiff, lifted his head, curled his upper lip, let out a string of high-pitched screams, hopped on the mare's back end and dug his forged steel shoes into the young girl's back. The stallion was just being a stallion. The girl was trapped. People screamed. The stallion hopped off and the girl fell to the ground with nasty gouges in her back." Rosy stood and stretched. "That's the best reason to choose a gelding."

Lydia stared at Rosy. "Liberty's a mare."

Rosy lifted one corner of our blanket. "Don't you worry, Lydia, we've got your back." Elle grabbed the other corner and together folded the blanket.

As Rosy removed Catch's hobbles, she continued. "Horses train people. It's amazing how fast horses learn. The more often an experience is repeated, the deeper it gets ingrained." She stuffed her hobbles into her saddlebag. "We get problem horses that have developed some bad habits. What bothers us most is that we can fix the horse, but when we return it to the owner, if the owner hasn't learned and changed, the horse will quickly resort to its old ways. Then we either get the horse back or the owner hires a new trainer. Horses are the easy part. Humans are much more difficult."

Sal tightened Thief's cinch. "And that's how you make the big bucks."

Rosy flashed Sal a sour look. "With a horse, you make the wrong thing difficult and the right thing easy." She cleared her throat. "One time, Ray and I watched a woman try to pick up her horse's hind leg to clean its hoof. The horse kicked at her. 'Oh, sweetie,' the woman said in a sappy voice, 'don't do that,' then she patted the horse's neck and fed it a carrot. She was about to pick up the leg again and that's when Ray lost it. He yelled, 'Mayday! Mayday!' Ray kept his cool as he tried to explain that she was teaching her horse to kick by rewarding its bad behavior." She looked at Sal, "We know about bad behavior, don't we?"

Sal retorted, "You lookin' at me?"

"There are lessons we could all learn," Rosy said, getting settled on Catch as we prepared to leave paradise. "Lydia, this trip will pay off in so many ways. One thing I do know is that you can't teach experience. You're learning more than you could have ever imagined."

A bald eagle floated overhead, then majestically glided out of site. We rode quietly for an hour then entered a narrow granite passageway with hundred-foot-tall walls that were covered with millions of tiny mica mirrors reflecting the sun's light.

Transfixed by the shimmering wall, Rosy whispered, "It's prettier than I imagined."

Halfway through the passage, a rock tumbled down from a wide opening overhead and landed in front of Catch. He shied, but Rosy kept stroking his neck and calmed him down. "Easy. Easy boy," she repeated.

Elle pointed at a big horn sheep scampering along the narrow ledge. "He did it!"

The goat stopped and looked down at us. Kitty shouted, "Check out those black horns!" Then chuckled, "They're not the only horny thing around here."

Sal picked up the bait. "Is sex all you think about?"

"Why not?" Kitty answered. "It charges my batteries."

Sal dropped her head, muttering, "I give up."

Elle was first to spot little stick figures, triangular tipis and what looked like mountains scratched on a south-facing granite wall. The tableau had a crudely carved four-legged animal hooked to what appeared to be a travois.

"What does it mean?" Lydia asked.

"Lucille said it's a migration story," Elle said. "Someone long ago intentionally etched it into stone."

We hadn't gotten far when a twisted cottonwood, probably downed

39

in a recent windstorm judging by its massive exposed root ball, blocked the trail. With no other option than to bushwhack, we had to detour quite a distance to get around the huge canopy, still full of shimmering leaves, and make our way through a maze of tangled undergrowth.

"I found it," Elle yelled. Later when the trail disintegrated into an old logging road, she checked the map. "This trail isn't shown on this map."

"If we keep heading east, we should connect with our trail," Rosy said. But instead of finding our trail, more riding led us to the edge of a weed-choked overgrown airstrip runway with faded windsocks, showing years of service. We wrapped our reins around our saddle horns, dismounted and walked to a small cement control tower and peeked through cracks in boarded-up windows. Rosy jiggled the doorknob. "Locked."

Elle unfolded our map and placed one finger on it and said, "Ok, we're here at this airport." She took a deep breath. "So we're not lost, but we definitely are not in the right place."

"This must have happened when we doglegged around that giant cottonwood," Rosy said, checking her watch. "It's pert-near four and time for coming up with Plan B."

Elle huddled over the map and traced a straight line from the airport to the east French Creek entrance. "Our horses can get their fill at the creek. Then we either finish the rest of the loop or take the wildlife highway and turn on an access road that will take us back to camp."

"Either way, we ought to be back by eight," Rosy said, sounding like a trail boss heading a cattle drive into a railyard.

Sal bellowed. "I hope this old body can take it." Elle tossed her the bottle of ibuprofen. She moaned, "Will I ever walk again?"

"You'll be good as new after a good night's sleep," Rosy said, helping her get settled back on Thief.

Sal groaned, "Promise?"

Rosy smiled, "I promise!"

As Kitty approached Rio, he reached his front legs forward and lowered his back, stretching like a cat waking from a nap.

Justice lagged behind. He was tired. I kept caressing his mane, feeling guilty about asking him to carry me even further. "You are doing great." My energy had drained, and I, too, felt weary.

Riding single file, we maintained a steady pace through a meadow blanketed with ferns. We slowed to a crawl when our horses had to maneuver through rocks jutting out of the earth like bones piercing skin. Each horse carefully placed their hooves in safe spots. Red and purple strips like ribbons were wrapped around the gradually departing sun. Rosy twisted around at the empty parking lot and wore an exaggerated look of puzzlement. "Can it be closed? Isn't this a popular trailhead?"

"Strange," Elle said.

Sensing water nearby, the horses, eager to satisfy their thirst, picked up their pace. Reaching the creek, they plunged in and we filled our canteens. We agreed it would be faster if we completed the loop. "How much longer?" Sal asked.

"Maybe two hours," Rosy guessed.

"Just shoot me!" Sal moaned as Rosy helped her stand.

We didn't get very far before we ran into a log jam that was so enormous that we had no option other than to turn around and take the Wildlife Loop road back to camp.

Nearing the parking lot, Justice stopped short and braced. Rio made a side-pass and dove deep into the undergrowth. Catch snorted. Liberty froze. Justice rotated his ears back and forth and drifted backwards. No one spoke. Directly in front of us, big, shadowy shapes moved. A giant herd of buffalo had taken possession of the parking lot while we went for water.

Rosy gasped, "Holy shit." Dumbstruck, paralyzed in our saddles, we could only listen as the milling buffalo herd thrummed with deep guttural snorts and grunts punctuated by ululating calves. After a long silence, Rosy spoke softly but loud enough for everyone to hear. "Do not panic. We've got to hold this together." She stretched her body up to appear taller in her saddle. "Do not let your horse go staring at any buffalo. Our horses won't tolerate prolonged tension. I guarantee you that you're sittin' on top a half-ton of fear." She paused. "Give no sign you are afraid. I'm serious, ladies. We just stumbled into a damn dangerous situation." She scanned the herd, looking for the bulls, then nodded to her left. "We'll steer clear of those old boys." My eyes focused on Rosy, waiting for a cue. Slowly, she raised her right arm. "Follow me. Move slow and steady. We have to stick together. We'll angle south and hug the edge of the timber." Rosy thrust her shoulders back and stared straight ahead. "Make no noise or fast moves. Nobody could survive a stampede. Come now. We're gonna get through this." As we began to skirt the herd, the whole herd, like a murmuration of starlings, shifted in unison. Before we could move away, they'd surrounded us. We all sat perfectly still. Steel-eyed Rosy waited for an opening. Again, she thrust her shoulders back, looked straight ahead, raised her right arm, pointing to the center of the herd.

My heart pounded like crazy. I oozed sweat. I tried to focus my remaining energy, my lifetime accumulation of personal power, everything I had into not freaking out so I didn't do anything that would spook Justice and trigger a stampede.

Rosy stroked Catch's neck and made soft clucking sounds. At first Catch resisted, but Rosy insisted he take the lead. The moment Catch inched forward, I thought, "Brave steed." With my eyes plastered on Rosy's back, I urged Justice to follow her and enter the herd. The smell of musk was so strong I swear I could taste it. Swishing tails, constant bellowing, snorting and pawing, the movement and sound of wild buffalo came from every direction. Knowing any eye contact could trigger an unwanted reaction, I guided Justice through the enormous beasts, praying that this would be our way out.

I kept repeating, "We are not a threat. We are not a threat. Do not be afraid." I swear I didn't draw a breath until we penetrated the herd and emerged on the other side. With the herd finally behind us, my heart raced. I breathed deeply. Completely overwhelmed, I exhaled loudly and leaned forward as far as I could to massage Justice's great neck with my elbows and the heels of my hands.

Rio snorted and threw his body around like he'd just taken a first in the show ring.

Lydia collapsed onto Liberty's mane.

Rosy rubbed Catch's shoulder. "We survived, big boy! You were totally amazing." She turned Catch around to face everyone. "You all were amazing. Ladies, we held it together!" She raised her right hand in a high-five gesture. "Can you believe we did that?"

I choked, "That was one of the most incredible things I've ever done."

Lydia tried to speak but couldn't.

With the back of her hand, Elle wiped sweat off her face. "That was amazing," she gasped, wiping her wet hands on Bond's mane.

Kitty looked back at the buffalo herd, then turned to the road ahead and did her best to lighten the tense mood. "I get it. That's why this is called the Wildlife Loop."

"Shut up," Sal raged. Anger bubbled up from her toes. "Trust me, I will never forget this day. Do you hear me?" She screamed, "I will never, ever go on another trail ride! Never!" Her voice cracked. "I can't take this. Earl was right. This ride was a stupid idea."

Rosy urged Catch closer to Sal, "Come on, Sis, you did great."

Sal's dam burst and she cried, "Shut the fuck up, Rosy."

Without saying another word, we rode along a two-lane paved road that cut through a vast grassland as the darkening horizon blended sky and prairie together. It was strangely silent. There was no traffic. Nothing moved except an eerie dance of prairie grasses. The whole world had stilled. When darkness consumed both the horses and women, Rosy switched on her headlamp.

I let Justice's reins hang loose and he shuffled in a circle. He was spent. Knowing I could not ask him for anything more, I dismounted and walked alongside him. The others stopped, but I told them to go ahead, that I'd meet them back at camp. I slowly plodded on. Lydia got off Liberty and walked with us.

"Shit," I said, stepping on a sharp rock. My reaction embarrassed me. Justice and the other horses had stepped on more rocks than we could count or know. I could not imagine how much Justice hurt. He'd carried me all day and into the night, trusting me, putting everything he had into lugging me around like a Sherpa hauling trekkers' gear. Deep down inside I understood with greater profundity than on any earlier trail ride that a well-trained, well-cared-for horse will serve its demanding human beyond the point of exhaustion.

Our pals were waiting by the creek just outside of camp. Cool water caressed their horses' tired legs. Elle stared at the unusually dead quiet camp. "Everything's gone dark. What's going on? No fires? No horses whinnying?"

A single dim light came from Ace and Lucille's RV. Minutes later, we saw a dull yellow kerosene flame swing from side to side as it came closer. Ace and Lucille were moving fast as they carried their lantern. "We were worried sick about you," Lucille cried, slowing down as she got closer. "Something really bad happened!"

My heart stopped. "My family?"

Ace set the lantern on a big rock. "Bad didn't happen just to one of us." He stretched his arms as if embracing the horizon. "Bad happened to all of us."

"What?" Rosy demanded, her voice sawn with sudden alarm.

"That aurora last night. You remember, the Northern Lights? Well it knocked out electricity." Lucille sniffled and wiped her eyes. "Electricity everywhere."

"Everywhere?" We asked in unison.

"That was a monster aurora," Lucille groaned, her dread infecting us with fear.

Ace wrapped an arm around his wife. "Got no lights, no internet, computers all fried, cell phones are dead. For all we know, there could be mass hysteria and panic in the cities. No internet, no TV, no radio. We're back to the stone age."

Cold as ice, Rosy demanded, "Just how do you know this, Ace?"

"Right after you gals left on your ride, Bill, the park ranger, rode over to tell us that a Rapid City ham radio operator broadcasting with a gas-powered generator in his garage, reported that the whole gal-darn country could be under a state of emergency. That beautiful aurora was the mother of all solar flares. Not sure which way to turn." Ace squeezed Lucille protectively. "Bill said that aurora supposedly zapped satellites, flipped the breaker on the grid and the power went off. He's waiting to hear the extent of it." Lucille pressed into Ace. "According to Bill, the governor declared martial law in South Dakota. I reckon it could be the same in Minnesota."

Ace's words hit harder than I could have ever imagined. I felt faint and pushed my head into Justice's shoulder. My mind raced. "Oh, my God! Are we stuck here? Powerless?" I wanted Mark. I wanted to be home.

Rosy stiffened. "When will it get it fixed?"

Ace looked like he was ready to burst into tears. "Weeks, maybe months. Bill said it's anybody's guess right now."

Rosy looked up at the starless sky. "Power is out everywhere?"

"I assume so. All Bill could say for certain was that a solar flare caused the aurora. Back in 1989 a solar flare knocked out Quebec's grid and it took six weeks to get the power back. That was just Quebec. According to Bill, who got it off a ham radioman said we could be talking North America."

"No!" Elle shouted. "This can't be happening. Everybody depends on electricity. How will people survive?"

Sal, still in her saddle, let out a long, slow caterwaul as she attempted to lift her leg and dismount. "Well that's the sixty-four-gazillion-dollar question now, isn't it?" When her foot touched the earth, her knees buckled and she collapsed. "This is fucking unbelievable. My trip through Hell just got worse." She got up and tottered, looking old and arthritic. Rosy offered to help but Sal pushed her away.

Rosy countered by touching her shoulder. "Don't worry, Sis, we'll figure this out. We'll get home somehow."

"Shit." Sal yanked free of Rosy and hobbled away. "Don't touch me. Don't even look at me. Don't speak to me. I hurt! I'm sore. I'm tired and I don't give a shitty shit about any of this horseshit. That includes you, Sis."

I asked Ace, "Where did the campers go? Is there a shelter someplace?"

"Not to the best of my knowledge. Not a shelter," he replied, head shaking, clearly unsure of what to say. "When Bill came over, we gathered all the campers and told them the bad news. One by one, they packed up and took off. When you gals didn't come back, we were beginning to worry we'd never see you again."

"We got lost," I said. "And we rode through a herd of buffalo."

Ace froze. "You rode through buffalo?"

Sal shouted, "Pure hell is what it was. Reckless endangerment by our trail boss."

Rosy followed Sal to her horse trailer and tied Catch to it and loosened his cinch. "We'll get through this, Sis."

"Another one of your false promises," Sal said, removing Thief's bridle.

Physically and mentally exhausted, we all moved on autopilot and took care of our horses. I loosened Justice's cinch to let him cool down before removing his saddle. I filled his grain dish, but he just stared at it. Never before had I witnessed him too tired to eat. I felt great relief when he lifted his head and accepted my affection.

Lydia and I crawled into our truck bed. She sat down on her cot with an unfeminine plop and picked at the dirt under her fingernails. Her voice quivered, "How will I ever get clean? I need a shower."

"A shower is the least of our worries," I said, stunned at her ignorance. "Pumps and water heaters need electricity." Melting onto my cot, I zipped up my sleeping bag. "Come tomorrow morning you can bathe in the creek," I said, burying my head in my pillow.

"I can't do that," Lydia sobbed, pulling her bag over her head.

"Go to sleep, Lydia." I said. Dizzy and confused, I wished I could cry. I couldn't stop thinking about Mark, home, our kids, our friends, our country. Oh, my God. How can we live without electricity? Will people go crazy? Will there be riots and looting and worse? Only a few hours ago, our greatest challenge after getting lost and riding too long and too hard, had been getting through a buffalo herd. We'd met that challenge. We did it. But this? Having no electricity would be harder, much, much harder. I tossed and turned. Why hadn't we met other riders? There were no vehicles. No airplane contrails. Was it true that the spectacular aurora had given birth to our demise?

Chapter 7

A Good Idea Gone Bad

Although the morning sun tried its very best to brighten our humble abode, Lydia and I were enveloped in the darkness of fear.

"I can't stand it." Lydia cried, "Please, please tell me that solar thing was just a bad dream."

"I wish I could," I said, staring at my truck topper's ceiling, my body heavy, my heart saturated with tears. I missed Mark. Our kids. Catatonic, overwhelmed by the unknown, I tried to contemplate a world without electricity. Could this actually be true? Are there really no cell phones, no computers, no grocery stores, no medical help? What if one of us got hurt or fell sick? How could we get home?

It felt like lightning hit me and I remembered Justice and jumped up, got dressed and hightailed it to the corral. Relief washed over me when I saw his grain dish was empty. My good old boy had survived yesterday's marathon. Momentarily comforted, I leaned into him and breathed in his smell.

Sal lumbered past on her way to deliver Thief's morning grain. Justice pulled his usual stunt of laying his ears back, thrusting his head forward, the curse of being an old crank who's greedy about food.

Sal snarled, "He is such a grump."

Takes one to know one, I thought, but kept my mouth shut.

A morning breeze gifted me with the aroma of coffee and the whiff provided a moment of normality.

One by one we gathered around the fire. We all wore yesterday's clothes. We had bags under our eyes and needed baths. We clutched our coffee cups, our eyes bathed in steam and smoke. We said nothing until Rosy broke the silence. Sober faced, she looked strong and yet, at the same time, fragile. "Gotta say, I'm struggling to wrap my brain around this situation."

"It's the worst possible fucking disaster ever," Sal growled.

Rosy sighed. "That's the truth." She sipped her coffee. "I thought about this all night. We need to talk about our options."

I poured everyone more coffee. "What are they?" I placed the pot back on the metal grill.

Rosy lifted two fingers. "One, we could stay here, but I don't think that's the best idea. Two, we head home." Her voice grew stronger. "I do not believe, not even for one minute, that someone will show up to rescue us. Everybody's gonna be busy taking care of themselves. The way I see it, we are on our own. We pack light. Drive as far as we can with the fuel we have. Ditch our trucks. Saddle our horses and ride home."

Sal choked, then spit coffee on the ground. "Are you crazy? I can barely walk after yesterday's ridiculous ride. Do you actually think I'd be able to ride all the way back home?"

"I believe you can do it." Rosy's voice cracked. "To tell the truth I don't think we have any choice." She stared at the fire, "I believe we all can do it."

Sal tossed her coffee dregs into the fire and hobbled away.

Elle shook her head back and forth. "If there's no electricity, that means there's no gas. So we really have no choice but to ride clean across South Dakota and Minnesota."

The sound of a horse at a full gallop grabbed our attention. A park ranger riding a palomino with a white mane and tail stopped at Ace and Lucille's RV. He dismounted, looked our way and touched the brim of his dark brown Stetson. He knocked on the door and Ace ushered him inside.

Sal came back and sat down. We waited. Our attention was glued to the RV like it was a TV. Finally, the door opened. Ace and the ranger walked over and he introduced Bill. We stood still as statues as Bill delivered a terse law enforcement report. "The National Guard's been called out. That aurora caused widespread damage. Blown substations. Fires. People in the streets. There've been reports of looting."

Rosy offered each of them a cup of coffee, then asked, "Any idea how long this will last?"

Bill wrapped his hands around the warm cup and blew on the black coffee until an eddy formed. He took a sip. "How long? Who knows, ma'am. Weeks, more likely months. Gotta be chaotic in populated places. I sure wouldn't want to be trapped in a big city. Know what I mean?" He looked around. "I guess one positive thing is that because this place is so remote we won't be as restricted as those in urban areas." He handed his cup back to Rosy. "I have to check on other people in the park. Thanks for the coffee."

After Bill and Ace left, Elle, the usually cool and competent woman who seems to know everything, paced like a caged animal. "Our lives are totally dependent on electricity. No computers. No banking. No stop lights. No elevators in high rise buildings. No refrigerators or freezers."

Lydia squeaked, "What will people eat?"

Sal sat next to her. "Each other. Whaddya think? Everybody'll turn into zombies?"

Lydia's mouth dropped open.

"Stop!" Rosy yelled, tossing a log onto the fire. "We need to talk about our needs. Food. Water. The right clothes and shelter."

Kitty raised her arm. "And our horses."

"And courage," I whispered.

Rosy rubbed her hands together. "Look. This is how I see it. We've got good horses. We can ride. We know how to camp We've got enough clothes and a fairly adequate supply of food."

Lydia's voice became unusually elevated and assertive. "Are you kidding? You want us to ride all the way home? Are you crazy? Why can't we just wait here? This situation won't last that long. Electricity will come back." She unfolded a tissue and blew her nose loudly, very un princess-like. "Tell me why we can't stay here and wait?"

Rosy made direct eye contact with her. "We can't wait. We have to take care of ourselves, and that means packing up and heading home." She took a deep breath. "We are not disaster victims and we are not going to act like victims. It drives me crazy how easily women accept the role of helpless damsels who need to be rescued. We are strong, powerful women, completely capable of figuring out how to safely negotiate riding home."

Sal stomped her foot. "Rosy, you are a fool. We are victims, damnit. This has been done to everyone, us included. We didn't bring it on ourselves."

Rosy snapped back. "Ok then, Sis, we're victims of circumstance, but I'm telling you we will not act like victims." The sisters locked eyes until Sal broke away.

Lydia persisted, "What if the power is only off for a few days? I thought we lived in a democracy and I vote we stay right here with Ace and Lucille."

Rosy raised her arms as if appealing to the gods. "Lydia, what if the power stays off for months? What will happen to us if we stay here when the weather gets bitter cold? When snow covers everything? What happens when our food is gone? This situation is nothing compared to how bad it could get if we stay here hoping things don't get worse. No. We can't wait. Really, we have no other choice than to head home!"

Lydia collapsed, her chest on her thighs. "I want to be home," she moaned. "I've had enough. I'm not a good enough rider. I'm not strong enough to do what you ask."

"Ditto." Sal echoed, sounding like a foghorn.

Then our Kitty bounded up. "Think of this as an unexpected adventure. Didn't we all agree we wanted an adventure?"

"Someone sit on her," Sal growled. "This is not the time for her pithy enthusiasm."

"No, Sal," Rosy snapped back. "Kitty's spot on. Attitude is everything. We gotta gather our strength, pool our resources, stay positive and work as a team."

Elle stood up and rested her foot on the bench, then leaned forward. "A big question is whether we can get more gas. I believe the chance of that happening is slim, but the more fuel we have, the shorter our ride." Her eyes turned toward our vehicles. "We filled up in Hermosa and that should get us back to the Missouri River." She reached out her hand. "Drivers, give me your keys." She ran from one vehicle to the other, checking our gas gauges. Returning, she dropped our keys on the table, hunched over and struggled to breathe. "The looters were busy. Two vehicles have no frickin' gas. My truck is still full." She sat down. "My gas cap was locked."

"How could anyone do that?" I sighed.

Rosy put a hand on my shoulder, emotionless, and answered. "It's simple, Maia. Just like us, they wanted to get home."

"Not like us," I objected.

"You're right," Rosy said, "They're worse than us. They wanted to get home so bad that they stole what they needed. From here on in our survival will depend on us taking care of each other. We don't have to steal. Least not yet. We're not going to rob banks, but make no mistake, we're a gang." She slipped her truck keys back into her jean pocket. "What just happened is that our long ride just got longer. We'll divvy up Elle's gas amongst our three vehicles. Instead of getting two hundred miles, we'll make about eighty. We'll find a place to park our rigs, then ride the rest of the way home." She took a deep breath. "We can do this."

Kitty flexed her bicep and struck a Rosy the Riveter pose. "Hell, yes, we can!"

"We're gonna need a hose to siphon gas," Rosy told Kitty.

"You got it, boss," and she took off to find Ace.

"This blackout's not going to be a picnic," Elle said. "Now we know what we've got for fuel." She paused, "I've taken survival training and I've learned that folks who keep their heads, those that keep cool, are survivors. Humans can survive three days without water and three weeks without food. Water will be our biggest concern, both for us and our horses. We'll need to be vigilant and not get too wet or too cold. We've gotta stay warm and dry."

Kitty returned carrying a length of pale green garden hose. "I told Ace and Lucille about our plan." A mischievous smile appeared on her face. "Now, who volunteers to suck it up?"

Sal gagged.

Elle spread a map out on the picnic table and slowly slid her hand eastward across South Dakota. "Our route home has to be based on continued access to water." She poked the map with her finger. "We drive to Hermosa and hopefully get more gas."

Rosy shook her head. "Maybe, maybe not."

"Maybe." Elle shrugged, "Maybe not. After Hermosa we take back roads that parallel the White River. It's a tributary of the Missouri." She surveyed our faces, making sure we were following her. "The horses will have water. We've got purifiers." She looked up. "Getting enough water in the Badlands will be our greatest challenge. After we cross the Missouri, we'll drop south and ride side roads. From then on, with all those ponds along the Interstate, water shouldn't be a problem. Before we get to Sioux Falls, we'll head north to avoid people.

"The Missouri River is still a hundred miles from Minnesota," I said, surveying the map. I tapped on little dots east of the Missouri. "These are Hutterite Colonies. Similar to Amish and Mennonites. They're known for growing lots of food." A surge of hope raced through me remembering how well our Amish neighbors live without electricity. Up with the sun. Asleep in bed when it goes down. They live off the land. Cook with wood. Horses provide transportation and perform field work. They work together as a community.

Rosy warmed her hands over the fire. "We'll pack our personal stuff in our fanny packs and saddlebags. We'll tie our rain gear and sleeping bags behind our cantles." She rubbed her chin. "We're gonna need to take a lot of supplies." Then rubbed her lips. "I don't think we can do this without having a pack animal and a set of panniers." She turned to face Kitty. "Where could we get a mule?"

Kitty smiled, "At the Livery Stable?"

"Bingo," said Rosy. "I hereby appoint you to have a chat with that Lance dude to see if you can persuade him to spare one."

Kitty jumped up. "I'll be happy to try. I'll ask Ace to go along."

"Wait." Rosy said. "Before that, we need to make a decision." Then asked, "Those willing to ride home, raise your hand."

Rosy, Elle and Kitty's hands shot up.

Sal's arm slowly inched up. "I don't know if my body can do it." She lowered her hand. "But I sure don't want to get trapped here."

I too raised my arm. Lydia's chest heaved in and out, but her hand remained down by her side.

Chapter 8

Ain't No Ladies Here

Rosy squeezed Lydia's knee. "Check with Ace and Lucille to see if you can stay here with them." Then she made a sweeping arm gesture, "Ladies, we are heading home!"

"Ladies," Sal grimaced. "Ain't no ladies here."

"That's not true," Lydia whimpered. "Lucille is a lady." Lydia squeaked one word out at a time between deep, tearful breaths. "Knowing. We'll. Have. Enough. Water. Is the. Best. Reason. To stay."

"We'll find water," Rosy said. "It's time we pool our cash. We're gonna need a chunk of change to buy us a mule, so get out your wallets." Collectively we had over two grand in cash.

Elle slipped off her watch and laid it on the picnic table. "It's worth about five thousand. My brother won it playing poker."

Rosy looked questioningly at Elle. "You sure you wanna give it up?"

Elle shook her head, "It never meant anything to me other than to tell time." She looked at Rosy's watch. "We only need one."

Rosy tapped her wrist. "Yeah. Mine cost all of twenty bucks."

Kitty shoved the cash into her fanny pack and secured the gold watchband studded with tiny diamonds onto her wrist.

Rosy lifted an eyebrow. "If possible, save the cash. Trade what you have to." She smiled, "If anyone can get us a mule, it's you, Miss Kitty."

Kitty smiled as she unbuttoned two shirt buttons.

Elle was helping Kitty saddle Rio when Ace trotted over riding Major, a red Dun with a black dorsal strip from his head to the top of his tail. With Kitty settled in her saddle, Ace gave her a cowboy nod and they cantered off, creating swirls of dust.

Lydia spread her pinecones out on a neighbor's table, nervously attempting to assemble a wreath. We led our horses to the creek. Bond followed Elle like a well-trained guard dog without needing a lead. Our fellow campers, in their haste to leave, left gifts of firewood, plastic chairs, tarps and one nylon tent. As we returned, our horses issued several loud whinnies, alerting us someone was coming. Rio pranced, with each step he bounced, his neck arched, his black tail held high. He kept turning around to check on the critter he had in tow. Brown canvas bags hung from both sides of the mule's gray stocky body. The mule had cute long ears. His whitish mane was trimmed short. His tail ended with a white wispy tuft. He had straight legs and hard, straight-sided hooves.

Kitty handed the mule's lead to Elle. "That sweet Lance latched onto your expensive watch like a trout hitting the right fly." She fluttered her eyelashes. "His first response was that he wouldn't sell a mule for anything." She winked. "So I gave him my best smile, took your watch off my wrist and laid it in my palms. He said he'd always wanted a good watch, like the rich guys that come to his place and ride his ponies."

Ace took off his hat and bowed to Kitty. "That woman was phenomenal."

Rosy thrust two thumbs up. "Thank you, Miss Kitty."

Lydia abandoned her pinecones and hurried over. She looked like a schoolgirl experiencing love at first sight as she touched the mule's ears. "What's his name?"

"Didn't come with a name," Kitty said, smiling at our princess. "How about Romeo?"

Lydia looked into the mule's big brown eyes. "Romeo, oh, my Romeo," she swooned. He blinked and fluttered his long lashes.

Lucille reached out her hand to Ace as he dismounted, then planted a kiss on his cheek. "Good work, honey."

He winked rakishly. "Kitty did it. Women do have their ways."

Kitty and Lucille both fluffed their hair.

"He's a solid, athletic pack animal," boasted Ace. "He's about 600 pounds and can easily carry a third of his weight. He'll be more sure-footed than any of your horses. He'll endure heat better, and drink and eat less." He patted Romeo's shoulder. This old boy is more like a goat." He brushed his hand over Romeo's mane. "I always wanted a good mule. I like how they solve problems better than a horse. Some say they like to ponder situations. Plus, mules have an extraordinary sense of smell."

Lydia stroked Romeo's smoky grey ears. "He's so perfect." Just then he opened his mouth and serenaded us with a long, drawn-out whinny that ended in a series of hee-haws. We all laughed as Lydia grinned from ear to ear.

Elle insisted we all take a look at the map of the Badlands she'd spread out on the table. "Look here!" she pointed. "This is a railroad corridor. It's a straight shot all the way across the Badlands straight to the Missouri River." She turned to Rosy, "Is it possible that we can ride the rails?"

"That could be a great option. I like that it's a straight shot and it's remote, but rails are hard on horses. Sometimes there's enough of a side bed running alongside to make it easier. We'll have to wait and see." She uncovered a platter of sliced roast beef, tomatoes, cucumbers, bread and hunks of ripe bananas she'd prepared while Kitty got Romeo.

Kitty had just finished eating when she leapt up like a spring. "I've got an idea." She grabbed Lydia's arm. "We all need to get clean." Lydia pulled away like a little kid resisting a parent. "Come on," Kitty tugged. "We're all filthy. Think about how good it'll feel to wash your body."

Lydia got up and helped Kitty secure Romeo in an empty corral. We gathered towels, shampoo, soap and our collapsible buckets. At the riverbank, Kitty stripped down to her sexy black sports bra and black G-string panties. True to her style, Elle wore a female version of gray male jockey shorts and an athletic bra. Rosy, me and Sal wore white nylon, old-lady panties, and riding bras that minimized bounce. Lydia was last to toss off her modesty. Then our Princess stole the show with her slinky blue Victoria Secret bra and matching panties.

Kitty was first to plunge into the creek. She let out a shrill scream when the achingly cold water hit her tender spots. Immediately we all understood that our time in the water would be a short-lived thrill. Kitty stood on the bank and lathered her hair, then I administered the rinse cycle by dumping icy cold water over her head. She shrieked.

Standing on the bank, naked, absorbing the warmth of the sun, Lydia cried, "I'm coming with you. I want to go home." Immediately we formed a circle and hugged.

Kitty's idea had provided a desperately needed reentry into the present moment. For a few minutes we were able to let go and not worry about our future.

Rosy took Lydia's hand on our way back to camp. "It feels so much better that you are coming with us. I want you to know I am impressed how well you've done on this ride. You and Liberty are a good team."

Lydia bobbed her head.

"Your riding is getting better every day. Don't fear, I trust that you are up to it." Rosy stopped. "And don't let Sal get to you. Remember, we each have our strengths."

Lydia choked up. "It felt like I was abandoning my herd. Especially now with Romeo."

Back at camp, Rosy added more wood to the fire, then looked in the direction of home. "We've got a lot to figure out." She took a deep breath. "For over forty years me and Ray have not been apart for more than a few days at one time. Not once. We've been a two-horse team. Sadie, our daughter, lives close by and she'll take good care of Ray. He'll be crazy with worry, but he knows we're competent and that one way or another we'll find a way to make it back. I'm certain that if he was trail-bossin' this ride, he'd do everything in his power to get everybody home."

Kitty sat cross-legged on top of the picnic table. "I don't have much of a family. I haven't seen my Mom in years. Haven't exchanged one word with my Dad since I was eight. Lost track of my only sister long ago and I don't even have a clue where she calls home." She looked at the corral. "Rio's my family." She turned to face us, "And you guys."

Sal zipped up her sweatshirt. "Earl's domestically incompetent. Computers are his passion, and that's pretty much it." She paused. "He is so screwed. He'll probably lock our apartment door, hop on his motorcycle and hightail it to his brother's place. He'll take care of Earl until I get home."

Lydia pulled a tissue out of her fanny pack. "Angela, our oldest, and our baby, Jessica, live in Texas near their grandpa. I pray they are together." She blew her nose. "Mom's gone. I was an only kid." She twisted the tissue. "I wonder if Richard will even notice I'm gone. He's got lots of buddies and a basement full of guns."

Sparks rose as Elle stirred the fire with a long stick. "Mom's ninety. For the last few years, ever since her mind went south, she's lived in a retirement facility. She'll be taken care of. My brother has my dogs. He'll pack up his family and head off to his second home along the Mississippi River." She pushed a log deep into the coals.

It was painful to think about my loved ones until I recalled a talk we had with our kids. If the world ever went haywire, everyone would try their damnedest to come home. Our garden would still be producing. Our pantry was pretty full. Mark hunts, so they'd have plenty of meat. The woods would provide enough firewood to cook and keep our house warm.

They could get water from the Root River that's within walking distance. I felt relieved believing my family could. . .no, would get through this. I also knew they'd be worried sick about us. "I just want to get home," I said. "I want us to make it."

"Words to remember," said Rosy. "Here's the deal. From now on we have to focus on what we have to do and we cannot spend any time or energy worrying about our families. We have to trust that our loved ones will get through this and they'll all be there when we get home." She waited as everyone nodded in agreement. "Ok, then." She sighed. "When do we leave?"

Lydia crumpled her tissue and tossed it into the fire. "Why do we need to rush?"

"It's not rushing," Rosy snapped back. "There is no good reason to wait. The longer we stay here, the faster we'll burn through our resources. We need to make it home before it gets too cold."

Kitty agreed, "The sooner the better."

"Turns cold?" Lydia shook her head. "But it's still early September."

Kitty rolled her eyes, "Riding home will take us a while."

Elle, her voice tense, said, "It's what's happening everywhere else that terrifies me. God only knows what we could run into. Country folks might get through this, but city people. . .city people scare me. Desperate people might turn to getting around on horseback with gas-guzzling cars, trucks and tractors out of commission. We'll have to keep our guard up at all times. Our horses are our ticket home. We avoid roadblocks. Watch out for military patrols. I believe we'll be okay traveling through the Badlands, but when we cross over the Missouri, we'll have to ride at night and stay clear of populated places to avoid being seen."

Rosy leaned back. "Elle's right. We need to think real seriously about not being seen."

Elle tapped her finger on the Missouri River. "We'll be vulnerable crossing the bridge."

"Cross in the dark of night," Kitty said brightly.

My mind flashed to a Western movie I saw as a kid, where the good cowboys padded their horses' hooves with rags in order to surprise some bad guys.

Sal sounded annoyed. "So, boss, when do we leave?"

"Lighten up, Sis, we've got a lot to figure out and we've got to get our stuff together."

Sal persisted. "Tomorrow?"

Rosy raised her voice. "I don't know, Sal."

"Can we give Justice at least one more day to recover from yesterday's ride," I begged.

"Justice is tough," her tone was rough and final. "He'll be fine. If we ride twenty miles a day, hell's bells, we'll make it home in a month. Some of the time we'll walk." She looked at Sal, "Exercise'll do us good."

"Is it time we take stock of what we have?" Kitty asked.

"Sounds like a plan," said Elle.

"Good," Rosy replied. "Elle, you're in charge of figuring out our camping gear needs and determining what personal stuff we can bring." Rosy spun on her boot heel and pointed at Kitty. "You evaluate our animals' needs." She pivoted so quickly she almost tripped over Lydia. Lydia flinched. "Honey, you take care of Romeo." Lydia smiled broadly. Rosy made her final turn and pointed at me. "Maia! You work with me to evaluate our food supply and get a plan."

"I can do that."

Rosy and I decided to make one breakfast bag, another for lunch and snacks and a third for big meals. She rubbed her belly. "We might eat less and might not like everything that's put in front of us, but with luck, we shouldn't starve."

Sal stuck a finger in her mouth, mimicking a gag. "I'm a goner."

Rosy snapped at her, "You know, Sis, the problem is not what goes into your mouth, it's what comes out of it."

"Lighten up," Sal retaliated. "I was just trying to be funny."

"Me lighten up?" Rosy shook her head. "Now that's a switch."

Sal retreated, unzipped her fanny pack, opened her flask and took a long swig before mumbling, "Witch."

"Watch it," Rosy said.

"I need everyone's attention," Elle said, then read her list. "Vest, one pair riding pants, a warm long-sleeved shirt, turtleneck, lightweight shirt, one change of underwear and something warm to sleep in." She turned to Lydia, "We need to blend into the environment, so leave all your razzle-dazzle, glitzy stuff behind."

Lydia looked hurt, "I don't have anything bland."

"I've got a beige shirt you can have," I said. "Don't fret, we will help you get a new wardrobe together."

Elle continued in the voice of a Girl Scout den mother, "Tie your sleeping bags and rain slickers behind your cantle. Bring your headlamp, hobbles and any extra gloves. Hook your canteen over your saddle horn.

Shampoo, soap, toothpaste and dental floss go in one communal bag. Put your toothbrush, identification, sunglasses, pocketknives, medications in your fanny packs."

Lydia wore a shocked expression. "That's it? That's all?"

Elle tossed up her arms. "Face it, Lydia, you are going to get dirty, real dirty, so I suggest you get used to it."

"I like getting down and dirty," Kitty replied with her usual sexual innuendo.

"Surprise, surprise," Sal snickered.

Lydia gasped. "My God, what about toilet paper? Will we have enough?"

"Sweetie," Elle lectured. "TP is for pooping. No pooping, then it's drip-dry. You'll be surprised how much TP you'll save."

A sensory image of my grandpa's two-hole outhouse drifted through my mind. It was dark inside with the only light penetrating cracks in the bare, weathered wood. A crescent moon was cut into the door. The smell. The wicker basket sitting in the corner filled with hulled corncobs. A Sears catalog with pages ripped out. Momentarily I felt comforted knowing that my grandparents lived long and good lives without indoor plumbing and running water.

Next, Rosy read her checklist. "Coffee pot, cutting board, nesting pots and lids, frying pan, portable peak stove, an extra pressure cap, tool kit, fuel containers, grill, hatchet, silverware, spatula, plastic bags, aluminum foil, six bowls, large spoon and a ladle will go into Romeo's pack."

"I've got the farrier kit, Bute, healing cream, superglue, vet wrap and two easy boots," Kitty added.

"Easy boot?" Lydia questioned.

Kitty explained. "If a horse's foot gets injured you slip it over a its hoof." She opened the first-aid kit and laid bandages, Benadryl, scissors, gauze, pain pills, vitamins, aspirin, matches and a space blanket on the table. "We'll bring the sewing kit in case we need to do some stitching."

"You mean I won't be wearing rags?" Lydia taunted.

"Not talking about stitching you a party dress, Lydia. We're talking about closing wounds or mending a tent."

Lydia stared at Kitty, looking hurt.

Kitty gave her a reassuring look, "Sweetie, nothing bad is going to happen to any of us."

Elle got her fishing pole and laid it by the tent we inherited from our long-gone neighbors.

"I'm taking my cot," I stated firmly. "I won't survive without it."

Elle looked at Rosy who puckered her face in such a way that I doubted I'd be able to take my cot. "I am the oldest," I protested, "and too damned old to sleep on damp, hard ground."

Rosy softened. "If you absolutely have to have that cot, Maia, then you'll have to figure out how to carry it because it's not going on Romeo's back." She took a deep breath. "Maia, a cot takes up a lotta precious space."

While I argued all the reasons why being the oldest warranted special dispensation, a shot rang from the woods. I froze.

We all relaxed when we saw Lucille smiling as she ran toward us. "That's just Ace. He went hunting. He's a crack shot. From the sound of it, I'll bet he'll bring some fresh meat."

Twenty minutes later, Ace burst out of the underbrush, his rifle wedged under his right arm, the business end pointed down. "We're gonna be eating good tonight, gals." Then said, "I could use some help."

Elle volunteered first. "I'm yours. What do you need?"

"Help getting that buck back."

"Holler if you need more help," Lucille said, and in a flash, Elle and Ace disappeared into the woods.

Lucille returned to their RV and came back with a rope, a saw, two sharp meat knives, several packing containers and towels and placed the butchering gear down on a neighbor's table. We watched as Elle and Ace broke through the underbrush with a long narrow pole slung over their shoulders. A small, grey mule deer hung by its legs, its brown eyes seeing nothing, its head and long ears dangling down, its black-tipped tail dragging over the ground as the eviscerated body oozed blood.

Lydia turned away dramatically and announced, "I can't do this. His ears are like my Romeo's."

Ace looped the rope around the dead deer's neck and tossed the other end over a tree limb. Together, Rosy and Elle hoisted the deer until it hung clear off the ground. Fresh blood dripped. Lucille handed Ace the saw and he proceeded to hack away, severing the deer's legs above the knees. Lucille carefully stacked the severed limbs at the base of a tree with all four hooves facing east.

Elle whipped out her pocketknife, pushed a button and the blade snapped in place. She cut around the deer's head, then down its chest, separating connective tissue between skin and carcass. Together, Elle and Ace peeled the hide until they were able to pull it off.

This once quick and agile mammal of the Great Plains morphed into a motionless carcass. Ace inserted his knife near its shoulder and worked it down along the spine, cutting close to each vertebra. He made a ninety-degree cut under the ribs, separated the loin and handed Rosy two bright red tenderloins.

"Don't get any better than this," the hunter-butcher grinned, using a white towel to wipe blood off his knife.

"Would it be all right if we made some venison jerky?" I asked.

"Help yourself." Ace replied wiping his bloody hands on the towel. "Take all you want. I shot this one for you gals," he grinned. "There's plenty of deer out there and I've got lots of ammo."

Rosy helped me trim off the waxy fat and connecting tissues. We sliced the venison into thin strips and marinated them in a soy sauce, garlic concoction we whipped up. Elle cobbled our neighbors' grills into drying racks, stacking one on top of another. We got a fire going and laid venison strips on the grates. Lydia gathered green wood to produce smoke to help flavor the meat. Lydia, whose demeanor suddenly changed from distressed and uncooperative to almost joyful, offered to take turns with me throughout the night to tend the fire and rotate our soon-to-be-jerky.

We wrapped potatoes, onions, and celery in aluminum foil and grilled them alongside the fresh tenderloins. Lydia spread out Rosy's finest blue-checkered tablecloth and carefully positioned each matching napkin. Sal uncorked several bottles of wine and we ate and drank like there was no tomorrow.

"What are your plans?" Kitty asked Lucille. "You staying here or will you leave?"

"There's no way we could make it back to our families in Georgia. Here we've got water, plenty of firewood and bullets." Lucille smiled at Ace. "We're staying put."

Ace returned Lucille's smile. "We've always wondered what it would be like to winter in these hills. Looks like our big chance has arrived." He pointed north. "If it turns out our RV doesn't keep us warm enough, there's a little log cabin just over that hill. Only a few people know it's there, so we'll be snug and safe."

Sal uncorked the last bottle of red wine. "Rosy won't let us take the wine with us, so I say let's drink up."

Kitty downed a healthy swig and then raised her left arm straight up. She shouted, "I say, let the adventure begin." Our defiant female warrior then proclaimed, "This might be the most exciting thing any of us will ever do." She lifted her glass to the gods.

"Have you gone completely mad?" asked Sal, refilling her glass.

Again, Lydia's mood darkened. "I'm scared. I don't know if I can do it."

Lucille wrapped an arm around her the way a mother would. "You have to head home, sweetie. It's your best shot. There's no good reason to linger here. You need to be brave." She squeezed Lydia until their cheeks touched. "Summon your courage."

"We'll need plenty of courage and a ton of good luck," Rosy added, as Lucille comforted Lydia.

Chapter 9

She Could Be Deadly

It was around midnight, under a waxing crescent moon, when I set the grates aside, fed the fire, sampled the drying meat and crawled back onto my cot. I awoke with Elle pounding on my truck window, yelling, "It's gonna rain!"

Thunder roared in the gray dawn. Cloud heads bubbled. Lydia helped me stuff three gallon-sized plastic bags with jerky. Rosy and Elle had just finished tightening the tarp ropes when the downpour began.

"Looks like we'll have enough time to get everything ready for our long ride," Rosy said, pushing a stick up into the tarp's growing belly and making water drain out of one corner.

Sal's coat covered her head as she slid under the tarp and plopped down. "I feel like shit."

Rosy handed her a cup of steaming hot coffee. "Poor sister."

Lydia ducked under the tarp, her shirt half buttoned, her hair a mess. She wore no makeup. Our Lydia no longer looked like a princess.

The drumming eventually blended with the staccato of dripping trees and the hiss of runoff. Everything glistened as yellow light rays wove through the clouds, gradually brightening our world of uncertainty. "I love that earthy smell," I said. "It's hard to put the feeling into words."

"The smell is called petrichor," Elle said. "It happens when rainwater hits dry soil and oils are released into the air."

Rosy and I went through all our food. We put oatmeal, all dry cereals, Biscotti, brown and white sugar, tea, coffee, hot chocolate, Tang and powdered milk in our breakfast bag. The jerky, salami, cheese, crackers, dried fruit mixes, fruit roll ups, granola, chocolate bars, candy, nuts, marshmallows and graham crackers went in our lunch and snack bag. Our third bag would contain our dried food meals of chili, beef stew, split pea soup, tuna casserole, curried chicken, plus three soup mixes, bags of brown rice, dried beans, salt, pepper and spices, flour and cornmeal. We'd first consume our perishables, the potatoes, cabbage, carrots, onions, oranges, apples, a couple homemade cookies, cucumbers, bacon, lettuce, milk, juice and a loaf of bread.

With our food bags figured out, our next task was to practice loading and unloading Romeo. Rosy circled Romeo, rubbing her hands over his back, checking for any tender spots.

Lydia scratched his forehead and swooned, "Romeo, oh, Romeo, how do I love thee?" She looked at Rosy, "See how he focuses on me?"

Rosy chuckled. "A mule's eyes are closer together than a horse's and that makes his blind spot smaller."

"Oh," Lydia replied sheepishly.

Rosy patted Romeo's butt before laying a thick pad on his back. "Packing a mule is so much easier than reaching over the back of a horse." Elle helped her hoist the wooden packsaddle frame on top of the pad. With their critical gaze, they made sure the packsaddle was squarely balanced. Rosy took the frayed leather pack strap, wrapped it around his body, then lifted his tail and snapped the croup to the buckle on the other side. She rubbed the front cinch latigo through her fingers, flattening it before threading it through a metal ring. She pulled the latigo until it was tight, then stepped back just in case our new mule was a kicker. Romeo brayed, turned his head toward Rosy, but did not kick. Using her shoulder, Rosy pushed hard against the packsaddle and it did not shift.

Ace slapped his thigh. "One thing everyone should know about a mule, is that you pull on a young mule's cinch until it starts to fart. With an old mule, you pull until it stops."

Lydia whispered in Romeo's ear, "Don't take that personally, sweetie."

Rosy and Elle lifted the well-worn canvas panniers and hooked them to the packsaddle. Using a half-inch rope, Rosy made a diamond hitch knot, secured the load and tucked each end into a corner. "Shouldn't move or flop around."

We used two of four tarps as liners inside the panniers and spread the other two on the ground. Our intent was to have two piles and divide our tents, horse supplies, camping gear and kitchen stuff into equal weights so both panniers would be balanced. Before leaving camp, we'd put our food bags on top for easy access.

"Not bad. Not bad at all," Rosy said, backing away, determining if Romeo's load was balanced. "All extra space will stow as many water containers as possible."

Elle saddled Bond and took Romeo's lead rope and they did a quick loop around camp. "That was easy," she said, handing Romeo's lead to Lydia.

Lydia gushed, "You are such a good boy."

We relieved Romeo of his burden and set the panniers on the ground. Then Rosy announced, "I think we're ready for our getaway."

"Almost," Ace said and handed Elle a .22 pistol. "You gals'll need a gun. It's a short barrel. Weighs less than a pound and has a range of about twenty-five feet." He gave her the holster and a box of ammunition.

Elle flipped open the cylinder to check if the pistol was loaded. Then asked, "Anybody ever shoot a gun?"

Kitty raised her trigger finger. "I have."

"Me, too." Rosy nodded.

Sal and Lydia vigorously shook their heads from side-to-side, and in perfect unison said, "Never."

"I sort of have," I said, remembering the day Mark decided I had to know how to protect myself and insisted I do a little target shooting. He'd set up several targets and was blown away when I hit the bull's-eye three times in a row. He said I had natural ability until I confessed that I was aiming at a different target.

Ace wrinkled his brow. "Here is the deal. To get this gun you all have to know how use it in case you need to protect each other." He led us across a wet, grassy meadow and unfolded a sheet of white paper with several concentric red circles shrinking gradually into the center. He tacked it onto a weathered wooden fence post and then paced back twenty feet. "It's pretty easy." He looked around, "Everyone must shoot it at least once."

Kitty took the pistol and held it with both hands, took aim and squeezed the trigger. After a thunderous report came a dull tick. Her bullet found its mark. Suddenly it became clear that Kitty could be deadly.

"See that?" Kitty smiled, handing the pistol to Elle.

Ace lifted up two thumbs, "Hot shot!"

Elle took aim. "Kaboom!" Another tick of hot metal sunk into the old post.

Ace clapped his hands. "That's two Annie Oakleys. Who's next?"

Rosy took a deep breath, stood tall, took aim and fired, but missed the target. "Guns were never my sport," she said, offering Sal the pistol.

Sal kept her hand down, refusing to hold the gun. "I tried shooting once. I couldn't hit the broad side of a barn."

Rosy pushed the pistol into her hand. "You will not stand in the way of us getting this gun." Without another word, Sal took aim, pulled the trigger and her hand recoiled as dirt jumped like a frog.

Lydia protested, "I'm not shooting that gun. I won't kill anything. Not ever."

Ace crossed his arms. "There's no way I can give you this gun unless everybody knows how to use it. That's the deal."

Sal shoved the .22 into Lydia's hand. "Ok," she said, "I won't stand in the way of us getting this weapon." Without really aiming she pulled the trigger. "Tick." Lydia broke out in a proud, sunny grin and handed me the gun.

"Here goes nothing," I said and took a deep breath. I surprised myself when my bullet hit inside an outer red circle.

"You've got yourself a gun," said Ace, clearly relieved we would not leave without firearm protection.

After profusely thanking Ace, Rosy announced, "We'll leave before dawn tomorrow." Nobody said anything, but an audible gasp came from Lydia. "I suggest everyone take this opportunity to chill out, rest up and get ready to hit the road."

Sal left to nap. Lydia gathered her pinecones and stashed them in my tack room. Rosy began dismantling camp. Elle picked up her fishing pole, and said, "I'm going fishing. Anyone care to join me?" Kitty and I grabbed our poles, put on our tennis shoes and followed Elle to where the French Creek bent and narrowed into a perfect V. Elle put a dry fly on her ultra-light fly rod, studied the current and evaluated the angles. Standing midstream, knee high in cold water, with a breeze keeping some flying creatures at bay, she cast her line and worked the rod from 10:00 to 2:00. The fly dragged out into the narrows and then, thoughtfully, she cast her line again.

With my left hand, I stripped line off my rod, let it run out, then steadily pulled it in, taking up the slack to make another smooth back cast. I brought the rod forward and set my fly down a few feet above a submerged log. Nothing happened. I cast again. The line went up and over my head, ran through my fingers and floated parallel to the bank. Suddenly my fly disappeared. Instantly I tightened my line and, without thinking, thrust the rod skywards and set the hook. A fish was on. I kept the line tight. The fish pulled, jumped, then suddenly my line went loose. I was left in awe at how hard a fish can pull and how quickly it can get itself off the hook.

Elle lifted a brown trout out of the water. It twisted and turned as she slowly pulled it in. "Looks big enough," she said, grabbing it securely. She removed the hook, and then in one quick motion rapped its head on a rock and tossed it onto the bank.

Downstream Kitty was angling for a hit. She looked so peaceful, as if one with the flow, watching water rush over rocks, gurgling and splashing as water creatures skimmed the surface. Funny how troubles can float away while fishing.

Our adventure ended with Elle landing two trout, me one and Kitty got skunked.

Elle sat down on the bank, flicked open her pocketknife and made a slit straight up one trout's belly and through its gills. She stuck two fingers into the cavity, pulled out its entrails, turned it over, slit the spine membrane and pushed blood out.

"That was slick," I said, watching her cleaning another trout. "How'd you learn how to do that?"

Cranking her neck, she looked at me while she washed blood off her hands. "My grandpa taught me to fish and hunt. Rest his sweet soul, I so loved him. He was a patient and kind and gentle soul."

Hiking back to camp, I felt sad realizing how much more I could have learned from my parents and grandparents. About who they were and how they lived. I remembered the old saying, something about youth being wasted on the young.

Back at camp, Rosy reached for our catch. "Look at that!" she said. "Fish for dinner." Our last supper was perfectly roasted, skewered trout with a carrot, lettuce and cucumber salad.

After we ate, Lucille and Ace joined us around our fire. Ace pleaded, "Promise you'll do everything in your power to stay safe. There could be dangerous folks out there."

"We'll do our best," Rosy vowed.

Lydia stood and placed her hands on her hips, "Why are we so fixated on running into bad people? Why can't we think about all those people that might help us?" She looked puzzled. "Just because people lost electricity doesn't mean they've turned into monsters. Don't you remember how many times disasters have brought out the best, not the worst, in people? There are lots of stories about neighbors sharing their resources and looking out for one another. People are basically good.

Families come together."

"Don't be naive," Rosy interjected. "Overnight our world changed. Remember our good neighbors that siphoned our precious gasoline?" She shook her head. "The less contact we have with people, the safer we will be. We stay out of sight, ride back roads and camp in isolated places." She put her hand on Kitty's shoulder. "And under no circumstances, can anyone join us, no matter how good looking. Period! No one else comes along."

Kitty threw her arms up. "Okay, okay, I get it."

At that moment Elle saw faint green aurora columns graciously drift together across the night sky. "It's back," she said.

Lydia screamed and darted straight to my truck. Although humble in comparison to the mother of all auroras and the solar flare that created a once-in-a-lifetime spectacular light show, I feared this one might pack another powerful punch.

After filling several plastic bags with our freshly made venison jerky, I crawled back into the safety of my truck shelter and lay on my cot for what might prove to be the last time. My head hurt with worry about making it home before we ran out of food. Would we find enough water? Can our horses make it? What about the millions and millions of people affected by the overwhelming aurora? How are people coping? Crazy with too many concerns, I found myself worried if my surge suppressor protected my computer. I almost laughed remembering the time I was washing dishes with my mother-in-law and we talked about what we'd do if our house was burning down. "God forbid," she said, and told me she would save her mother's china and grab her photo albums. I'd take my computer and run for my life.

Then I thought of how frightening it is that computers have come to control almost everything and dictate our lives. As a society we've put all our eggs in a digital technological basket. Without the universal Internet that bind us together, without that virtual glue, we as a people are untethered, homeless, orphaned. I tried to get control of my thinking, but random fears kept coming. What about old people in care facilities? People in hospitals? Would nurses and doctors be able to do their jobs? What about city people? What will everyone eat? Will banks be ransacked? Prisons unsecured? Prisoners on the loose? Military weapons? What about the nuclear warheads and the launch codes? Schools, stores and factories? Trains and planes? My God. "Stop," I shouted. "It's not the end of the world!"

Lydia bolted up. "Maia, what? What?"

"It's ok. I'm ok. I was having a meltdown," I said as I tried to catch my breath and calm myself down.

Lydia lay back down and sounded small when she said, "Maia, I think Rosy is making this situation even worse." She sniffled, "Why won't she even consider that good things just might happen to us? Where's her faith in humanity?"

"She's carrying a lot of weight," I said. "She feels responsible for everything and, more than anything, she wants us all to survive this journey."

"Look at how great Ace and Lucille have been," Lydia said. "I remember my grandparents talking about living through the Great Depression and how neighbors helped each other. I'm putting my faith in believing in the goodness of others." She blew her nose. "That's what I'm holding onto."

Chapter 10

Let's Ride

"Who, who cooks for you?" screeched a barred owl from an ambiguous perch, piercing my sleep. Crisp, cold morning air hit my lungs. My eyes popped open. Snug as a caterpillar embraced in a cocoon, I carefully rolled over in my sleeping bag, attempting to trap my warmth. Too soon, fear flooded back. All at once, I dreaded a future of unmerciful heat, relentless wind, lack of water and dangerous people.

It was dark when I buttoned my shirt, pulled on my riding pants and slipped my still-warm feet into cold boots. Lydia shifted on her cot. "Good morning," I mumbled. She said something I didn't understand, then quickly pulled her sleeping bag over her head. I barked, "Get up. It's time. We have to go."

Elle, our human bellows, was attempting to breathe life into last night's smoldering coals. A strand of hair fell over her eyes and broke her rhythm as the wind swirled erratically, making her task even more difficult. Then, like magic, her determination won out and orange flames licked the air. With one hand she steadied a hunk of wood, gripped her hatchet's worn leather grip and raised it up and, in a series of swift, rhythmic motions, chopped kindling.

"You ready for today?" I asked, watching her add splintered sticks to her enlivened fire.

She paused, sucked in a deep breath, lifted her chest, and inhaled the morning air. "Today, tomorrow, the next day and the next, until we make it home. We have no choice other than to take it one day at a time."

Kitty poured everyone a cup of coffee. Rosy rubbed her hands over the fire, then placed them on her cheeks. Pointing at a bucket of grain, she said,

"Give that to Justice. He needs it most."

Sal shuffled over in her flannel pajamas with her sleeping bag draped over her shoulders and sat down. "I'll have a three-egg cheese omelet, hash browns, a couple links and wheat toast with grape jelly."

"Get dressed!" Rosy growled. Sal stared at her sister. "Right now!" Sal spun around and left without saying another word. Rosy marched over to my truck and shouted, "Lydia, get your butt up right now." Morning light grew as we hovered together around the fire. "Finish your coffee, ladies. It's time we load up and move on." She softened her tone. "Come on, now. We can do this."

Elle jumped up, went to her slant load trailer, pushed her dividers to one side to make room for Romeo and then tied Rio and Bond short. With the path cleared, Romeo jumped into the trailer. When Justice spotted the grain bucket, he hopped in my trailer. Liberty followed eagerly.

Lydia refused to let go of Lucille when the time came to say goodbye. "I'll never forget your kindness and generosity," she said, finally breaking away.

Ace clasped Elle's hand tight and gave her a box of bullets. Elle choked up, fighting back tears. "You two have been so great."

Lucille blew Lydia a kiss. "You help take care of these brave cowgirls and keep an eye on that cute little mule." Lydia forced a smile.

Rosy stood next to her truck door. "Do not use your air conditioning. It reduces mileage. Remember: three short beeps is the signal for you to shut off your engines." She got in her cab, rolled down her window and commanded, "Let's do it!"

Lydia sat in the passenger seat, clutching her frilly pink satin pillow. "I'm afraid everything's gone crazy."

"You're not the only one," I said.

The little town of Hermosa was due east and we each had less than a third of a tank. Exiting the same road we enthusiastically entered days earlier, I prayed we'd be able to purchase more gas, even if it was sinfully, outrageously expensive.

Rounding a corner, three bighorn sheep with corkscrew horns traversed a steep, rocky slope. It was strangely comforting how they were oblivious to our human crisis. It was silent in the truck, each of us staring at the road. Halfway to Hermosa, we saw two men sitting on a front porch of a run-down ranch house and they followed us with their eyes. I waved, but only one waved back. "Looks like life goes on," I said, hopefully.

Lydia squeezed her pillow, "I think so, too," she said. "That was a good sign, right? People sitting on the porch watching the sunrise, waiting for electricity to come back on."

"It may be a long wait."

At Hermosa, Rosy pulled into the station we stopped at a lifetime earlier. A sign hung from the front door. "Nothing's left. Go away."

My prayers evaporated. Rosy honked three times and we pulled over.

Kitty jumped out the passenger side of Elle's truck and briskly walked to a middle-age man wearing greasy coveralls and a red baseball cap that was leaning against an industrial-sized garage door. As we followed her, we saw a dim work-light shining through a crack in the door and heard the hum of a generator. Kitty stopped less than a foot away from the man, squeezed her waist to exaggerate her curves and said, "We're heading home. We sure would appreciate if you could spare some gas."

"You and everybody else I reckon," he said, squinting through dirty glasses. "There's no gas anywhere, ma'am. Gas was gone the first day the lights went out. Damn regrettable mess, but what you gonna do?" He stuffed an oily rag into his back pocket then carefully nudged a pack of Camel straights from his breast pocket, slipped out a cigarette, tapped it on his black thumbnail, then wedged it between his cracked lips. "Phones, radios, televisions, computers, everything got zapped. Fires everywhere from those power surges. Lootin' and shootin' in Rapid City I heard." He reached into his hip pocket for a lighter. That's when we saw his handgun. He sucked hard on his Camel and exhaled a mouthful of smoke enveloping his face like fog. "A military truck out of Rapid City drove through yesterday broadcasting that everybody's supposed to stay put. Shelter in place, he called it. A state of emergency is in effect."

Rosy asked, "Anyone give any idea how long this will last?"

The man blew a smoke ring. "Nope. My guess is it won't be over any time soon."

Kitty ran her hand seductively along her neck, sliding her finger down her chest. "You sure you don't have any extra gas you'd consider trading?" She inched a finger inside her shirt. "We have cash."

He grinned, revealing a mouthful of brown teeth. "Sorry Ma'am. Can't do you like that. Wouldn't be right. We got no fuel to spare." He flicked ash from his lit cigarette. "Good try, though."

Kitty cocked her head. "You real sure?"

"Give you a piece of advice, ma'am. You better watch yer pretty self. This is a damn bad situation. People are doing desperate things 'cause they're scared they're gonna die before things get better. If I were you, I'd button my shirt and steer clear of strangers." He took another deep drag. "Good luck to ya," and turned away.

Rosy led our caravan out of town on a little-traveled backroad toward the west end of the Badlands. My fuel gauge was leaning towards empty when we turned onto a gravel road and a black buggy rumbled toward us at a fast trot. A woman dressed in black held the reins of a sorrel Quarter horse and averted her eyes as she hurried past. I watched her disappear in my side mirror in a cloud of dust.

When the road eventually forked north and south, Rosy flashed her left turn signal, stopped and again beeped three times. Sal climbed out of the truck and moseyed back to Elle. I got out of my truck and joined them. Rosy asked, "Which way, left or right?"

Elle opened our map, then threw up her arms as if needing divine guidance. "This intersection isn't shown on the map."

Sal stomped her foot and kicked up a little gravel storm. "We can't afford a wrong turn. We're almost outta gas. Will somebody make up their damn mind?" Watching her little tantrum was like witnessing a pimple about to pop.

"Don't be an ass, Sis!" Rosy yelled, climbing back into her cab. Sal got in and slammed her passenger door shut.

Drawing in a deep breath, I prayed Rosy would make the right choice. Worried if we were headed in the right direction, I was also concerned that the personal dramas could get us turned around and we'd get hopelessly lost. I put the truck in gear and followed.

Lydia pounded her fist on my dash. "What a bitch! Doesn't Sal ever think about anybody but herself?"

"She's too self-absorbed for that."

Lydia clung to her seat belt like it was an emergency parachute and confessed, "I'm getting really tired of her, Maia. We don't need any more of her negativity."

Minutes seemed like hours. Mile after mile, I dreaded the sputter and stutter of my truck's last gasp for gas. We passed weather-beaten buildings that years before could have been thriving ranches. My mood was lightened when we passed a row of fence posts capped with old cowboy boots, tall, short and flashy ones. A metal cattle guard spanned the roadway and caused my wheels to vibrate wildly. Our horse trailer lunged forward then jerked us backward.

Seeing cattle clustered around several wooden windbreaks, I said, "Looks like they've got food and water. Yup cattle are a good sign."

Topping the crest of a hill, the distant Badlands silhouettes looked like dragon's teeth. Below, a narrow green ribbon threaded through a seemingly endless tan world. My gas gauge registered empty. I could barely breathe, fearing I'd run out of gas in a few hundred feet. To conserve fuel, I shifted into neutral and coasted down a long hill. Reaching the bottom, the road leveled out. A mailbox stood at the entrance of a one-lane road near an old black and white railroad sign.

Rosy rolled down her window and pointed at the railroad tracks before pulling onto a flat grassy meadow. Elle and I followed and formed a wagon train circle near a stand of huge, gnarled cottonwoods. "Looks like the end of the road," I said, turning off my engine. The cool dawn had given way to the warm morning sun. We stood in silence, suffering from what felt like a 'What-do-we-do-now?' paralysis.

"Well, this is it," said Rosy, breaking our trance. "Let's check out those tracks." Our spirits were buoyed when we found the railbed contained new ballast that recently had been graded. "That'll make it a whole lot easier on our horses."

Elle snapped to, "Gotta check our horses."

Rosy stared at the nameless mailbox and peered down a narrow gravel road. "Maybe we could stash our rigs on private property?"

"Won't hurt to ask," I said.

Sal didn't look at anyone as she unloaded Thief and led him away. No one called after her.

Rosy saddled Catch and asked Elle to ride with her. Elle saddled Bond and slid the pistol into her fanny pack. Rosy took the cash and they rode off, carrying our hopes with them.

While Kitty and I ran a picket line between the trees, Lydia asked for help picketing Romeo. "No need," Kitty replied. "Ace said because mules crave companionship, Romeo has no desire to be left alone." She smiled at Lydia. "We're his herd now. He'll be totally loyal."

Sal led Thief back, tied him to the picket line, then busied herself gathering firewood.

Lydia gathered rocks and started constructing a fire ring. Cradling an armful of kindling, Sal suddenly dropped her load on the ground. "Not there," She snarled and pointed to her feet. "Our fire ring goes right here."

Lydia squatted down to pick up her rocks and muttered, "She's such a jerk."

Sal had come up from behind and heard Lydia and reached out, pushed her shoulder and snarled, "You want to say that to my face?"

"Sure," Lydia said, dropping her stones, barely missing Sal's feet. She shoved her face into Sal's. "You are the most self-centered, insensitive female I've ever met. You are a real bitch." Then punched Sal's shoulder.

"Oh no," I thought to myself, fearing Sal would whoop Lydia's ass.

Sal grabbed Lydia's wrist, twisted it, forcing her to spin around, then pinned her arm behind her back. Sal hissed, "When me and Rosy were kids—Rosy was the sweet one, I was the brat—I damn near broke her wrist one time when I did this." Sal tightened her hold. "All right, little miss princess, now's your turn to kiss my ass."

Lydia reacted fast and somehow twisted free. She reached up, grabbed a handful of Sal's hair, and pulled so hard that Sal lost her balance. They both fell onto the ground. Lydia scrambled like a high school wrestler, wrangled Sal onto her back, and then flipped her over, grabbed her arms and forced Sal's face into the ground. Sal wiggled, twisted and screeched, but Lydia kept diggin' in deeper. "You bitch," Lydia growled, breathless, shedding more of her princess veneer.

When I couldn't stand it anymore, I grabbed Lydia and pulled her away. "That's enough," I barked, holding her tight. "You two are acting like spoiled rotten kids."

Sal yelled, "She started it."

Lydia trembled and started to bawl. "I want this nightmare to be over."

"We all want that, Lydia," I said, relaxing my hold. Our eyes locked. "You got in a fight, little sister. I didn't know you had it in you."

"Me neither," she sniffed, her face smeared with dust and tears.

Sal didn't say anything, got up and stormed away.

Kitty came closer. "That was somethin', Lydia, but there's somethin' you need to know about Sal." In hushed tones, she told us that Sal had been in alcohol treatment three times. "The last time she went cold turkey and completely freaked out. Just like this. Rosy told me she's terrified of having to go through all that again."

"I never knew her drinking was that serious," I said.

"That explains why she is such a thoughtless bitch," Lydia said, watching Sal walk toward the tracks. "Why didn't you say something sooner?"

"Loyalty, I guess," Kitty said, softly.

We picked up Lydia's stones and piled them where Sal wanted. I twisted handfuls of dry grass into spirals to start a fire. Careful to use only one match, I cupped my hands around the flame and was relieved when the grass lit and the fire took hold. We heated up our leftover venison, carrot and potato stew.

Our watchdog horses whinnied, signaling us Rosy and Elle were returning. "Well, we got the right place to stash our vehicles," Rosy said, dismounting.

Kitty held Bond's reins while Elle loosened his cinch. "Reed and Kelly live about a mile down the road. They're a great couple. Reed thought a hundred dollars a month per rig was a great deal, so we gave them six hundred for two months. We trust that our rigs'll be totally safe there." She hooked her hat on her saddle horn. "One less thing to worry about. God-willing, by November this'll be history and we'll come back and retrieve our rigs."

"What did Reed and Kelly know about the aurora?" I asked.

"Reed said a friend rode his motorcycle over from the Ellsworth Air Force base in Rapid City. He warned them about the state of emergency and said there'd been something like an enormous earthquake on the sun that overwhelmed the earth's magnetic field and seriously damaged sections of the electric grid."

"Sweet Jesus," I said. "Did you get any idea how long it will take to get the grid up and running again?"

Elle looked away and swallowed hard. "Who knows? Months probably. He said there've been reports of big power surges in the cities, powerplants exploded, substation fires, transmission lines burned."

Rosy leaned against Catch. "Dealing with the infrastructure damage will be complicated and take time. Reed said it was possible that some satellite systems were protected by a warning system that triggered them to shut down ahead of the solar flare that could've prevented some major damage."

"That sounds positive." I said. "So it's possible some of the world could be working?"

"It's possible, but Reed didn't know any specifics," Rosy replied. "His real warning was that the military is in control and martial law's been declared." She looked at each one of us. "He stressed that no one is allowed to move around."

"Well, we're not the only ones breaking the law," Elle countered. "I'd bet there are lots of people wandering around, trying to get home. What we know is that we've got to stay alert and out of sight."

Rosy looked around. "Where's Sal?"

"Not happy," Kitty said, then paused. "She freaked out and got into a cat fight with the princess. It was stupid. It was over where we should build a fire ring," Kitty looked at Lydia, "The fight ended with our princess pinning your sister's ears back."

Rosy squinted at Lydia, "What?"

Lydia blurted, "I don't know what got into me. Guess I saw red."

Kitty shook her head. "I haven't seen females tangle like that since my mom got into it with one of Dad's girlfriends."

All heads turned when Sal reappeared and headed straight to Lydia. I held my breath until Sal crumpled on the ground and dropped her head in her own lap. "I'm sorry," she choked. "This is too fucking hard. I'm so sorry."

Lydia laid her hand on Sal's head. "We both got crazy, Sal. This situation is way too intense. I can't stand it either. I can't scream loud enough or cry hard enough to express how I feel. I'm sorry I didn't know you were dealing with a whole other issue."

"Anger is sometimes the easiest way for fear to come out," Rosy said, helping her sister stand.

Kitty stirred the pot of stew, ladled a bowlful and handed it to Sal. "This should help you feel better." Then said. "Remember you have five girlfriends on your team."

Sal accepted the bowl but kept her head down as she thanked everybody.

Elle gulped, "There's more." She choked, "Sorry to say. It's not good. Reed said the White River is more like liquid cement and its not drinkable."

I stiffened. Another bomb dropped. "That was our water source!"

Sal lifted her head up, "What are you saying?"

Shocked, looking betrayed, Lydia asked, "Does that mean we turn around and go back to Ace and Lucille?"

"No," Rosy snapped back.

My heart raced. "I need you to explain this."

Elle went on, "According to Reed, the White comes northward into South Dakota from Nebraska and as it passes through the Badlands it picks up eroded sand, clay and volcanic ash making it a dirty, chalky white goo. The closer it gets to the Missouri, depending upon rainfall, it can get cleaner. He tried to comfort us by saying that there's water in the Badlands and the best way to find it is to look for green. Grazing cattle let you know water's nearby. Watch for metal stock tanks that glisten in the sun. In some places ground water is not far down. There are lowland ponds that have pipes that bring up fairly clean water. Kelly suggested that when we find water, we should cover our buckets with cloth, pour the water over and give it some time for the crud to settle out before using our purifiers to filter it."

Lydia asked, "So we're still heading home?"

"There's no other choice," Rosy answered, gathering our bowls and stacking them together. "It's time we put everything we're not taking in our trucks. We'll drive to Reed and Kelly's and shed our trucks and trailers."

I saddled Liberty and put her in my trailer to ride back and save my old boy Justice a few miles. Justice carried on when his best buddy Liberty disappeared into my trailer. When I got in my truck cab, I saw Lydia's red hat, her yellow rhinestone satchel and frilly pink satin pillow on the passenger seat. Her flashy red boots were purposely propped up on the truck floor. I followed Elle and Rosy down the one-lane road. A border collie and a German shepherd ran along the side ditch, their tails whipping the air. A tall man I took to be Reed stood next to an old gray barn. He pointed to a flat spot by another outbuilding and signaled for us to park parallel to each other. After we parked, we unloaded our mounts, locked our doors and handed him our keys.

"Everything will be safe here," he said, slipping the keys in his pocket.

A woman wearing a yellow dress was hanging out clothes in the side yard of a two-story home that had tall windows and an expansive wrap-around porch. She bent down and picked up a large bag and came toward us, her black ponytail swishing left, then right. "Hi, I'm Kelly," she smiled. "So you gals are riding horses back to Minnesota?" She shook her head. "You are brave at a time like this."

"It's our only option," Rosy replied.

She presented Rosy with a bag of apples. "Just picked. Aren't perfect but they'll taste pretty darn good as you make your way across that hot desert." She held a hand in front of her face, attempting to block the sun. "That sun's a killer. Some days it's so hot, it feels like my skin's turning to leather and by nightfall, it's so dang cold we have to fire up our woodstove. This is a land of extremes. Weather around here can change real fast, so be ready."

Reed leaned against the hitching post and stroked Liberty's forehead. He cautioned, "Say all of a sudden it starts to rain like hell, or you need protection from the sun, check out train trestles, but beware, rattlers, porcupines and other critters, like shelter too. Right now, rattlers are shedding. They're in their blind stage. A scared snake'll coil up and strike at just about anything." He wrinkled his brow, "I hope you've got a gun."

"A .22 pistol," Elle replied.

"Ain't much, but a .22's better than nothin." He rolled his eyes. "We've got some pretty nasty critters and plenty of rough characters around these parts."

"That's true," said Kelly. "But it is also true that most of the people around these parts are good folks that know how to take care of themselves." She locked eyes with Reed. "Ranchers have fuel storage tanks, just like us. If we're careful, the fuel we've got should keep our generators working for weeks, maybe even months. Some ranchers have wind turbines and solar panels and live off-grid."

Reed suggested we consider riding the old stagecoach trail that lies east of the village of Interior. "It might be easier than following the White River." Then he warned us, "Another thing that holds true around here, is that most people don't care much for strangers." He shook his pointer finger for emphasis. "Play it smart when you run into folks. Do what you did with us: tell them who you are, what you're doing and make it crystal clear you are not a threat." Reed crouched down to pet his dogs and I felt a pang of loneliness for my dog, Will. I stood tall and fought the urge to cuddle his furry pals, and told myself not to think about home.

Rosy drank everything in, then said, "We'll be careful. Promise. We'll return as soon as we can." She settled in her saddle, waved goodbye, pointed down the road and then said, "Let's ride!"

Trotting away, I looked back and remembered the day Mark and I bought our trailer. Mom and Dad were about to move into an assisted living home, and Dad begged us to bring our horses so his grandkids could ride on his land one last time. Mark called the Featherlite Company factory, and the salesman said he'd give us a good price on a two-horse slant, bumper-pull that had a nice-sized tack room. The first time I saw it, it took my breath away. I gasped at the Minnesota Vikings purple striped sides and purple roof. Even the hitch was purple. Mark thought it looked like a whore house and wondered if our horses would even load into such a gaudy space. After we wrote the check, we laughed all the way home thinking about how easy it would be to find our trailer at our county fair.

Rosy raised her arm and I snapped out of my reverie. We broke into a full canter and Liberty came alive. Not only we were eager to return to the others, it was a way to release tension.

Back at camp I tied Liberty to the picket line and gave Justice his last bowl of grain. He performed his usual: ears back and thrusting his head forward, displaying the curse of getting old and food greedy. I laid my head on his warm neck, drew in his smell and remembered Mark always saying that the scent of a horse was very expensive perfume. I sucked in a deep breath and as I exhaled I tried try best to push thoughts of home out of my mind.

Chapter 11

Water is Life

"No bitchiness. No cat fights. Period." Rosy waved her arms as if holding an imaginary baton in her hand, conducting her personal orchestra. Her eyes cut to Sal, then darted to Lydia, me, Kitty, then Elle, her right-hand gal. "We are a tribe. Each one of us must maintain a positive attitude."

Sal placed three fingers on her forehead in a mock girl-scout salute and croaked. "I'll try. Really, I will. I promise."

Kitty tossed a wet stick on the fire creating little smoke cyclones that spiraled up.

Lydia whimpered, "I'm still scared. I don't know if I've got what it takes."

"Get it together, Lydia," Rosy said using her trail boss voice, sounding like a politician speaking through a bullhorn on the courthouse steps. "We are all scared." She drew in a deep, long breath. "Our decision to ride home was unanimous. We decided to take control of our destiny and not become victims." Rosy pointed her baton eastward. "Our way home is on horseback."

Lydia unfolded a fresh tissue and pressed it against her eyes. "I know. I know."

Rosy stirred the dying fire with a stick, separating the coals to help it go out. "Time to pack up."

I'd just secured my cot behind my saddle when Rosy came over. "Leave it," she demanded.

"Leave it here? Rosy, I need it." I lifted my elbows over my head, then swiftly yanked them down to my side. "These old bones cannot endure sleeping on hard ground."

"You are not taking your cot and that is final. I don't give a dang about your age. Shoot, I'm almost as old as you. Maia, you are not special, not this time. We all sleep on hard ground!" Rosy glared at me. "Plus, you can't afford that use of space on Justice and he doesn't need to carry any extra weight."

I glared back at her, defeated, I sighed, "Fine," knowing I'd lost the showdown. I unloaded my cot and laid it next to Sal's fire ring.

Ignoring my dramatic concession, Rosy circled Romeo, carefully evaluating whether or not his panniers were properly balanced. "A difference of a few pounds from one side to his other could throw off his load. If he gets a sore back, we'll be in an awful fix."

Selfishly I wished Rosy cared that much about my back. Fear surged though me as I lifted my body up onto my saddle. I understood how Lydia felt. I, too, was fearful of not being up to the journey. I stroked Justice's mane and neck and with as much brevity as I could muster, I bent down and whispered in his ear. "Old boy, we're about to have the experience of our lives."

Rosy adjusted Catch's reins, sat back, looked ahead and ordered, "Let's do this."

I pushed my hips forward and made a clucking sound to urge Justice on. Our departure was simple. No trumpets blared. No flags waved. Nobody looked back. We all fell in line on a relatively smooth railroad bed and entered uncharted territory.

"Can we trot?" Lydia asked.

Rosy shot back, "No! That would jostle Romeo's packs. Trotting could cause his load to slip, and if he got off balance he could get hurt. Then what would we do?"

"Got it," said Lydia.

Behind us was a landscape of tall trees and abundant water. Ahead was a desolate wasteland of pink, beige, gray and brown sand, gravel, volcanic ash and formations embedded with fossilized remains of a long-gone inland sea. Layer upon layer of mudflows created formations as voracious winds and rain perpetually gnawed and reshaped this earth. This was a silent place. No people. No buildings. A place without sharp edges. A majestic, breathtaking, expansive land of freedom that lifted the eye upward. An unfenced openness. Somehow the Badlands felt feminine. It was like an unveiling of the senses.

I soon became mesmerized, lost in a meditative state, listening to the puck-pock, puck-pock, one-two of our horse hooves hitting the hard ground, beating time like a human heart.

The constant shifting of colors reminded me of the time Mark and I ventured down into the Grand Canyon for a week-long pack trip. The Grand Canyon is a gigantic hole full of colorful rocks where light continuously changes. Being in the canyon was like being inside of a kaleidoscope. Shadows danced and rocks changed shape as our trusty mules hauled us up and down steep rocky trails. Our guide told us about a new trail spur, built after two riders had been struck dead by lightning on the old trail. Their bodies had been recovered, but the horses and all their tack was left where it fell. He said it was easier to build another spur than to deal with their spirits.

Overhead, turkey vultures soared gracefully, lifting on updrafts with their heads angled down, ready to delve their featherless red heads into any available foul-smelling, decomposing flesh.

"They're eyeballing us," said Sal.

"Their job is to clean up the dead. They're not interested in you," said Rosy. "You're too tough."

"That's right," Sal smiled. "I'm a tough old buzzard."

"Me too," said Lydia, flexing an arm muscle.

With the hot sun beating upon our backs, the ever-present wind came in bursts, sometimes in gusts, and the surges helped cool us down. It moved the grasses, passed through vegetation, pushed clouds around and, at times carried the strength of a woman done wrong.

Sweat dripped from under my hat and trickled down my face. When Sal wiped her face, she smeared the fine dust into what looked an ochre tattoo. "This is no fun."

Kitty winked at her, "Oh, hell, unbutton your shirt, Sal. Live dangerously. Let some air in."

"Yeah, instead of always letting it out," Rosy chuckled.

Sal, her mood once again prickly, countered, "Buzz off, Sis."

When the smooth railbed ended, deep ballast ruts forced us to traverse from side to side. We maneuvered around high steel rails and ragged wooden ties that for decades resided on the ground and still exuded the smell of creosote.

An engine somewhere to our south caught everyone's attention. Elle lifted her binoculars and scanned the horizon. She pointed, "It's a friggin' motorcycle hightailing down that north-facing escarpment."

"Best we get out of sight," Rosy said heading toward a spindly clump of trees crowning the northern slope. We waited under shadows in gloriously cool shade.

"Maybe Earl's coming to rescue me," Sal said. "Not."

"A motorcycle would be a fast way to get home," I said, pensively. When the rumbling biker turned west, we eased our herd back up the embankment.

Ahead, a thread of mirage-like green wound through a sea of beige. Relief! Green equals water. Our horses spread out along the tiny little stream and satisfied their thirst. Kitty and Elle filtered water and refilled all our containers.

"Water is life. Water is life," I kept repeating over and over.

Kitty took her hat off, reached down and used it to scoop up water, then plopped her hat back on her head. Without any hesitation, everyone followed her lead. A palpable "Ahh" filled the air, as us horsewomen cooled off.

"Water is life," I said aloud, feeling rejuvenated.

Just as Sal left to duck behind a sand hill to relieve her bladder, Rosy reminded her, "Watch out for rattlers." Finding my own bathroom, a light breeze lifted a whiff of my body odor into my nostrils, and I yearned for my bathtub, for a long, long soak, for scented candles and all the comforts of home.

On a nearby grassy mound, a black-tailed prairie dog rested on its back legs, its nose straight up, ears twitching, black eyes bulging, issuing a series of sharp, chirping barks, then sniffing the air before--in a flash!--disappearing in its burrow. Seconds later, it peeked out.

"Too cute," Lydia cooed.

"Cute?" Sal growled. "They're like rats."

"In the Lakota language, they are called *pispiza*," I said, "They're considered a respected relative that know about plants and medicine. To some, *Pispiza* are healers of the land."

More prairie dogs emerged from their burrows, stretched, groomed themselves, then groomed each other. They crouched up and presented their rear ends to each other before turning and kissing. Two *Pispiza*, tails twitching with excitement, tangled, biting and kicking like Sal and Lydia. As quickly as the fight began, it stopped. Whatever their differences, they let them go and stood next to each other nibbling clumps of grass.

Rosy winked at Sal. "We could all learn from those little rascals."

"Healers," said Sal, bending at her waist, wrapping one arm around her middle, sweeping the other arm with a flourish. "Touché, Sis. Consider me healed."

"A healthy prairie depends, in part, on a vibrant prairie dog community," I said. "They've been systematically poisoned for at least a hundred and fifty years and their population has been cut in half. Plenty of folks still use prairie dogs for target practice." I shook my head, "Senseless killing makes my gut ache."

Lydia stared at the little dogs, "I don't understand it."

"Me either," I said.

Refreshed, we saddled up and skirted the stream until it dipped down into a deep ravine that carried it beneath a railroad trestle. Slowly we maneuvered the horses down a bank of loose stones, knowing they couldn't cross the trestle bridge. At the bottom, Justice pawed the way he does when he's fixing to take a bath.

"No!" I yelled, forcing my heels into his ribs, discouraging him from rolling.

Climbing up the other side of the bank, Liberty braced, hopped to the right and attempted to back down. "You piss-ant," said Lydia, shortening her reins and holding firm until backing down was no longer Liberty's main concern.

Romeo's panniers shifted as he climbed the embankment. Stopping at the top, Rosy and Elle rebalanced his cargo. Lydia planted a kiss on his muzzle. "Do you think that maybe, that sometime, I could ride him?"

Rosy smiled, "When we get home, we'll see if we can make that work." She touched her index finger to her lips, turned and said, "Our princess has fallen in love with an ass."

Not the first one she's fallen for, I thought.

On a game trail, heading back to the railroad bed, Romeo skillfully protected his load from wiry branches and downed trees.

"Smart boy," Rosy smiled.

A high-pitched screech came out of an old cottonwood snag, then came the heavy sound of wings flapping. A heartbeat later, a golden eagle dove low, then quickly climbed, effortlessly heading downstream.

"It's leading the way," I said. How appropriate. Eagles are high flying, two-legged brave creatures that symbolize looking ahead, not back. For many people they represent a connection to the Creator and truthfulness.

The moment the little stream turned toward Interstate 90, some twenty to thirty miles to our north, and the railroad went east, we knew water would have to come from unknown sources.

Rosy checked her watch. "Almost six." The blazing red sun was about to dive under a purple blanket when we dismounted to walk alongside our horses.

Sal howled when her feet hit the ground, her knees buckled, and she fell. "I'm not taking another step. Enough is enough. Sis, please, call it a day."

Rosy helped her up. "You gonna be ok?"

"Not if we don't stop right now."

"You're right," Rosy said, "We'll camp here."

I could have kissed her. Kitty actually did. Lydia let out a whoop and began to free Romeo of his load. A raw, nickel-sized fleshy wound was on his spine. She gasped, "This is bad, isn't it Rosy?"

"Yes, dear. Get the salve. We've gotta take good care of your beau; he's our ticket home. Before we pack up tomorrow, we'll cut away some of the felt on his saddle pad to take pressure off his wound."

In order to wake up at first light, we pitched our tents facing east. After hobbling our horses, we laid out our blanket and balanced our saddles on their horns to they could serve as our armchairs. Sitting in a circle, we leaned against the hairy undersides, ate leftover stew and listened to our shuffling herd while watching the silver crescent moon rise in a ceiling of stars.

Elle asked, "How many miles do you think we did today?"

"Got a late start. I reckon maybe twenty," Rosy said, looking tired, physically and emotionally, yet relieved we'd gotten through our first day. "We'll do more tomorrow." She scraped her bowl clean with a finger, then popped her finger in her mouth. "We drove about eighty and rode another fifteen, so maybe twenty, about a sixth of our way home."

Sal rubbed her knees. "Is this a pep talk?"

"Yep," Elle said, stretching her legs out. "Ladies, we are astounding. It was a good day!"

Lydia picked up a tiny flower that glowed white on the barren ground. "How do flowers live here?"

"How does anything live here?" Sal grumbled. "This is hell. We could die of thirst and, sister of mine, what would you do with a dead body?" Her agitation grew. "What if someone steps on a rattler? What if one of us gets bit by a black widow or recluse spider? What happens then?" Her voice quivered, "Rosy, I really need a drink!"

"Not gonna happen, Sis," Rosy said.

"You can get through this," Elle said, "None of us can let our fears control us."

"You'll make it." Rosy said, picking up a stick and snapped it into six pieces, three short and three long sticks, then held the tops so they looked even. "This being our first night, I say we take turns keeping watch over our herd. Long sticks pull first guard tonight, and whoever's up keeps the pistol."

Rosy got the first shift, Kitty second and I won third.

Lydia and Kitty crawled into our tent, each claiming a side, leaving me sandwiched between them. The hard earth pushed against every contour of my body and I longed for my comfortable cot.

Dead to the world, I shot up when Kitty shook my foot. "Your turn. All's well."

As I sat up, my hips hurt. Without waking Lydia, I crawled on my knees and emerged out our tent into the dark cave of night. I switched my flashlight on to check for rattlers and accidentally caught Justice's eye. He turned his head away as if to say, "Let me sleep."

Resting back in my saddle armchair, I felt comforted by the quiet. I spotted the Big Dipper hanging crooked in the northern sky. Peering into the darkness, I searched for the Milky Way, but clouds kept me from admiring the spinning galaxies and solar systems. A coyote yipped, and from the opposite direction came a string of long, moaning howls. All around, coyote packs responded. Alone. Peaceful under a magic sky, I felt the intensity and great power of this seemingly desolate place.

I like people. I like being around people. But I recharge my batteries best alone. I'm like the horse that stands alone in the pasture a little distant from the rest of the herd. At times, constantly being around people has been challenging. I remembered a conversation I had with my friend Nancy before coming on this ride. I said I was going with five other women. Nancy blanched, "Is it a vacation or a group encounter?" I heard her say, "Are you crazy, Maia? Don't do it." If only I had heeded her warning, she would have saved me from this disaster. My mind wandered to Mark, the kids, our families and the suffering of others. I had to keep telling myself, "You're here. Don't go there."

Darkness was about to surrender to light when I heard Romeo's loud, jarring, foghorn brays. With each in and out breath he got louder and more intense. Then came the unmistakable sound of kicking, and everyone dashed out of their tents and sprinted towards him. His back legs were aimed square at Rio's rear end.

Rosy grabbed his halter and pulled him away, yelling, "Anybody hurt?"

"Don't think so," Kitty replied, taking control of Rio as he snorted and pawed the ground. Quickly they examined Rio's and Romeo's legs and breathed sighs of relief finding neither one seemed to be hurt.

"Holy Jesus!" Kitty pointed at fresh red blood coloring the desert floor. A rattlesnake had contorted into a ball and we stood and watched as it became lifeless. "They weren't kicking at each other. They were acting as a team." Kitty pushed her head into Rio's shoulder, "It's comforting to know we've got two snake killers."

Lydia was walking over to see the snake when Elle said, "Don't go near it. Don't touch it!"

"But it's dead," she said.

"Yes and no," Elle said. "It sounds crazy, but I read an article in the Smithsonian magazine that a dead rattlesnake's head can be just as dangerous as when it was alive. Its head can maintain the bite reflexes for hours after death because its nervous system can respond to stimulus without needing the brain to send a signal." As she talked, one by one we backed up and left the snake alone. She continued, "The article told about a guy in Texas who decapitated a snake with his shovel and minutes later he bent down, picked up the severed head and it bit him. The guy almost died."

"Good to know," I said.

As we packed up, a black and white bird with long iridescent tail feathers reflecting the bronze-green of morning light landed nearby, pecked the ground and squawked, "Maag, maag."

"What in God's name are you doing in this remote place?" Kitty asked the bird.

Sal imitated a southern drawl. "Tryin' to stay alive, Miss Kitty. Just like the rest of us."

Lydia smiled, "Our first visitor was a snake and now we see this beautiful bird."

"Magpies are not only pretty, they're smart and crafty, like crows," said Elle. At that exact moment the bird raised its head and looked at her as if acknowledging her compliment.

As we moved on, dawn backlit the dark Badland peaks and, for a moment, they looked like sentinels or a choir of coyotes locked, frozen in a howling stance. Lydia rambled on about how she believed that God was right beside us.

"Love ya, Lydia, but you are delusional," said Sal. "You and your God shit. Face it, there is no God and no life after death. I hate to be the one to tell you but there's nothing more. Nada. When we die, it's lights out." She raised her voice, "Forever."

"Chill out, Sis," snapped Rosy. "Don't start. Lydia's entitled to believe whatever she wants. Everyone's entitled to search for themselves."

"Search for what?" grumbled Sal.

"For answers, Sal. To find peace inside."

"Peace inside?" Sal said, snidely. "What kind of new-age bullshit is that?"

Lydia smiled at her, "You'll know it when you find it."

Elle pointed at black dots on a khaki hillside. "Remember what Reed said? 'Cattle means water.' It's likely a pond is somewhere nearby."

Two strands of barbed wire blocked our way. Rosy and Elle dismounted and laid the wire down. Our thirsty critters wasted no time getting to a small reservoir hidden behind an earthen dam that spanned a shallow draw not yet eroded into the ravine. Lack of rainfall was evident in the rings of dried, cracked brown mud surrounding the cloudy, greenish water. Elle rubbed the pondwater between her fingers. "We'd be insane to try to filter this enough that we could drink it." She wiped her hands on her pants. "I'm not willing to risk it."

With the horse's thirst satisfied we re-attached the barbed wires. The temperature was dropping quickly as dark clouds consumed the western front. A flush of birds rose. Wind whipped. A storm was brewing. Grit filled the air. We pulled our bandannas up over our noses and looked like bandits in an old western movie. Within minutes what began as a sweet rain intensified, and the ground turned into slippery grease that made walking impossible. Gunk, like chewing gum, clung to our horse's hooves.

"This is damn dangerous," yelled Rosy. "Somebody's gonna get hurt." Her words no more than left her mouth when Justice's right front knee buckled, and he veered sideways. Luckily, he caught himself before slipping and suffering a leg injury. Dismounting, we stepped down into sticky goo that covered our boots. Rain slammed our backs and poured off our hats as we covered our saddles with black plastic bags. Elle grabbed the bucket from Romeo's pannier as everyone scurried for protection behind a hundred-foot-high table rock, pyramid-like formation. Unfolding our space blanket, we each held a corner intending to divert the downpour into our bucket. The horses stood, butts facing the driving rain. The clouds gradually receded and shafts of sunlight broke through. "That was intense," I said, as we drank the rainwater and watched our horses drain the puddles dry.

Rosy lifted Catch's right front hoof and attempted to chisel the gunk-cement with her pick. "This is some awful shit," she complained.

Kitty attempted to pull clumps of matted horsehair out of Rio's long black tail. "I should just cut his tail."

Elle dug through the first aid kit for our scissors. "Do it," she said, handing Kitty the scissors.

Three cuts later, Rio's tail was shortened by half. Kitty backed away to assess the results. "That's better," she said, holding up the scissors. "Now do me."

Rosy cocked her head, "Seriously?"

Kitty wove her fingers through her black curly locks. "I'd rather have short dirty hair than this god-awful stinky mop."

Lydia snatched the scissors out of Kitty's hand. "I'll do it. How short do you want it?"

Kitty held two fingers an inch apart. "Butch. Always wanted one."

Lydia and Kitty spread a tarp on the ground. Kitty wiggled around until she got comfortable. Lydia primped and snipped and combed with her fingers as Kitty's curls fell.

"You look like a boy," Sal snickered.

Kitty fluffed her new do. "Part of me always wanted to be a guy."

Lydia wrinkled her brow. "You'd like facial hair?"

Kitty stroked her cheeks where a beard would grow. "Protection from the elements."

"Ick!" Lydia looked like she'd just sucked a dill pickle. "What an awful thought. I can't imagine growing a dirt collector on my face."

"Beards hide wrinkles," I said.

"Spare me," Lydia groaned.

Elle waved the scissors around. "Who's next?"

I raised my hand. "My turn. But if you don't mind, I'd like Rosy to do the deed."

Rosy coughed, "Me?"

"Yes, you. You've been grooming horses for the show ring for how many years? You're not afraid to clip an old palomino mare, are you?"

"Gimme those scissors." Rosy said, then wove her fingers through my blondish hair. "How short?"

"Really short, but with style."

Lydia, our self-appointed stylist, moved in to get a closer look. "Give her a shag with bangs."

"Shag with bangs coming up," Rosy announced like a short order cook at 2 a.m. "Get your butt over here, Maia."

Rosy's blades were sharp and her cuts swift. My gray roots quickly took center stage as my blond hair topped Kitty's pile of black. With a sweeping hand gesture, I shooed imagined locks over my shoulders.

"Up for another?" Elle said, kneeling in front of Rosy. "Do mine like Kitty's."

Again, the clicking scissors went to work. Elle's blond hair topped my contribution. When Rosy finished, Elle rubbed her head. "Oh, that feels so much better." She stood up, "Thanks, Rosy. Salons were never my style."

"I guess I'm up," said Lydia. "I'll do my own. Maia, please hold the mirror." At first, Lydia carefully guided the blades into her shoulder-length red hair, but then, acting as if possessed, she started to snip and shear with wild abandon. When finished, Lydia reminded me of a grayish brown thistle with prickly red ends.

Kitty shimmied her shoulders. "Sister, you look like a rock star."

Lydia dug into her fanny pack for lipstick, painted her mouth, rubbed her lips together, looked in the mirror and kissed her reflection. "I like it."

"Well, hells-bells. My turn," said Rosy, positioning herself cross-legged in front of Lydia who went to work without saying a word. When the deed was done, Lydia offered Rosy the mirror, but Rosy declined, slipped her hat on and placed her hand on Sal's shoulder. "Remember when you were little, and I cut your hair?"

Sal jerked away from her touch. "Mom cried when she saw how bad you butchered me."

Rosy squeezed Sal's shoulder. "Promise I'll do better this time. Everybody else's done it, and everybody else is glad they got clipped."

Sal covered her eyes and clamped her mouth shut. Rosy wasted no time culling her sister's hair. When finished, Sal looked at her image. "If we get rescued tomorrow, I will be so pissed." Her face reddened. "Wait, I didn't mean that."

Rosy chuckled, "Now, that was funny."

Sal pulled her hat over her eyes. "People will think we're a gang of dykes."

"I, for one, don't give a damn what people think," Kitty said.

"Who cares, anyway?" Elle replied. "News flash, Sal. We're alone in the middle of nowhere."

Slowly I surveyed my pals. No question, we did look different, but hair was secondary. We looked stronger, better defined. Then again, maybe it was just that our heads looked bigger.

"Well, it's time we finish clippin' our horses' tails." Elle said, taking the scissors to our horses as they grazed on the dominant perennial short grasses. When the last tail was trimmed, I tossed the black, red, brown and Goldie-locks mix of hair like a salad into a blended clump. "Birds will love this nesting material."

"Quiet," Elle said, turning her focus to the south. "I hear bellowing."

"Oh geez," Sal said, "Don't tell me we've got more buffalo."

"Sounds like cattle," said Rosy.

Kitty hopped on Rio and rode up the nearest rise. Returning she said, "A cowpuncher's pushing a cattle herd." She smiled. "I'll bet that dude would know where we could find water."

"Do we risk it?" Rosy asked, her face tight with uncertainty. Exhaling a deep breath, she nodded, "It's worth the risk." Then asked, "Only one person?"

"I only saw one," Kitty said, stepping off Rio.

Elle looked at Rosy, "We do need to replenish our water supply and our horses are getting thirsty. If it's okay with you, I'll ride over."

"I'll ride with you, Elle," I said, quickly.

Nearing the herd, I flashed back to our riding through the herd of buffalo at French Creek. I stroked Justice's mane and reminded him of how magnificent he'd been maneuvering through those big scary beasts.

Two border collies headed straight toward us until the cow puncher whistled. Immediately, they crouched down. We slowed our pace as we rode toward the lone rider. As we approached, we saw that the cowboy was female. My jaw dropped. He was a cowgirl. She gestured a hello by touching the brim of her hat, but her right hand never moved off of the scabbard strapped by her thigh. Lifting my hat to say hello, I was embarrassed by my short hair.

The woman was small like Kitty and seemed powerful. She wore a blue denim shirt and faded jeans. She had weathered dark skin and brown hands. Her eyes squinted in the sunlight. Her stocky gray quarter horse had a short back and a thick muscled hind end and shoulder.

"We're just passing through on our way home to southeastern Minnesota. We need to find water for our horses," said Elle. "Can you tell us where we can find some?"

She pointed south. "You'll find a water tank at the bottom of that hill a couple of miles from here." After an uncomfortably long silence, she asked, "Just the two of you?"

"We're six women, six horses and one mule," Elle replied. "The rest are waiting on the other side of that rise." We explained we were on a trail ride in the Black Hills when the aurora happened and we figured our best bet was to ride our horses home. I pointed to the western end of Badlands, "We left our rigs with Kelly and Reed. Maybe you know them?"

She placed her right hand on a very large saddle horn on her well-used saddle where a lariat was attached by a leather strip. "I know them. Good people."

"It's been a long, hard day," I said. "Do you think it would be okay if we camped near that water hole?"

"Nobody around to care much about what you do as long as you don't cause no trouble."

"Thanks for the help," I said, lifting Justice's reins to turn him away.

"Hold on," she said, and leaned back on her high cantle. In a deep, yet soft voice, she said, "I heard my heart speak." Elle shifted her eyes to look at me. The woman looked like she'd just come out of a trance. "Name's Stella."

I reached my hand out to hers, "I'm Maia." Then Elle shook her hand.

"It's not our way to abide strangers, but you gals strike me different. If you want, my place is closer. You can get water there."

In unison, Elle and I said, "Sure would. We'd be much obliged."

She pointed at Elle, "You go fetch the others." Then looked at the road, "Follow this and it will bring you to our place." She turned to me, "You come with me." Elle wove out of the herd, and when clear, Bond broke into a full gallop.

"This is Justice," I said. "We are the oldest of our group."

She patted her horse's thick black and white mane. "This here athlete is Pete." She chuckled, "My husband rides his brother, Repeat."

I laughed, suddenly realizing it had been a long time since I felt joy and the release of humor.

Stella's agile, attentive dogs kept the herd together as we moseyed down a graveled country road. "We're all pretty scared," I confessed. "We're doing our best to get through this, but it sure is challenging."

She looked around, scanning the landscape. "This is the most beautiful place on this planet. Nature surrounds us. It looks barren, but it has riches beyond what an eye can see. This land is alive." Her dogs funneled the cattle through an open gate, and when the last cow was through, she signaled Pete to side pass and parallel the gate, then reached down and latched it shut.

We rode past wooden sheds, discarded machinery overtaken by tall grass and a large old barn. Smack at the end of the gravel road stood a simple, small weathered ranch home. Off to one side was a garden with kale plants the size of small Christmas trees, bright orange pumpkins and yellow squash, tomatoes still green, and corn stalks sprouting randomly between the rows.

When Stella dismounted, she stood maybe five feet tall. Her dark skin, high cheekbones, black eyes and strands of coal black escaping from her hat suggested a deep connection to this land. Loosely wrapping Pete's reins around her horn, she opened the corral gate. Justice smelled water and lunged for the tank. The old saying that you can lead a horse to water, but you can't make it drink only applies when a horse isn't thirsty. Justice was thirsty and couldn't get satisfied quick enough.

We were standing by the tank when she said, "It's getting late and I think it would be okay with my husband if you overnighted over by the orchard."

"Thank you," I said, holding back tears.

We waved at the others as they rode side by side coming straight toward us. Sal dismounted and fell to the ground. Her hat fell off and exposed her new do. Rosy hopped off Catch and tried to help her sister stand. Sal reached down, grabbed her hat and quickly covered her head. Elle burrowed through her fanny pack and tossed Sal the ibuprofen bottle. "Take two." Rosy said, handing her a canteen.

"There's a hand-pump on the back side of the corral," said Stella. "It's pretty good drinking water."

I introduced Rosy. "She's our trail boss." Rosy tipped her hat. "You met Elle. She's good at figuring stuff out."

Elle beamed. "And not bad at hunting."

"And so much more," I added.

Eventually Sal was able to stand straight. "She's got problems from sitting too long in the saddle, but she's a fighter." Sal made a limp fist.

"Gal in the buzz cut is Kitty." Kitty tipped her head. "Our crack shot and good negotiator."

"Lydia, she's in charge of Romeo."

Lydia rubbed his ears. "He's our savior."

"Lydia's quite a fighter and is holding up pretty well considering this is her first long ride."

"Sure isn't what I expected," Lydia said, rubbing her back into Romeo's shoulder.

I explained that, while we waited to dry out after that downpour, we gave each other haircuts.

Stella smiled. "I noticed."

Everyone gushed gratitude when I told them about her offer. She pointed to the southeast of her home. "An orchard is down over that slope. Feel free to harvest any fruit on the ground and gather downed branches for a fire." She shook her head, "Just don't go wanderin'. These days we see lots of rattlers. After you've finished unloading, put your herd in the corral." Then she gripped her saddle horn and in one fluid motion rotated her body like a trick rider up into the saddle. "My husband Chip should be riding in from the south before dark. Make sure you tell him I gave you permission to camp here." With that, she rode off, then tied Pete to a hitching post in front of her little white house and disappeared inside.

Out of earshot, Lydia asked, "You think she's Indian?"

"Yes. I believe she's indigenous to this land," I replied.

"She seems so strong," Lydia said.

"That's the truth," I said.

"Ok, ladies, it's gonna get dark soon," said Rosy. "First thing is water." Like our horses, we greedily gulped as much as our bellies could hold.

Sal limped as she led Thief to the corral. "Rosy, please try to convince me that a shot of whiskey wouldn't be great medicine."

"Be strong, Sis," Rosy replied, taking Catch's saddle off.

Carefully removing Romeo's panniers, Rosy breathed a sigh of relief seeing his sore had sealed.

Free of his saddle, it didn't take Justice long to find the perfect spot to roll after spinning circles on his forehand. He bent his front legs at the knees, tucked them under, leaned forward, bent his back legs, folded them and plopped down with a thud. He rolled to one side, kicked his legs out and rolled again, momentarily balancing on his backbone, pushing his body into the earth, ridding himself of itchy, sweaty, matted hair. Unable to completely roll over, he stood and repeated his frolic on his other side. When finished, the old boy stretched his forelegs, pushed forward, hopped up and shook like a dog shedding water. Horse protocol is that when one horse rolls, all the others follow. Rio was next to hit the dirt. Romeo ended up being last.

After we got our herd settled in the corral, we staked our tents and Lydia and I gathered soft, bruised, yet delicious bug-bitten apples, leathery pears, sweet, juicy plums and a few sour grapes. Kitty gathered sticks, then placed our grill down and made a fire. She filled a pot of water, added some jerky and a handful of rice as we cut fruit into small chunks. We'd set our saddles up near the fire and were resting when Stella came carrying an armful of kale. Kitty reached out and accepted her gift. "My, oh my, what a great addition to tonight's soup."

"Sounds like we need a stone," I said.

Kitty raised an eyebrow, thought for a second. "Stone soup?" She looked around, "I reckon we'll need a tasty stone for that."

Lydia wrinkled her brow. "What are you talking about?"

"Stone soup," I explained. "It's an old European folktale. A group of hungry strangers wandered into a village looking for food, but the villagers refused them. So the strangers put a stone in a simmering pot of water and began sampling the soup. One by one curious villagers came by and the cook would say how his soup could use just a pinch of salt, or a potato or whatever. Gradually each villager added an ingredient until the pot was full and everyone enjoyed a bowl of stone soup."

Lydia seemed confused. "And?"

"And. . .stone soup brings people together, people who don't have much to eat. Everyone contributes something, even water and stones. Everyone shares the feeling of community."

Lydia got up and strolled through the orchard and found a half-buried white stone. She brushed it clean like an egg and slid it into the roiling pot, then stirred with the flourish of a magician casting a spell. "Perfect," she said, then laughed. "This cook is stoned."

Stella removed her broad brimmed, sweat-stained hat and her long, jet-black hair cascaded over her shoulders. Lydia ran her hands self-consciously over her new hairdo. We eyed each other uneasily, a little jealous of Stella's full head of beautiful hair.

Rosy offered Stella a bowlful. "Plum delicious," she said.

Stella's widow's peak was like my mom's. Mom too had black eyes. I remembered Mom was born somewhere west of the Missouri River. Perhaps it could have been someplace near here.

After slurping the most delectable soup ever concocted, Rosy asked. "What do you know about what's happening in the world?"

"Hopin' you could tell me," Stella said. "We don't know much. We've had power go out before, but nothing like this. We're independent folks; we'll wait it out." She twisted a strand of hair and stuffed it behind her ear. "Root cellar's stocked. Got a gravity water system and a cistern. Won't go thirsty any time soon. Two generators in the shed. Don't use them much. Good-sized fuel tank out back. Just topped it off last month." She turned her eyes toward her cattle, and smiled. "Got lots of meat."

"Sounds like you've got this figured out," I said.

"It keeps us busy taking care of what's needed around here."

Just then a small green frog leapt onto Lydia's boot. She jerked back like she'd been struck by a rattler. She squealed, with her lips pressed together. "What. Is. That?"

I picked it off her, held its middle and stroked it with my finger. "It's a leopard frog," I said, stretching out one leg. "Frog legs, anyone?" I laughed, "Supposed to taste like chicken."

Stella chuckled. "You'd need a pond full of those little guys to feed six hungry women."

Rosy winced. "We're not that desperate."

"Not yet," Sal groaned.

Lydia wrinkled her nose. "Yish."

Setting the little guy down, for a moment it seemed stunned, then leapt away.

Stella jumped up when we heard horse hooves pounding dirt at a fast trot. "Gotta be Chip."

Seconds later, a lanky-built cowboy rode in wearing a long sleeve western shirt. He looked permanently sunburned. He wrapped his reins around his saddle horn, then stepped down off a horse that looked exactly like Stella's Pete. A dead calf was strapped behind his saddle. Its legs hung down both sides. A floppy Stetson shrouded Chip's face, allowing him to avoid eye contact while Stella made introductions. Chip was about as tall, dark and handsome a cowpoke as I'd ever laid eyes on. Even handsomer than Lance.

Rosy kept her eyes drilled on Kitty as if to say, "Don't you even think about it."

Kitty shoved both hands into her pant pockets, pre-empting her usual slipping a finger down her cleavage when in the company of a man.

Rosy offered Chip a bowl of soup. "It's tasty."

While he ate, Stella told our story, finishing with, "We wish you gals good luck."

"We'll need it," Sal said, stretching out her legs.

Chip looked back at the calf. "Had a broken leg. Glad I found it before the coyotes got it."

Stella lifted an eyebrow. "Or a lion."

Sal emitted a sound somewhere between a squeal and a gasp. "Lion?"

Chip stirred his soup. "Don't see big cats often, just their leftovers. Plenty of 'em out there."

Sal froze the way Lydia had when the frog landed on her boot. "You talkin' mountain lions?"

"Trust me, they're more afraid of us. They steer clear of people."
He licked the spoon and handed his empty bowl to Rosy. "I'd be more
concerned about stepping on a pancaked rattlesnake or ending up in
quicksand than about running into a big cat."

Sal slunk down. "Pancaked rattlers."

Lydia gasped. "Quicksand?"

"Mud in suspension," said Stella. "Bottomless, for all intents and
purposes." She patted Chip's leg. "Remember the time we went looking for
strays along the Upper White?"

He nodded. "Yeahhp. Coming back across the river, pert-near to the
bank when my horse dropped right out under me."

"Tell you, that was intense," said Stella.

"Holy shit," yelped Sal. "There's quicksand around here?"

"Rivers, creeks, sometimes in some ponds, places you'd least expect."
Chip wagged a finger. "Never ride alone, and always, always, always carry a
rope."

Stella scanned us. "You gals have ropes?"

Elle answered, "We do, and from now on mine's gonna be within easy
reach."

Chip tipped back his hat and lifted his eyes. "Play it safe around water.
Stick to game trails. If you get into quicksand, keep your body horizontal.
Don't struggle. Don't go thrashing about or you'll sink like a stone."

Elle used a long stick to stir the fire and sparks swirled upwards. "Reed,
the guy where we left our rigs on the western slope, told us that White
River water was not drinkable."

Stella said, "We call the White River Makhiziita Wakpa, meaning dirty
white water. As you get closer to the Missouri and away from the eroding
Badlands, the water usually gets cleaner and certainly good enough for your
horses."

Chip responded dryly, "S'pose it's better than drinkin' dust, but not
by much." He looked away. "You need to know that there's water around
here. Keep a lookout for green, especially on hillsides. A natural spring can
ooze out of a slope."

Stella handed Rosy their empty bowls. "There's food and there's water
if you know where and when to look." She paused. "My people have lived
here for a long, long time. This land may look dry and barren, but it has
always nourished our bodies and our souls." Her face brightened. "For
thousands of years my people understood and embraced bio-diversity.

They thought of how to feed all species, not just humans. They understood the give and take of reciprocity. We take care of the land, water and air and it gives us food, clothing and shelter. We've got hackberries. Roasted hackberries make a delicious coffee-like drink. With black chokecherries we make a soup called Wojapi. Buffalo berries are like chokecherries, but more tart. You know what a prickly pear cactus looks like?" She asked and we nodded. "Ok. Burn off the thorns or dig them out, slice the flesh like a green pepper and eat it."

Chip smiled at her. "Mmm. It's pretty tasty."

"Plants are medicine," she said. "For thousands of years, my ancestors hunted buffalo, tanned hides, dried meat into jerky and made tools." She looked east. "Ironic you gals are from Minnesota. My people traveled there, tapped your maple trees, grew corn, beans and squash. Rich soil you have in the Upper Midwest. We fished your rivers and lakes. Harvested nuts. Hunted waterfowl. Stalked prey in the forests and across the prairies. My ancestors came back towing travois heavy with supplies wrapped in buffalo skins. Intently, she looked at each one of us. "We are connected by the land regardless of borders. Your land fed my people." She breathed in the cool night air. "This land can feed your body and spirit as it does ours."

I could not contain my excitement. "This was the story we saw carved in the stone pictographs in French Creek," I said.

"I've been there many times," Stella said. "It is a sacred place." All around coyotes began to howl. We listened to their cries. Then, Stella told us, "Ever since the night of the bright lights, their cries seem longer and deeper."

"You saw the aurora?" I asked.

"Yes." With the depth of a shaman, she said, "It was amazing. It did so much more than just shut off electricity."

Everyone's eyes darted back and forth. "What do you mean, so much more?" I asked.

Stella remained silent, then acted as if she heard something move in the darkness and nodded at Chip. Abruptly they stood up and went to Chip's horse. With one foot in his stirrup, he asked, "Gotta weapon?"

"A .22," replied Elle.

Stella gently lifted a spider off of Chip's leg. "Iktomi," she said, tenderly placing it on the ground.

"Iktomi?" I asked.

"The trickster," she replied. "Watch out for him. She looked at the sky, "Remember, if you need guidance, ask the ancestors. Sometimes they come calling." With that they disappeared into the night.

We sat in our saddle chairs and gazed at the star-filled night sky and the rising halfmoon.

I dozed off until Kitty playfully elbowed me. "Nuh-uh," she teased. "No sleeping. I have a question."

"What? What?"

She pointed at four bright stars that made the shape of a square. "What's that called?"

"Pegasus," I replied. "The flying horse. Pegasus was born from the blood of Medusa when she was beheaded. Legend has it that whenever Pegasus' hooves touched the earth, springs were created."

"Springs?" asked Lydia "Like water?"

"Not just any water, special inspirational water," I replied. "Like the water inside of us."

"That's ironic," she replied. "I love the idea of being watched over on this long ride by a flying horse that can find water."

Rosy got up, "I'm plum tuckered out."

It was pure heaven to have enough water to brush my teeth and wash my dirty face. After our usual round of saying goodnight, I changed into my sleepwear and retreated to our tent. Deep-throated hoppers serenaded us as we settled our bones on the hard land. I zipped up my sleeping bag, then, as tired as I've ever been, I was wide awake. "Lydia," I said, "I've figured out my dream."

"What dream?" she asked, sounding three-quarters asleep.

"The dream I had the night of the aurora."

"Yeah?" She rolled over, "Like Stella said, that aurora did more than shut off electricity. What was your dream about?"

"A two-headed horse."

Then she asked, "Is Pegasus like Medusa?"

"Medusa had one head, Lydia, and snakes for hair, and a stare that turned people into stone. The horse in my dream had a head on each end of its body so it could run in either direction without turning around."

Lydia stifled a giggle. "How did it decide?"

"I don't know," I said annoyed. "It was a dream! I think the two-headed horse was a symbol. He ran back and forth and back and forth through our horse camp. I think it means we could have just as well stayed in camp instead of heading home."

"That's weird," she said. "You think the two headed horse is with us now? Think he's telling us to go back?"

"No."

Lydia took a deep breath. "Good, because we have to believe we made the right decision."

"I think so, too. In the morning, we'll head into the sun."

"I'm ready. Night, Maia."

"Night, Lydia."

I tossed and turned as Kitty's breathing grew louder and turned into muted, whistling snores. Stella roused in me a cellular ache for a deeper and more intimate connection to land and its real history. Her widow's peak, her dark eyes and dark hair was like Mom's. Over the years I have often wondered why my Mom's mother, my grandmother, told her to stay out of the sun and keep her skin covered so her skin wouldn't turn dark too fast. My older sister has maintained that in the late 1800's my grandma and her sister, my aunt, were taken by train from South Dakota to southwest Wisconsin to work as free labor on the family farm. My mother and my aunt were small in stature and fine-boned in comparison to their so-called stocky, Germanic-looking brothers and sisters. Like Mom, Grandma had a widow's peak, high cheekbones, black eyes and hair that stayed black as coal until just before she passed on. It remains a mystery why my pregnant grandmother left Wisconsin to give birth to her first baby, my mom, in South Dakota.

As a kid, my skin got so dark and reddish in the summer that my family, neighbors and playmates often called me a little Indian. I'd play on the hills behind our house and make clay pots with my bare hands and dry them in the sun. When I had my children, people made the same comments about the color of their skin. I rolled onto my side. Am I just another white person hoping to claim Native ancestry? Or is it deeper than that? Am I hungry to reach back to where I came from and find out who I am?

Chapter 12

Making Dew Do

The early morning baby-blue sky had not a speck of white when we exited our tents. Mooing and bawling cattle serenaded us as we readied to leave. Stopping to say thank you and goodbye, Stella gave each one of us a brown paper lunch bag. "Last night we divided a shoulder into six pieces and made you sandwiches. Veal's pretty tender. Just took it off the grill. Meat's still warm."

Chip sauntered over carrying a shotgun with the barrel pointing at the ground. He handed it to Elle, "This old pump-action Winchester twelve gauge is pretty darn easy to shoot."

Elle unzipped her fanny pack. "How much you want for it?"

"Naawp," he drawled. "Bring it when you come back for your rigs."

"I shot a gun just like this with my grandpa," said Elle, examining the Winchester. Tucking the stock against her right shoulder she peered down the barrel over the site. "She's a beauty."

"Give her a test run," said Chip, pointing to an old rusted sign nailed to a fence post. "That's about twenty yards away." He handed Elle a shell. "Always make sure the safety is on before loading it."

Elle placed the shell in the open port, moved the slide forward, raised the gun, aimed, pushed the safety off and pulled the trigger. The gun spoke with a deafening roar. The recoil slammed her shoulder back as the smell of gunpowder filled the air. "Damn!," she hollered.

"Good work," said Chip, "You hit it."

Elle pulled the slide back, ejected the spent shell casing, and engaged the safety. Examining the peppered sign, warped with holes, Chip said, "This is what happens at twenty yards. The closer you are, the denser the pattern and the more lethal. At forty yards, pellets scatter and lose potency. Get too close to a bird, snake or rabbit and you'll blow it to smithereens. Too far away, you'll end up empty handed."

With profuse gratitude, Elle accepted Chip's shotgun. "Having both a pistol and a shotgun feels much so much safer. The pistol is protection from others and the shotgun will be great for hunting."

"They'll both kill," Chip said. "It's always good to have options."

Rosy asked, "Whadda you think would be better, if we took the stagecoach trail or stayed along the rail corridor?"

"It's possible you could run into people along the tracks. That'd be my guess." He turned to Stella. "What do you think?"

"Stagecoach trail is pretty isolated. Every couple of years it's used by those Rendezvous folks and sometimes ranchers use it to check their herds. Right now, until this situation gets resolved, most ranchers are letting their cattle graze freely."

With sincerity, Chip said, "You gals be careful."

"You heard him," Stella said, walking alongside of us. "There's a campground a little north of Interior that has a hand pump and an open shelter that could be a good place to rest up and get more water."

As the distance grew between us, Stella yelled, "Hopefully the White will get cleaner as you go downstream a piece."

Not far down the road, I turned back and already the ranch had disappeared into memory. A sudden gust of cold swept over us from the north and Justice braced. He snorted, blowing at something invisible. I rubbed his shoulder, "What's that about?"

Lydia, bringing up the rear, asked, "Did we get lucky or what?"

"We sure did," I said. "More strangers helping."

"I'm beginning to feel more confident that good, principled people will emerge from the darkness of this disaster," Lydia said.

"I don't understand why Rosy is so afraid. Why can't she be more trusting?" I said, signaling Justice to get up alongside Rosy and match Catch's pace. I summoned my courage, "What if we head for the Interstate? We can ride along the frontage roads."

Rosy raised an eyebrow.

"Remember all the ponds along I-90? I'll bet that water will be a lot cleaner than what's around here."

Rosy kept her focus straight ahead.

"There's waterfowl. Pheasants. More food. We'd have plenty of time to duck out of sight when we hear vehicles coming."

Rosy didn't utter a word.

Lydia brought Liberty up and rode on Catch's other side.

"Will you just think about it?" I pleaded. "There's no gas, so there shouldn't be much traffic."

"Too risky," Rosy grumbled. "We are in a whale of a dangerous situation, Maia. Gas or no gas, strangers are our biggest threat." She urged Catch to pick up his pace.

As she put distance between us, I raised my voice. "Why can't you just consider it? We've already seen goodness surface. Reed and Kelly. Stella and Chip. People in desperate situations aren't necessarily bad."

She yelled back, "They aren't necessarily good, either!" She urged Catch to increase the distance between us. "No. We're staying the course. Our number one priority is to avoid people."

"We're people," I shouted. "So far everybody we've encountered has been helpful."

Rosy pulled Catch's reins back and stopped. She shot back, "So far, everybody we've encountered have been ranchers. They've got nothing left to lose in this no-man's land. No. We have to be invisible and not spend half our time ducking out of sight."

Lydia said loudly. "But what if things aren't as bad as you think? Rosy, what if you're overreacting?" Her voice cracked. "If we ran into more people, maybe we could find out what's really happening." Lydia reached down, tenderly stroking Liberty's mane. "Why are you so afraid?"

Rosy loosened her reins and Catch moved away. "I'm calling the shots here. If electricity was back on, don't you think we'd hear more vehicles and see airplane vapor trails? People would be out moving around. We don't know what's going on in people's heads at a time like this. No, we can't risk running into the wrong people." She raised her voice, "Case closed. Discussion over!"

I thought about the story of the two wolves. The one that's fed is the one that grows strongest. I couldn't help but wonder about our alpha she-wolf. The one that's afraid to share the responsibility of making decisions. Is she feeding her fear?

Lydia and I fell in line and followed Rosy's lead. She paused at the outskirts of the Badlands' little village of Interior. We saw the Crossroads gas station's sign and, as we walked past, it appeared abandoned. Next door, in the overgrown parking were dozens of what appeared to be empty RV's.

"Could be people ahead," Elle said. "Rosy, how we gonna handle this?"

"We'll ride the edge south of the main road toward Highway 44." Interior appeared to be a ghost town. One-story buildings, empty lots, rows of mobile homes, a boarded-up church, an old schoolhouse and a weather-beaten sign advertising a bar and grocery store. A hollow, ping-ping-ping came from a shredded American flag that slapped against a metal pole in front of the shuttered post office.

Lydia kept looking around. "Where is everybody?"

No one answered. Fear of running into anyone, instilled in us by Rosy, outweighed curiosity as we rode through the deserted village.

Like Stella said, the campground was empty. We ducked under the shelter, filled our water buckets and everyone took good long drinks. We refilled our water containers while our herd munched on grass. "Great people," I said, savoring the most delicious tender steak sandwich I'd eaten in my entire life.

"We sure did get lucky running into them," Lydia added.

Sal rubbed her belly. "Delicious steak."

High noon found us back in the saddle, listening to Sal relentlessly complain about suffering from heat stroke. Poor Sal. Always suffering.

Crossing the northside of the two-lane Highway 44, heading east, about thirty feet away, a person slid a rifle barrel out of the driver's side window of a green Chevrolet Impala. I felt Justice tense.

"Gun!" Elle shouted, pulling her shotgun out of Chip's old scabbard. Rosy jerked Catch's reins and he spun around. Kitty dropped Rio's reins when she trained her pistol on the Impala.

The first gunshot sent everybody scattering. Rio veered and dumped Kitty. Thief bucked and sent Sal flying. With the second shot, Justice burst into overdrive and, luckily, I stayed in the saddle. Dismounting, I hugged the ground, scared to death. Kitty rose up, retrieved her pistol and ran to Elle, who was already lying down with her shotgun aimed at the car door. Kitty almost reached Elle when a third shot rang out and she let out a holler. She hit the ground hard, yet immediately began crawling toward Elle, dragging her body while holding the pistol in one hand. Our horses clustered together, heads held high, ears focused, watching.

The driver's side door popped open and a shirtless guy emerged. Gaunt, wearing overalls that sagged, he grimaced and seemed to be waving at us with his shotgun. He wobbled, leaned back against the car, lifted a bottle, took a swig, then tossed it in the air. We heard it hit the ground.

"Should I shoot him?" Elle hissed.

Rosy crawled in between Kitty and Elle. "Wait."

We watched the gunman lift his head toward the sky, curse, drop his gun and collapse backwards. Nobody moved. After a few minutes, Elle rose up with her shotgun tight to her shoulder.

Romeo was drifting, walking like a drunken sailor because his panniers shifted. Lydia jumped up and ran to him. Rosy shrieked, "Get down!" Motioning wildly for Lydia to protect herself. As Lydia dropped to the ground, she managed to grip Romeo's lead.

Minutes seemed like hours as we waited for any movement to come from the shooter. I got into a low-profile stance and crept to our horses to get them further away should the gunman come back to life.

Lydia brought Romeo over and we tried to push his panniers back in place. "Why would anybody do that?"

"Fear? Meanness? I don't know, Lydia." I said, trying to hold up the panniers. "When people lose hope, they can do horrible things."

Rosy and Elle helped Kitty in her struggle to stand. Bent over, clearly in pain, clutching her right thigh, she moaned, "Fuck! He shot me!"

"First aid kit," Elle demanded.

Kitty pushed her shoulders back, angry and deadly, then hoisted her pistol sideways like a drug dealer in a crime movie, staying focused on the green Impala.

"What are you doing?" asked Rosy.

Kitty snapped, "I'm gonna kill that son-of-a-bitch!"

Elle pushed Kitty's hand down and tried to take the gun away. "Put that down. Give it to me. Please."

"No. That asshole could have killed us. He shot me." Finally Kitty relaxed her grip and Elle took her gun.

Elle and I wrapped Kitty's arms over our shoulders and helped her hop out of range. "Let me look at your wound, Kit," said Rosy helping her lay down. Kitty rested her head on my lap while Rosy removed her boots and bloodied jeans. A flesh wound grazed her outer thigh. It looked like someone had slashed her with a shard of broken glass.

Sal pulled her pants down. Already her hip showed early signs of potentially deep bruises.

"Can you hold on?" Elle asked Kitty.

"No problem," Kitty said. "Go check out that bastard."

Elle approached the car cautiously, her shotgun leveled at the shooter lying motionless on the ground. She yelled back at us. "Don't worry about this sniper, Kitty. If he tries to get up, I'll blow him away." She kept her gun aimed at the crazy stranger. "You hear me, asshole? You stay put."

"Wait!" yelled Rosy and ran toward Elle. After quickly inspecting the Impala, Rosy backed out of the passenger side door, holding a bottle in one hand and a handful of shells in her other. "We got some tequila." Then asked Elle, "Think he's alive?"

"Drunk! High! Looks dead as a doornail," Elle said, lowering her gun. "Like he OD'ed on whatever's in that syringe."

Rosy ran back to Kitty with the tequila bottle. "Need a drink?" She twisted the bottle cap and handed it to Kitty then locked eyes with Sal, "Need some medicine?"

Sal dropped her eyes to the ground and shook her head. "No thanks. I'll tough this one out."

Elle kept backing toward us with her gun pointing at the creep. She knelt down next to Kitty and opened her Swiss Army knife. Rosy lit a wooden match and Elle slowly moved the blade over the flame.

Kitty, cheeks ashen, gulped tequila, "Got a stick for me to bite?"

Rosy untied the bandanna from around her neck, twisted it like a thick rope and carefully placed it in Kitty's open mouth. "Bite down on this. Better than a stick."

Elle dug three small BBs out of Kitty's thigh, then bandaged her wound.

Kitty looked up, "More tequila."

Lydia cried out asking for help to uncinch Romeo's panniers. His bandage was drenched with fresh red blood. As Elle rebandaged him she urged us to check our horses to make sure they didn't get hit with any scatter shot. I took Rio to Kitty and asked, "You gonna be ok?"

"Just a bee sting," she said. "Just a nasty sting," as I guided her foot into the stirrup, then gave her a leg up. Slowly she swung her leg up over the saddle and attempted to get comfortable. "No sweat. It's just a scratch."

With Sal settled on Thief, Rosy looked at the car, lifted her reins and ordered, "Let's get the hell outta here." She glared at me and Lydia. "I warned you. I told you people are dangerous." She narrowed her eyes, "I don't want to hear one more word from either of you about how great people are. Not one fucking word."

"Reed warned us," Elle said. "He said there were some really bad actors around here."

"That sure scared the shit out of me," I said humbly.

Lydia's voice shook, "Everything happened so fast. I've never had anybody shoot at me. That was the most horrible thing I've ever been through."

"Freaked all of us out," I replied. "Rosy you were right! People can be damn dangerous."

Lydia moved Liberty next to Kitty, "You gonna be okay?"

"I'm tough," Kitty said, shifting around, trying to adjust. "This won't get me down."

Rosy pointed at a shadow at the base of a distant hill. "We'll rest there a spell. I need to take another look at Romeo."

Kitty resisted help as she dismounted, arguing, "I can do this." Elle spread our blanket down on the ground and Kitty stretched her body out, insisting, "I'm fine."

"Not me," Lydia said. "I'm a total wreck. Someone could have gotten killed."

Sal dropped to her knees, slowly getting her body horizontal. Elle tossed her the pain pills, then gave Kitty the bottle. Comforted by the welcoming shade, we watched our herd graze and relived every detail of that ambush.

"It was so weird," I said. "Right before the first shot, Justice acted skittish, like he knew something was going wrong."

Lydia narrowed her eyes. "You saying he sensed danger?"

"Absolutely," Rosy said. "We see it all the time. Horses try their best to warn us. The problem is, we either don't pay attention to the signals they're sending, or we don't know how to interpret their cues." She rolled on to her side. "From the hooves to the brain, a horse's body is an amplifier. Horses can feel an earthquake before it happens. They can anticipate storms long before we can. They can hear predators and footsteps a long way off. Horse's senses work in concert." She sat up. "They are not just geniuses, they're downright clairvoyant. Maia, Justice knows when you're happy, doesn't he? Scared? Even threatened?"

"He sure does," I replied, watching my old boy munch the dry prairie grass. "He's my barometer, my compass."

Rosy raised an eyebrow. "A good friend of ours owned a stable. Nice place. Clean. Horses treated good. Well, along comes a fella that called himself a horse trainer. Our friend said that every time this guy'd walk down the center aisle, as he passed every single stall, every single horse made aggressive gestures toward him."

"Like what?" asked Lydia.

"Like biting. Screaming. Low and behold, one day the police came to the barn and arrested that guy on suspicion of murdering a woman down in Iowa. That dude had shot her and run over her with his truck for supposedly cheating on him. He's doing life in Anamosa."

We all tried to rest, each lost in our own private thoughts. When our two wounded puppies felt sufficiently rested and Romeo was taken care of, we helped Kitty and Sal back in their saddles. Riding parallel to the railroad, Catch stopped short when a barbed wire fence blocked our way. With the shotgun clenched in one arm, Elle peered through her binoculars, scanning the landscape.

"What the fuck?" Sal barked. "Why is a fence in the middle of nowhere?"

Elle aimed her shotgun at a wooden shack tucked into the hillside that had car parts strewn everywhere. "Somebody's put claim to this land."

"Think it's the asshole that shot me?" Kitty said, touching her hip.

"Could be," Elle said, dismounting, laying the wires down and standing on the barbed wire while everyone passed safely over.

Kitty aimed her pistol at the cabin. "Got to be illegal something."

Sal brightened. "Mary Jane?"

"Worse," Kitty added. "Could be seriously dangerous drug dealers. I bet this hole-in-the-wall hideout had something to do with what happened at the crossroad."

Lydia whimpered, "I am getting more and more afraid. What bad thing is gonna happen next?"

"We'll get through this," I said, nervously looking around. Our horses picked up on our anxiety and stepped up their pace.

Our once clear baby-blue sky was now alive with puffy white, constantly changing clouds that had flat gray underbellies. With clouds passing overhead, we'd get momentary relief and cool down as the wind slammed against our backs. At times, the beauty of the Badlands overwhelmed me and I was able to embrace the wonders of nature. Although this land seemed inhospitable, it had mind-blowing grandeur. Table rocks banded with color felt like altars to the gods. The timberless landscape had domes, gullies, pyramids and mesas with bands of yellow, lavender, magenta, ocher-gray, pink and red layered sediments. Outside of time and away from to-do lists, our only expectation was to keep moving as one.

Catch traversed back and forth between the trail and the railbed depending on which surface was easier. Bank swallows circled above a wooded thicket and Rosy commented, "The White's close." Bushwhacking down the bank, we stood parallel to each other and stared at water that looked like a vanilla malt.

Kitty groaned, "Aw, shit," summing up what we all felt.

"We've got enough water for a day or two," Rosy said. "It's the horses that worry me."

Elle walked to the river's edge, squatted down and scooped up a handful of the milky water. She smelled it, then rubbed it between her fingers. "It's grit." We got our pails and filled them with the white water and offered our horses a drink, but even though they were thirsty, they declined.

Justice pawed the ground, like he was trying to get water from down under.

"What the hell?" said Rosy. "He might be trying to tell us something. What do we have to lose? Let's dig."

Twenty feet away from the sandbar we dug down using our nesting pots. Putting my hands into the earth felt great. I had a job. Digging. Reaching down. Feeling wetness. Two feet down water began to bubble up that appeared to contain considerably less sediment. Again, we offered our horses a drink, but again they refused.

Rosy suggested we secure cloth over a bucket to serve as a sieve, then pour the groundwater over and continuously scrape the grit away so it could filter through. "Then, if we boil it, that should do the trick."

Sal and Lydia were gathering firewood when we heard them scream, "Snake!"

Elle grabbed her gun and ran in their direction, but by the time she got to them, the snake had slithered into the dense thicket.

Lydia cradled a load of firewood and dropped it next to our digging spot and stretched her arms out wide. "That rattler was this big."

Kitty raised her brow. "That big, huh?"

Lydia widened her reach. "Bigger even."

Selecting the driest twigs, we got a robust fire going, then picketed our horses before setting up our tents. We took turns digging and straining the groundwater and began the boiling process. Even though the day had been long and hard, we took turns fueling the fire, straining the muck in order to satisfy our herd's thirst."

"I want to see your bruise," Elle said to Sal. Sal unzipped her pants. Her butt looked like a purple grape. "You need a pill?"

"Two," Sal said, pulling her pants up.

Elle checked Kitty's wound. "Looks good. Painful?"

"Naaw," Kitty said, as she crawled into the tent. "Just a scratch."

Lydia and I agreed to do the second shift. Lying in our tent, I kept envisioning rattlesnakes slithering outside the too thin walls.

Before long, we heard Elle wake us with a soft, "Your turn." Night was pitch black when we saw the glow of the fire. For what seemed like hours we boiled and then presented water to our herd.

As the morning mist rose, we fed the fire and offered our horses the final results of a long night's work. Lydia held the bucket for Romeo, and said, "This was way too much work. It would be so much easier if we rode along the Interstate and took advantage of all those ponds."

"I agree," I whispered.

Kitty spun around and glared at her. "Do I have to remind you about yesterday's asshole? Someone could have gotten killed!"

"Sorry," Lydia said. "It's just."

"Don't fucking go there," Kitty warned. "We do what Rosy says. She's boss."

Elle handed each of us an empty gallon-sized plastic bag. "Fill this with any vegetation, then put it on top of your saddle bags, so during the day the sun will distill it."

"I've heard of making do," I said smartly, "But making dew do takes it to a new level."

"Funny girl," Elle chuckled.

Riding a game trail that turned into a willow thicket, Sal reached out and pushed a baseball bat sized branch out of her way. It slapped back and smacked Liberty's head. Liberty freaked, but Lydia held on and stayed in the saddle.

Rosy was livid. "Never ever push on a branch. Damnit anyway, Sal!" She turned to Lydia, "You ok?"

"I'm ok," she stuttered. "Thank God my sweet Liberty didn't get hurt."

"I'm sorry, Lydia," Sal apologized, "I wasn't thinking."

Lydia narrowed her eyes. "You sure you were not trying to do me in and get my TP?"

"Hadn't thought of that," Sal said, smiling sheepishly.

Back on the trail, clear of the thicket, we walked, stopped, ate something and sometimes dozed off while our mounts grazed on greener grass.

As the temperature rose, Kitty used her hand to fan herself and lamented, "Remember air conditioning?"

"And turning on a faucet and running water," I said.

"Clean sheets," Lydia added.

As the relentless sun baked us like a Badlands pie, Sal let loose a stream of complaints. "It feels like a hundred and ten, my lips are blistered and cracked and I want a fan."

Rosy urged Catch next to Sal, his thick tail swishing back and forth. "I'm your fan."

"Shut up!" Sal barked. "You make my butt hurt."

"Everyone, stop!" Elle shouted, "There's no point dreaming of home and its comforts. We've got a long way to go and it's no use torturing ourselves."

Spotting a downed willow extending over the river, Lydia and I shinnied out onto a thick branch and dangled our bare feet in the cold White River goo. "That felt great," she said as she walked back to join the others. Lydia reached down and picked up a small rock, rubbed it against her pant leg, then lifted it up to capture the sun's light. "I think this is jasper."

Lydia showed Sal saw her jasper and Sal removed her hat and bowed. "I believe our princess knows her jewels."

"Technically, jasper isn't a jewel, it's a gem," explained Elle. "It's probably quartz, which is an impure form of silica. The red comes from iron. Green jasper, heliotrope or bloodstone is the birthstone for March babies." She looked at Lydia. "When's your birthday?"

"March fourth," Lydia smiled and slipped the smooth red stone in her pocket. "I found my touchstone."

Sal looked flabbergasted. "Elle, how do you know all this . . .this stuff?"

"I listen," Elle said, "and I read."

Rosy, Elle and Kitty decided to ride ahead to search for better water. They hadn't been gone very long when we spotted what at first looked like a dust devil but turned out to be Rio, returning at a full gallop "We found an old homestead," Kitty panted. "Old windmill with blades turning like it was yesterday. Hopefully, we can get the well pump to work."

We got to the homestead and we all took turns pushing the iron pump handle up and down, up and down, but our efforts proved fruitless and our pail remained empty. Elle looked defeated. Luckily, we satiated our thirst with the drops of dew from our distiller bags.

Back on our way, the wind sounded like a flute playing "Taps" as we circumvented through deep ravines. Unfamiliar sounds, as though the earth itself was breathing, came from all around. Eager to end another long, hot day, we found a flat spot to stop and didn't move for a bit until Elle loaded her trusty gun and left to hunt for our supper. Her stride, opposite of defeat, showed strength and conviction.

Rosy held up a dried cow pie. "Pioneers called this 'prairie gold'."

Sal shook her head, "Looks like shit to me."

"One person's lemons can very well be another's lemonade."

We heard a shot and waited. Elle showed up with a jackrabbit about the size of a big housecat slung over her shoulder. Its hind legs hung down. Its grey and white tail bobbed like a flower being blown about in a playful breeze. Its long, black-tipped ears still flopped.

Sal pinched her nose. "That's roadkill."

"It's protein," Elle replied, making a slit across the rabbit's back with her knife blade. She wiggled her fingers through the slit, pulled the hide off, rolled the carcass over, slit its belly, removed its organs, pushed it flat, cracked its pelvis and picked embedded pellets out of the raw muscle. She pointed to an embankment. "This little guy was distracted as he drank from a little spring oozing out." She sharpened a nice straight stick and shoved it into the carcass for us to roast for tonight's meal, then led us to the natural spring and we proceeded to set up camp.

Slowly Kitty stood up. "I'm feeling pretty good, so I'm gonna hop on Rio and go look for firewood," She unsaddling Rio, wrapped a rope around her waist, grabbed his mane, and slid her body onto his bare back. Returning, Rio was in total carriage mode as he proudly pulled a snarl of flash flood debris.

Rosy whipped up an apple-plum sauce to serve with roasted rabbit. Comfortable in our saddle chairs, we watched the first quarter moon gradually appear in the dusky lavender sky. Behind us, the darkening Badlands ridge reminded me of the edge of a serrated knife.

"Never thought I'd eat jackrabbit." Sal said.

"First for me, too," Elle smiled, and with that, supper was served.

Rosy slid back into her saddle chair. "Getting through the Badlands is our first hard part."

Sal glared at her, "I pray you are speaking truth."

Kitty poked Rosy, "The first hard part?"

Rosy sighed, "There'll be more hard parts. More long days and nights. Our next big challenge will be crossing the Missouri River bridge."

The moon was high in the sky when Lydia pointed. "See those five stars?" She shook her shoulders, like she was showing off a piece of jewelry. She fluttered her eyelashes like a silent movie starlet. "That constellation looks like a diamond necklace." She sighed, "Last year Richard said he'd buy me a new diamond piece for our anniversary, but it never happened."

"That's Auriga," Elle said, pointing at the brightest diamond in Lydia's necklace.

Rosy scanned the sky. "And there's our new horse barn and those little stars are our horses."

"That's Cepheus." Elle said. "Cepheus, the king of Ethiopia, was married to Cassiopeia and had a daughter, Andromeda. Ever heard of them?" She waited. "Andromeda's a galaxy. Our closest neighbor. She was so beautiful that Poseidon, the guy with the trident, decided to send a tidal wave. The only way Cassiopeia could save Ethiopia was to chain Andromeda to the rocks and wait for a sea monster to eat her."

Lydia clutched her imaginary necklace. "Stop it. That's awful."

"Hang on," Elle said. "Perseus was sailing back from killing Medusa, the lady with snakes for hair and a stare that turned men into stone. Perseus took one look at Andromeda chained to the rocks, was smitten, slew the scary sea monster, saved Andromeda, and then they married."

Kitty rolled onto her side and sank an elbow into the ground, resting her head in her hand. "Anyone see that bright star next to Rosy's barn?" She laid back, "That's my Rio."

Sal stared at the millions of stars. "I see a brand-new shiny ivory Jaguar that would get me home fast."

"And where would you get gas?" Lydia asked smartly.

"It's electric," Sal replied. "Don't need gas."

Elle contemplated the night sky. "By God," she said, "why am I seeing a tent? A tent? I'm wishing for a tent?" She shook her head as if trying to dislodge the image.

"The Big Dipper is mine," I said. "I see it as a big question mark."

"What's the question?" asked Rosy.

"No end to questions," I replied.

Lydia sniffed the air, then covered her nose. "Who's blowing wind?"

Rosy pointed at Sal. Sal rolled onto her good hip, lifted her other cheek and let one rip.

"Two can play this game," said Kitty, farting loudly, then grabbing her gut. "Jack the rabbit could solve our energy needs."

Rosy joined the chorus with a belch that sounded like it came from her toes. "Blazing Saddles has nothing on us."

"You are all outrageous," said Lydia. "You're acting like kids."

Kitty struggled to breathe. "Well, all I can say is it's about time we had a good laugh."

Sal sat up, "How about we light our farts?"

"Stop, right now," Rosy yelled. "We can't waste a single match."

Sal farted in response.

Our laughter faded and we got back to our usual tag team approach to get enough water for the horses and hopefully refill our containers.

Early the next morning while packing up, I said, "I had another dream."

"Let me guess," Sal snickered. "You were being chased by a two-headed, gas-passing rabbit?"

"Not funny," I said. "No. This time it felt more like a vision. Everything was perfectly quiet. We were on a narrow trail when several ghostly, cloud-like figures came straight toward us. The last one rode a pinto horse pulling a travois with a body wrapped in a buffalo robe."

"Well, for Christ's sake, I don't like that at all," Sal said, setting our lunch bag on Romeo's panniers.

"Me, either," Rosy said, securing the ropes.

"Is it just me or is anyone else having wild dreams?" I asked. Then everyone acknowledged they too were having crazy dreams.

It was an enormous relief when we began to run into tributaries to the White River where the water was clean, and everyone got their fill. Prairie dogs provided entertainment as they perched on their grassy observation posts. Suddenly they'd rush toward each other, stop, kiss, crouch down, smell each other and nibble on the surrounding vegetation.

"They are so adorable," said Lydia.

"They're rodents," grumbled Sal.

"Why do you insist on calling them rats?" Lydia countered.

"That's right," said Elle. "One night those adorable little rats might be dinner."

Lydia winced. "I'd rather starve. I'll never eat a dog."

Elle shrugged. "Your choice."

A red tail hawk circled overhead, and a prairie dog issued a shrill warning. Instantly all the others disappeared into their maze of underground tunnels.

As the day rolled on, Kitty asked, "Remember Dale Evans, Queen of the West?"

Elle smiled. "Wasn't she the only female to gain fame during the cowboy era?" Then paused. "Interesting her name was more male than female."

"It was a man's world then," Rosy said.

Sal patted Thief's shoulder. "Still is."

Kitty tenderly stroked Bond. "Her horse was Buttermilk. Roy's was Trigger and their dog was Bullet."

"Roy Rogers was my hero," I said, nostalgically. "Those were the days. His cowboy motto went something like, don't drink, smoke, shoot pool and never spit."

"Does anybody remember any of the Cowboy Wisdom sayings listed on the poster in our office?" Rosy asked.

Sal laughed. "Don't squat with your spurs on. Never slap a man who's chewin' tabacca, and my favorite, the quickest way to double your money is to fold it over and put it back in your pocket."

Rosy eyed her sister. "I like the one, never miss a good chance to shut up." She winked. "The other one is when you're throwin' your weight around, be ready to have it thrown around by somebody else."

"How about this one?" asked Sal. "If you get to thinkin' you're a person of some influence, try orderin' somebody else's dog around."

Kitty raised her hand like a student wanting to be called on. "I liked the one about the three kinds of men. The ones that learn by reading, the few that learn by observation and the rest have to pee on the electric fence for themselves."

Rosy laughed, "That's so true."

"That's good," Lydia said. "I remember the one about lettin' the cat outta the bag being a whole lot easier 'n puttin' it back in. And the one saying, if you find yourself in a hole, the first thing to do is stop diggin'."

"Mark always liked the two theories of arguin' with a woman. Neither one works."

Elle was last to share Rosy's poster's wisdom. "Always drink upstream from the herd, and never kick a cow chip on a hot day."

"You guys did great," Rosy said, pleased.

For the next several hours, we went back and forth recalling our favorite western tunes. Collectively we remembered the words to Happy Trails to You, Home on the Range, Tumbling Tumbleweeds, Don't Fence Me In, Mule Train, Back in the Saddle, Goodbye Old Paint and Cool Water.

At day's end, with our horses busy grazing we settled back in our saddle chairs. Kitty held up a strip of jerky and she looked like Groucho Marx smoking a cigar. She tapped her make-believe cigar, pretending to flick ashes away. "What's the secret word?" But, instead of waiting for anybody to answer she said, "Sex," and ripped the jerky in half with a quick snap.

"Home," said Lydia. "I miss my girls. I'm afraid something bad has happened to them."

"You gotta believe they're okay," I said. "Don't go to that fear place. Fear devours courage."

Lydia kept rubbing her new touchstone. "Everybody's fine. Everybody's fine."

"My life would have been so different if I'd had kids," Sal muttered. "I would have been an awful mom. It was hard enough taking care of myself. Besides, with Earl, I woulda felt sorry for our kids."

Kitty hunched over. "Rio's my kid, the purest love I've ever known."

"I know, I know," Sal interrupted, "He's something big to love that goes between your legs."

Rosy smiled and said, "Miss Kitty, you are so bad."

"Funny," Kitty replied, "that's what Dad always said." She looked away. "Rio changed my life. After I got him, something broke loose in me. It's hard to explain. I felt more whole." She paused. "Rosy, you said once if I gave my heart to a horse that it could change my life. Well, you were right."

Elle choked up. "Bond has so enriched my life. He's helped me embrace the relationship thing."

Lydia asked, "Is that why you named him Bond?"

Elle cleared her throat. "When I got Bond, he had this long, sophisticated, very impressive pedigree that got tangled on my tongue. Changing his name was pure inspiration." She took a deep breath. "I never considered getting married or having kids." Her gaze turned upward to the sky. "Way back I did have one love. It's been over thirty years and yet still feels like yesterday."

Nobody said a word. This was the first time Elle revealed anything deeply personal. "I remember every detail of that night. A friend called and asked if I'd like to go canoeing and camp out overnight. We'd known each other for a long time. Sounded like fun. We paddled all day on the Yellow River in northern Iowa. That night, the moon hung above the horizon, just a sliver shy of full. We made a campfire, cooked and talked for a couple hours before crawling into a tent. Somehow, we melted into each other in a perfect blending of body and soul. Throughout all these years a day hasn't gone by that I haven't thought of her." Elle looked at the ground. "Last summer I was shopping at the co-op and, suddenly, there she was.

We stood, dumbstruck. When we hugged, it took away my breath. She was soft and loving, and again, I felt our hearts join. A guy stocking produce commented about how lovely and happy we looked. We went to a coffee shop to have a chance to catch up. She said her grown kids were living their own lives and doing well. She said her husband proved to be a challenging partner. With grace and loyalty, she said she still loved him. She was surprised I'd never married. I told her she was an impossible act to follow. She suggested we meet again, but I declined her invitation, knowing if we were together again, I wouldn't be able to bear another parting."

"I don't understand. Why not see her?" Kitty urged. "You have nothing to lose."

Elle snapped, "Kitty, she's married."

Kitty rolled her eyes. "Sounds like a pretty unsatisfying, rotten marriage."

"It's a line I won't cross. If she were single, it might be different."

"Who knows what really goes on between two people?" said Lydia. "Marriage is about making do."

Kitty stiffened. "Making do? Not me. I prefer being single."

"Love is complicated," Lydia said.

"Tell me about it," said Sal.

Rosy stood. "Ladies, it's time to blend our bodies with Mother Earth so we can move out early tomorrow morning."

Chapter 13

Moving On

Iktomi waited patiently in his dew-filled web outside our tent for the arrival of his next delicious dinner guest. "What trick do you have in mind for today?" I asked, as I watched Lydia emerge from a ravine after performing her morning constitutional. She wore a sour scowl, but quickly changed her demeanor, using a surprisingly sweet French accent, announcing she was out of toilet paper. "Anybody willing to share their papier hygiénique, si vous plait?"

Kitty tugged her ear lobe. "What on earth do you have that would get me to part with such a treasured possession?"

Lydia squinted. "What treasure?"

Kitty lifted an eyebrow. "Perhaps your diamond earrings?"

Lydia slapped her thigh. "Toilet paper for diamonds?" She glared at Kitty. "Both?"

"Both," Kitty said, pausing between each word, "every. . .little. . . sparkle."

Lydia removed the jewels from her fanny pack.

Kitty dug into her saddle bag for her stash. "Girl, you gotta learn the drip-dry technique and collect soft grasses during the day."

"Wait a minute," Rosy said. "If we need those earrings for negotiation, regardless of ownership, they'll be forfeited. Agreed? Understood? Kitty, you agree?"

"Got it, boss." With the toilet paper exchange finalized, Kitty rotated her head from side to side, showing off her new diamond studs as Lydia stuffed TP in her saddle bag.

Elle held Bond's bridle up and he lowered his head to receive the bit.

When Elle lifted her head, she saw a white ribbon cut across the bright blue sky. "Look!" she said.

Lydia's face lit up like she'd been saved. "It's a plane! It's a plane!" she screamed. "That means the world is working!"

"Probably military," Rosy said, bursting Lydia's balloon. "It don't change anything. We move on. We've got many miles to cover today." Gradually the white contrail separated into faint wisps and then evaporated into an ocean of blue.

The rolling, undulating hills at the east end of the Badlands were a mix of green needle, thread, cordgrass, gamma and buffalo grasses with prairie coneflowers, white milkwort, and butterflies, moths and more birds. Too soon the morning became unbearably hot and mirages played with our senses. "This sun and water-sucking wind is turning me into jerky," Sal whined. "Biting beasts lurk everywhere. The asshole in the Chevy coulda killed us. Kitty got shot. I got no hair. My butt looks like a purple grape, my body stinks and I can't even think about alcohol." She lifted her arms up as if appealing to the gods. "This is Hell's slow burning fire and, Lord, I'm a sinner." She lowered her head, "We need rain." With the temperature unbearable, we escaped the heat by ducking under an old wooden trestle. Its underbelly contained proof of previous tenants: snake skins, spiders, webs, scat, bones and feathers among the debris. The remnants of rain.

Kitty called out to a magpie that landed nearby. "Hey, bud!" She flaunted her new sparkles. The bird looked around, hopped over to a horse deposit and stuck its beak into nature's hot lunch.

Rosy chuckled, "That's what I call making lemonade out of lemons."

I stripped down to my underwear, walked out into the open, then slowly stomped my bare feet up and down on the hard earth.

"What in hell are you doing?" Rosy puzzled.

"Rain dance," I said.

Lydia took off her shirt, pants, boots and socks. Standing tall, and with exaggerated purpose, she stomped her left heel down hard, then lifted onto her toes, momentarily perched, before repeating the same movement with her other foot. We mimicked each other's movements, bending at our waists, rising up tall, constantly turning in a circle, repeating our moves.

Rosy threw up her arms. "You two have lost it."

As the others cheered us on, with Tai Chi precision, we pleaded, "We need rain. We need rain."

Everyone except Rosy chanted the chorus, begging for rain. Rosy sat under the trestle rolling her eyes until we all fell still.

Elle, lean in profile, placed her hands on her hips and flexed her biceps, assuming a body builder's pose. "Rain or no rain," she roared, "I want you to know this has been the most challenging adventure I've ever faced. I feel better and tougher than I have in years. I love being outside of time. No longer am I caught in the loop of money and acquiring things I don't even miss. Truth is, stuff, material shit, never made me happy. We don't own material shit, it owns us."

Sal looked incredulous. "You're not saying that crawling across this desert, dying of thirst and turning into dried prunes is good?"

Kitty joined Elle and assumed a karate profile. "I feel alive. Freer than I've ever known. These last few days have been rich. I feel one with the land. One with nature. And being with the most incredible women ever!"

"Aw, bull," Sal snorted. "Romantic drivel is what that is. Heat stroke must be affecting your brain. You can't convince me you don't miss your cell phone, your GPS, your computer. Get real. Remember hot showers, clean sheets, washers and dryers?"

Elle extended her arms toward the sky, opening them wide. "Hear ye, hear ye! I'm getting my batteries charged. I don't need no damn hair dryer or microwave oven to cook my food!" She lowered her arms. "I've no need for a flat screen TV as long as I've got you to entertain me." She motioned toward our horses. "They are living great lives. They get to sleep under an open sky, get plenty of exercise and dine on delicious grass. They are stronger than ever because we are stronger than ever." She lifted her right arm like Rosy the Riveter, "We are all strong!"

"Conserve your energy," Rosy said. "Trust me, you are not going to make it rain." Just then the wind picked up and clouds came in from the west. Lydia and I smiled at the pitter-patter of a light rain on the wooden trestle.

Rosy smiled back. "I guess I shouldn't doubt the power of strong women."

"Maybe Iktomi pulled this off!" I mumbled.

The temperature dropped as Kitty and Elle rode ahead to scout for water. They came back and reported a black Angus herd clustered around a man-made pond appearing to be fed by an underground pipe. Nervously, we followed, scanning the landscape, wary about running into somebody and enduring another ambush.

Elle volunteered to fill the buckets and stripped down before entering the water. Butt-deep, halfway to the middle, she shouted, "Toss my rope," her voice taut with urgency. "This goo might be hiding quicksand."

Rosy tossed her a lasso and cinched it to Bond's saddle horn just like in Western movies. Elle looped the rope under her arms, balanced a bucket on one shoulder, then slowly sidled over to a pipe level with her armpits that spewed water. Our water brigade was relieved to find the water surprisingly clear. With enough purified water and our containers full, our spent crew called it a day. Even though prairie gold was all around, we fired up our peak stove and feasted on rehydrated dried chili. Settled back in our saddle loungers, and watched the rising of the soon-to-be full moon.

Our conversation turned to our vulnerability about crossing the Missouri River only a few days away. "Safety's number one," Rosy said sternly. "Once on the other side of the Missouri, we'll stay clear of people and avoid populated places. We'll ride at night and sleep during the day."

It was deadly silent when Elle whispered, "Something's moving." She switched on her headlight and her beam caught the yellow eyes of a large animal that quickly vanished into the darkness.

Lydia clutched her chest, "What was that?"

Sal whimpered, "A mountain lion?"

"Could've been," said Rosy. "More probably a bobcat. If it were a lion, Romeo and the horses would have gone wacko and I didn't hear one hoof stomp."

I went to Justice and buried my face in his neck. Elle came over and patted my back, "You're doing good, pal. Even though this is not easy, I think we are all getting better at managing our fears. I really believe we'll make it home."

"You hear that, old boy?" I said, "I'm counting on you to get us home and reunite with your buddy, Black Jack." I crawled into our tent, embraced the hard ground and listened to the sounds of night. I tossed and turned, worried that this marathon was too hard, and that my old boy was tired and sore, and this ride was taking its toll. I thought about asking Elle if I should give him a dose of Bute but knew that drug could be hard on his gut.

Early morning, packing up, I told Elle how I was concerned that Justice was getting weaker. "Don't, Maia," she, said, lifting Romeo's panniers. "Justice is doing great." When I saddled him, I kissed his nose, looked into his giant amber eyes and prayed Elle was right.

Late that afternoon, we happened upon remnants of a time past. Weathered boards, bleached gray, strewn around a long-gone farmstead was what remained of a shelter that was once a dream home to pioneers.

Those brave souls that had ventured to the Great Plains packing hopes and dreams. Rusted metal odds and ends, a horse plow and an old truck frame lay in tangled grasses surrounded by an overgrown pasture and skeletons of neglected fruit trees. One, however, still had apples that were pretty dry and shriveled.

I tried to imagine what it was like for homesteaders to live here. How they were brave or desperate enough to leave their homelands and believe they could survive?

Lydia sighed, "The utter loneliness would have driven me crazy."

"I'd have shot myself," Sal said.

Lydia and I waded through tall grass as we made our way to the old apple tree. My boot hit something. I bent down into earth's basket and picked up an old wooden cross with a carving that simply said, "Wife."

Lydia poked around and found another smaller cross that once marked another grave. "Baby Boy," Lydia sighed. "This is so sad."

"If only we knew the real history of this place," I said.

Respectfully, we laid the crosses back exactly where we discovered them. Looking around I wondered if my mom was born in a place like this. If I'd stumble across her birthplace, how would I even know? Would I sense it the way Justice sensed danger?

Balancing in the low-slung crotch of the gnarled apple tree, I took off my shirt and tied the sleeves together to make a container. Slipping apples into my shirt, I was eye-level with a mud-lined bird nest and about to lower my apple-filled shirt to Lydia when I noticed movement below in the grass. "Lydia," I shouted, "Don't move. Snake to your right."

The serpent rattled its tail and lifted its triangular head. Lydia froze and stifled a squeal. "Listen to me," I said. "Slowly, very slowly, move left. Slowly," I repeated. Lydia followed my orders and when clear of the rattlesnake, I yelled, "Run! Get Elle and Kitty!"

Lydia ran like a bat out of hell. I watched the rattler's forked tongue lick the air. I tossed an apple and it landed near its head. The rattler struck, recoiled, relaxed, stretched and began slithering away. Just then, Kitty came, stopped about fifteen feet away from the snake, fired her pistol and nailed that rattler. It twisted and contorted into a ball. She fired a second shot and blew its head off.

"I'm coming down," I said, easing my legs to the ground.

Everybody ran to see what was happening and stayed away from the snake, debating how to deal with its potentially lethal head. Elle lifted her shotgun, took aim, fired a shot and blew its head clear away. Feeling safe, she bent down and lifted the headless, lifeless snake's body chest high. "Feel it," she said, pushing its body toward me. Slowly I reached out to touch its greenish dark brown scales. It felt rough and I jerked my hand back. "It feels like extra-coarse sandpaper."

"Most snakes are smooth," Elle said, cutting off the rattle, shaking it, then tucking it into her hatband by her rabbit's foot. She stretched the dead snake's body out on the hard ground. With her hunting knife, she slit the snake end to end, and scooped out its innards with her fingers. Kitty helped pick the pellets out. Slowly Elle slid her fingers down her knife blade, then wiped it clean. Then proudly said, "We'll be adding snake to tonight's meal."

Sal laughed, "Didn't someone once say that rattlesnake tastes just like chicken?" She waited a minute, "So this time we turn snake into chicken?"

"It will be great if everything we're gonna eat will taste as good as chicken," Rosy said.

"Howdy, pardners," Kitty said, then presented us with her cheerful morning greeting of, "Daylight in the swamp." Bright-eyed and talkative, as we left camp, she asked. "So, what's your favorite movie?" We all agreed that *The Jerk* and *Blazing Saddles* topped our lists. She smiled, "Remember *The Big Chill*?" And everyone agreed it was a great movie.

Elle asked, "So, what's your most treasured book?"

Rosy brightened, "*Bridges of Madison County.*"

"Hands down, my all-time favorite is *A Sand County Almanac* by Aldo Leopold." Elle paused, "I sure do miss reading something other than maps and signs."

"I never really got into reading books," Kitty said. "Magazines worked better for me."

"*The Bible* was the most important book ever written," Lydia said.

Sal stuck a finger in her mouth and did a fake gag. "Right. Another book written by men wanting to hold onto power and money."

"Don't do that," Rosy said. "Remember, we each have a right to our own opinions."

"Well, I like fiction," Sal replied. "I like that it takes me away. It's an escape." She chuckled. "Anyone ever read Janet Evanovich's books? I love Stephanie Plum and all those crazy characters. It's light reading and makes me laugh."

Book titles raced through my mind. Literature was my college major. The course on Steinbeck was such a fabulous gift. *The Grapes of Wrath* was a powerful and timely piece of literature. I then said, "Anything by Dr. Seuss. I've read *Horton Hatches the Egg* and *The Lorax* over and over again to our kids and grandkids." I took a deep breath, feeling the ache of missing our grandbabies.

Rosy moseyed Catch closer to Thief. "I think we might have a problem." Sal looked stricken. "I think I heard a clink coming from Thief's back right leg." Rosy dismounted, lifted Thief's rear hoof and groaned, "He's got a few nails loose."

Elle got out the farrier kit from Romeo's pack. Then, acting as Rosy's attending nurse, she passed instruments to her boss. Rosy crouched down with her forearms planted on her thighs and Thief's hoof secured between her legs and scraped away the hardened clay with an oval farrier's knife. Using the nippers, she removed two loose nails, then swapped Elle the nippers for a hammer. She held each shoe nail with its head angled out to carefully hammer it into place.

"Cutters," she commanded again, sounding like a surgeon. Handles first, Elle gave her the cutters and she clipped the protruding nail ends, filed each one flat, then pressed them tight to the hoof. Struggling to stand without help, Rosy showed her age. "Watched Richard, our farrier for years, but this was my first time doing it myself. Richard always cautioned that a horse could go lame if a nail went soft or got pounded in at the wrong angle."

"You did good, Sis," said Sal.

"Thanks."

Kitty told another one of her stories while Rosy and Elle did a quick check of each of our horse's shoes. "There was this young mom looking to buy a horse and brought her five-year-old daughter to Ray and Rosy's stable. That day Rio was getting new shoes. The child, her eyes big as saucers, asked innocently, 'What kind of shoes? Tennis shoes? Ballet shoes?'" Kitty giggled. "Can't you just imagine what her mind saw?"

"Sounds like a great kid's book," I said.

Kitty beamed. "I can see it. Rio, my man, with his picture on the cover."

"Let's see if we can make that happen when we get home," I said.

Our attention was drawn to a dozen or so antelope bounding up the south-facing hill.

Lydia asked if there was any difference between antelope and pronghorn. "No difference," Elle replied, rubbing her belly. "They taste the same."

Lydia shook her head. "You see food. I see beauty."

"You'll come around, sweetie," she said, putting the farrier tools back in the leather case. Hearing a pheasant call, she grabbed her shotgun and headed off into the grasses. After the report of her gun, we watched as she emerged carrying her quarry. The rooster had a neat white ring circling its neck and a red crest, the color of a wine bottle topping his head. She laid it on the ground and, within minutes, its iridescent dark green and purple feathers were pulled from its still warm body as she cast them into the wind for a final flight.

"We'll camp here," Rosy said, sounding like a chuckwagon cook of a hundred years ago. Elle twisted dry grass into rolls shaped like little bird nests, lit a match, cupped her hands and blew until smoke rose. Soon the smell of supper drew us together.

Sal belched after devouring her share of roasted pheasant. "Tasted like chicken."

"Worked for me," Kitty said, licking her bowl.

Lydia was unusually quiet while we ate, then slipped away. I got up to follow her, telling the others that something about Lydia didn't feel right. I found her in our tent curled in a fetal position. "What's wrong?" I asked, sitting next to her.

She sniffled, "I can't stop thinking about my family, Maia." She blew her nose. "If only I knew they're okay."

I rested my head in my hand. "Do you believe in telepathy?"

She rolled over and faced me. "Huh?"

I took a deep, long breath. "I want to believe that we can communicate telepathically."

"You mean like sending your thoughts to others?"

"Like that. In my lifetime, telepathy has happened so many times that I can't deny it. It's something I can't say I understand. Sometimes I'll think about somebody and they'll show up knocking on my door, or the next day I'll find a letter from them in my mailbox or they'll call. So how about trying this, when a loved one comes to mind, in your head, say you love them and tell them you are on your way home."

"That's ridiculous."

"Lydia, our culture is addicted to communicating using gadgets. Computers connect us in ways that stagger my imagination. What if the human mind can outdo all of that? What if it's possible to elevate our consciousness, our awareness, and in some way free ourselves from technology? Just maybe we have the baked-in power to communicate by ourselves." I sat up. "We need to learn to trust our own abilities. We trust computers and electricity. Isn't that ridiculous?" I paused. "Why do we not trust our own powers?" Lydia stared blankly at me. "You think I'm crazy, don't you?"

"I trust you, Maia, but telepathy?" She rolled onto her other side. "Yes, I think you're a certifiably crazy loon from Minnesota."

"Won't hurt to try," I said, lying down. "I try to do it with Mark and the kids. I'll see when I get home if they felt it."

"I'm trying, Maia. Believe me, I'm trying, but I'm not getting any mail. Nobody from home is calling."

"You believe in a god you cannot see. Prayer and Divine messaging is ancient telepathy."

"That's true," she whispered.

I thought, it's strange how fear, like an imaginary prison can creep into consciousness. Until sleep took me, I kept repeating, "I'm praying you are all okay and know I'm on my way."

Like a pastel painting, the early morning sky had hues of soft pink and gentle lilac. "Look," Lydia said, as a blazing white ball traveled north along the eastern horizon. Elle lifted her binoculars, "Meteors are flashes in the pan and quickly move across the sky. I'd guess it's a comet." She handed the binoculars to Rosy. "If we see it tomorrow, it's a comet."

Sal crossed her arms. "Oh great! Aren't comets considered bad omens? Don't they forecast catastrophes?" She uncrossed her arms. "Like we need any more bad luck."

"Don't buy that omen crap," snapped Elle. "That's just fear-based nonsense. A comet is a hunk of ice and rock wagging a fuzzy tail. No way can a comet predict the future, especially a disaster." She paused. "Well, unless it's gonna hit earth."

"Don't go there," Rosy said. "We've got enough to worry about."

As we rode on, we discussed the concepts of infinite space and watched tall blue stem grasses dance on the high rolling hills. Ahead, Canada geese, with their landing gear down, circled, then disappeared behind a hill.

Elle squinted, "I'll bet there's a pond." With the shotgun in her hand, she crept toward the honking. Her meat harvester sounded, and we hightailed it to the pond in time to see all but one of the flock dash across the water and resume flight. Elle stripped down and, like a hunting dog, swam to retrieve her bird.

Kitty had a sly, playful look on her face as she stared at the pond trimmed with browning cattails. Promptly she took off her boots, belt and hat, yet still wearing her shirt and pants, she plopped in the water, then twisted and turned like a washing machine. With the moves of a stripper, she exited like she was strutting across a stage, slipping out of her wet clothes, tossing them to dry on wild rose and honeysuckle bushes.

"What a great way to do laundry," exclaimed Lydia, and promptly followed Kitty's example.

Elle handed Rosy the goose and we helped gut and pluck. Rosy lifted a hunk of raw meat and triumphantly proclaimed, "This here is pure protein."

Sal groused, "If I eat anymore wild birds, I'll grow feathers."

"Then you could fly home," Lydia giggled.

"You are so funny," Sal replied.

Dragonflies hovered. Chirping crickets and cicada joined the swooping whoosh of nighthawks and the dance of lightning bugs. Wispy, eerie-looking clouds stretched across the night sky and clouds bundled together, some taking the shape of critters incarnated in a totally different realm.

"Anyone ever see a ghost?" I asked.

Sal squawked, "No such thing."

"Well, I saw one," I replied, smartly.

Lydia lifted an eyebrow, "Do tell."

"Mark and I were on a trail ride in the Canadian Rockies that Ray and Rosy had arranged. We were with two local guides and a huge group of riders. One night, camping about four hours north of Whistler in British Columbia, we all gathered together around a big campfire. Abruptly, Mark stood and left without saying one word. I was annoyed because we'd agreed to stay up and talk with our new friends. Fifteen minutes after he left, I excused myself and walked toward our tent. The night was bright with a full moon. Everywhere little white ground flowers glowed. Halfway up the hill trail to our tent, I stopped and looked up. Fifty feet directly in front of me was the figure of a tall man, dressed in black wearing a cowboy hat. I thought it was Mark and called his name. The figure moved closer, yet became hazier, fuzzier. It's hard to describe. 'Mark?' I said, but there was no reply, just a thick, almost loud silence. I was confused, but not scared. Gradually the fuzzy figure floated backwards."

"Like off the ground?" asked Lydia.

"Like a foot off the ground. Poof, then it disappeared. I spun around, hoping it would turn out to be a shadow cast by someone I hadn't seen. Better yet, by Mark. Nobody was anywhere around. I got to our tent, unzipped the flap and saw Mark lying on top of his sleeping bag with his hands balled into tight fists pushing down hard on his chest." Fear was in his eyes. He gasped, 'Sharp pain, Maia.'

I lay next to him and we held each other. We were in the middle of nowhere with zero possibility of getting any medical help. Somehow, we both fell asleep. Thankfully, the next morning Mark felt better."

Lydia held her hands on her heart. "That's so heavy."

"Way too weird." Sal shook her head from side to side.

"It was weird. But I did see something that night. Since then, whenever people talk about ghosts, I listen. It was pretty unbelievably weird, but I'm telling you it really happened."

Rosy shook her head. "Over the years on these rides I've seen, heard and felt so many oddball dang things. I don't doubt you for a minute, Maia. Far's I'm concerned, it was one more brush with another reality. Life can be mysterious as all get out. Brutal. Merciless. Beautiful. Yet at the same time filled with wonderment. It sure does have the power to hold our attention. We gotta give it that."

Chapter 14

Harvest Moon

"Thar she blows!" Elle shouted, as a glowing egg cut a south to north path straight across the eastern horizon. "Wonder how long it'll be with us?" She passed the binoculars to me. "Good omen, Maia?"

"Time will tell," I replied, watching the comet race away.

"Pack it up, ladies," Rosy barked.

Sal parroted, "Pack it up, ladies."

Rosy spun around to face her, "Don't mess with me."

Sal lowered her head, muttering, "Are we getting a little edgy?"

"Yes," Rosy grumbled.

The closer we got to the Missouri River, the more moisture we felt in the air. We were grateful to no longer be breathing grit. Rosy signaled us to ride side by side so she could run through her plan for crossing the bridge. "First we find a high perch on one of the bluffs and check out the Lewis and Clark bridge to see what's happening on the river. We lay low until it's dark and quiet, then we cross the bridge like mice. Once on the other side, we'll hide out somewhere near the big overlook."

"Sounds good," said Elle. "It's smart we have enough time to witness our first real interaction with civilization."

"I'm nervous about riding across that long stretch of concrete," I said. "What if Justice freaks out? What about vehicles and roadblocks?"

"Don't worry about Justice. We've all been through a lot. Our horses trust us," said Rosy. "We're a gang. A band of sisters. We've got no choice but to take this risk."

"Don't fret," Elle said. "We'll be careful. If the bridge is crawling with drunken drug addicts, or the National Guard, we'll wait till they clear out."

We rode south by southeast until intersecting with a gravel road that headed due east. Checking the map, Elle determined that gravel road would be a clear shot to the Missouri. Above, a flock of mallards, flying in a rag-tag loose line, quacked as they headed south.

Romeo's load heaved and swayed as he climbed the bluff to our vantage point. The top was not so much a promontory as a perch. Below, the glistening turquoise river chiseled with sunlight took my breath away. It seemed as though a lifetime had passed since we crossed the Missouri on our way to Custer. The I-90, two parallel concrete ribbons, curved north at the western approach, stretching over a long embankment before crossing the main bridge near Chamberlain. It looked empty. Downstream, a rust-brown railroad bridge stretched across the river. The no-frills Lewis and Clark Memorial Bridge rose above the navigation channel. Distinctive rock outcroppings decorated the east bank, offering positive proof of where glaciers stopped their advance. East and west banks are different in geology and in spirit. Eastern South Dakota is a land of endurance tended by hard-working farmers. Western South Dakota is magical ranch country.

Settled on our perch, we kept watch. No boats were on the river. No trains crossed the railroad bridge. We saw several trucks speed across the concrete bridge. Elle, Kitty, Lydia and I decided to hike down a game trail to the river and took a fishing pole and various water containers. The river edge had piles of flat shale. Kitty picked up a flat hunk, slid it through her fingers, then skipped it three times before it entered its new underwater residence.

With our boots off, we rolled up our pant legs, then ventured into the icy cold water and struggled to hold our own against the strong current.

I sighed, "It feels great to have clean feet."

Lydia picked her toenails, "I sure could use a pedicure."

Kitty found a wiggly creature and drove a hook into its little body. She tossed her line into the fast-moving water and snagged a bluish catfish. Swiftly she swung it onto the bank. It flopped its deep-forked tail back and forth, as if angling itself back toward its watery home. Its wiry whiskers gyrated as Kitty tried to remove the hook. After a frustrating struggle with the three-pound fish, she picked up a rock and, in one swift motion, crushed its skull, then threaded a stringer through its mouth and swung her catch over her shoulder, looking like Huck Finn.

Elle was first up the game trail back to our perch when all of a sudden, a cloud of stinging monsters swarmed around us. "Bees!" she shrieked.

As bees enveloped her, Lydia freaked and ran in no particular direction, slapping at the air and hitting her own body. Kitty twirled the catfish over her head as she bolted to escape the swarming cloud. I ducked through underbrush and gradually climbed up the hill. I heard Elle yell, "Somebody get Lydia's fanny pack! Quick!"

Lydia was sprawled out on the ground, her chest heaving, having difficulty breathing. Elle held the Epi-pen as she knelt beside her. "Want me to do it?"

Lydia choked, "Wait." Already her hands had swelled with red welts.

Rosy caressed Lydia's hair. "Don't worry. We'll take care of you."

Elle took Lydia's pulse. "If you start to lose consciousness, I'm administering this epinephrine," then ordered, "Somebody get the first aid kit." Sal handed her the kit and lifted a canteen to Lydia's lips as Elle dropped 100 mg of Benadryl into Lydia's mouth.

Lydia closed her eyes. Romeo stood next to us, as we waited to see if the Benadryl would help his Lydia. Lydia tried to speak, but suffered a dry, horsey throat. "We are going to cross the river tonight," she insisted and tried to sit up. "It's just a bee sting."

"More like a dozen stings," Elle said, urging her to lie back down. "We have plenty of time. Relax. We'll cross when you're up to it."

"Damn right," Lydia groaned. It was at that very moment that it became crystal clear that the fashion princess who showed up at Rosy's barn dressed to the nines to go on a horsey ride had transformed into a real, down-to-earth cowgirl.

To avoid a fire that might be seen, we lit our camp stove, heated a pot of water and cut Kitty's fish into small cubes. Daylight was fading fast when Elle used the binoculars to check the river scene. "A boat's coming really fast upstream toward our side of the bridge."

"Probably fishing," I said.

"Looks more like a heavy-duty tug than a fishing boat," she said. "Like it could be military. Funny. It's the same color as the water." She spotted a black pickup truck parked near the end of the bridge with two guys sitting on the truck gate reading something." She paused, "Something written on their truck door." She squinted, "Looks like, 'Prairie Power.' Yeah, that's what it says in bright copper-colored letters. 'Prairie Power.'"

I asked, "Prairie Power? Could that mean electricity is back?"

Rosy focused on the activity below. "Not for one minute can we fool ourselves into thinking electricity is fixed. I don't think anything will ever be normal again."

"I can hope, can't I?" I said.

"Sorry," Rosy said. "This situation makes me nervous." She turned to Elle, "What's happening? Can you tell what they're doing?"

The boat slowed down and hovered near the bridge. The two guys on shore waved, then sprinted down a trail toward the boat. Two men on the boat launched a motorized heavy-duty, dingy-like amphibian raft. Another man remained on the boat while the others drove the raft ashore. Four men quickly worked to unload packages about a foot square and stacked them at the water's edge. "Whatever's in those packages must be incredibly heavy, because it's taking two guys to carry each one," said Elle.

When the raft was completely unloaded, two men returned to the boat and hoisted the raft back on board. While the boat disappeared downstream, we watched the two men on shore make at least a dozen trips back and forth and shove the packages onto their truck bed.

Hearing a convoy of trucks coming down the hill toward the bridge, the two men abruptly stopped, turned toward the approaching sound and jumped in their truck. The driver made a sharp turn east and the truck's back tailgate dropped open and something fell on the ground.

"What the fuck did we just witness?" stammered Sal.

A shiver ran through me. "Oh, my God," I said. "Something about that sure didn't feel right."

Elle lowered her binoculars. "I wonder what fell out of their truck. Let's see if we can find it when we cross the bridge."

We ate boiled catfish chowder and watched the sky turn deep blue, as several pink lights appeared on the eastern slope. Then an enormous, pumpkin-colored globe began its rise. We all commented, "It's so huge!"

"When the moon appears bigger than usual it's reached perigee," said Elle. "That's a highfalutin' way of saying it's as close as it's gonna get to earth."

Transfixed, Kitty said, "It's gorgeous."

Although big and beautiful, the moon cast no warmth.

"The Harvest moon is a symbol of abundance" Elle said, stretching her arms out. "It also means winter is coming."

"That's sobering," Sal said.

With the moon directly overhead, Rosy told us it was time to saddle up. "See any vehicles, keep walking. Don't make eye contact. Pretend you belong. If you feel your horse is getting nervous, whisper its name. Stick together. We can do this."

I saddled Liberty and helped Lydia get settled. "You okay?" I asked.

"I can do it," she said, caressing Liberty's mane.

Rosy took Romeo's lead rope and we ventured down a game trail, stopping several times to detect if anybody was nearby. Reaching the bridge, Elle's eyes were drawn to something flapping against a pilaster holding up a thick parapet rail.

"Wait," Elle yelled, hopping off Bond and picking up a standard eight-and-a-half by eleven book. "This might help us figure out what we just witnessed." She stuffed the book under her butt. "At least it will be something else to read."

Lined up single file, nose-to-butt, we waited for Rosy's signal. She raised her right arm just like she did when we went through the buffalo herd. Catch stepped onto the bridge, and Rosy turned around. "Stick together. We can do this!"

Justice and I were at the end of the line and I imagined if someone could have looked down at us from a small plane we could have looked like a caterpillar, slowly inching forward along the rail as we crossed the bridge. The hollow pock-pock of our horse's hooves reverberated on the concrete deck, for a moment, I regretted we hadn't covered their hooves to soften our sound.

Backlit by silver moonlight that reflected off the black water like diamonds, the moon cast enough light for us to see the swift river current racing, creating dark whirlpools and eddies, brush-stroked with white highlights, madly twirling around the enormous concrete bridge pillars. The steep, man-made dike created pools that channeled the river under the main bridge.

Last to leave the bridge, we'd covered the distance in less than twenty minutes without any incident. Luckily, we saw no one. My entire body was tensed to the point of rigidity. I sucked in a deep breath and I felt a release and then Justice did the same.

Hightailing it past a gigantic walleye sculpture, Kitty made a fly-casting gesture. "Next time, let's go fishing."

"Next time," Rosy replied, "we are getting our trucks and trailers, turning around and heading home."

Sal spat and it hit the concrete pavement. "Trust me. There will never be a next time."

Chapter 15

Lightning Strikes

Kitty was the first to spot a hiking trail sign that pointed straight up the hill to the Overlook. Cottonwood leaves rattled and cast winks of moonlight as our caravan climbed the hillside. At the top, the fifty-foot-tall stainless-steel statue of Sacagawea called "Dignity" embraced us with open arms. Moonlight shone like a beacon on the blue and white star quilt wrapped around her. We dashed to the hand pump and drank water without having to filter it.

Relieved to find the parking lot empty, we decided to play it safe and take turns keeping watch. After helping Lydia get settled, I secured Justice to the corner of a cement shelter and spread my sleeping bag out on a precast picnic tabletop. Clouds drifted across the moon, blocking its light and I fell into a deep sleep. It was completely dark when I jerked with a quick spasm triggered by the sensation of falling. Justice was a few inches away and nudged me with his head, preventing me from tumbling off the table and onto the hard ground. I got up and wrapped my arms around his neck and thanked him for being such a great pal.

While I took my turn, Elle woke and perched on her concrete tabletop bed with her sleeping bag draped like a heavy shawl over her shoulders, staring at the eastern sky. Behind us, fog rose up out of the river gorge as sunlight revealed fields of corn and soybeans that glistened golden. Robins issued their morning wake up calls. Pheasants crowed.

"Here it comes," Elle said. "We've got ourselves an awe-inspiring comet."

Rosy checked her watch. "I think it's showing up a little later and looks like it's getting duller."

"Fine with me," snapped Sal, plopping down next to Elle. "Too spooky. Makes me nervous."

Elle opened the book she found at the bridge. "Check this out." The cover was titled, "Prairie Power" and appeared to be an engineer's book with smooth ivory drafting vellum gridded sheets. Page after page had equations, sketches, electrical diagrams, calculations, with incomprehensible words and highly detailed pictures of wind turbines with thick wires and cables. One highly polished page showed a metal object the size of a big wedge of cheese with one blunt side. She pointed, "Look at this." A turbine displayed a slice straight through a gearbox connected to blades labeled 'wings' and a shaded edge labeled 'nickel' and a small "Inverter" sketch. "Interesting," she said, turning another page that revealed a centerfold. "Kitty, check out this centerfold."

Kitty peered over her shoulder.

Elle chuckled, "Fooled you. Not that kind." They laughed and closed the book. "I'll bet those cheese-like wedges were in the boxes those two men loaded in their truck."

"It's all too weird," Rosy said, unfolding our map. "We need to decide what backroads will safely get us around Sioux Falls and into Minnesota.

"We still have four hundred miles before we get home," I said. "If we ride twenty plus miles a day straight through, we should be home in three weeks."

"Doubt that's gonna be possible," Rosy said, pulling her hat down almost to her thick, graying eyebrows. "Lucky if we make it back in a month."

Lydia tried not to scratch her itches and whimpered, "The worst is behind us. Right?"

Rosy looked worried. "Can't say that for certain."

I tapped a finger on the map and pointed at a linear scatter of little black dots. "These are Hutterite Colonies and they grow tons of food. They're kind of like the Amish, except they use tractors and have electricity."

"That means they're in the same boat with everybody else," said Sal.

"I guess," I replied. "That could be true, but they know how to do things the old way. I wonder if they might sell us some food."

"We'll see," said Rosy. "We need to get outta here before we run into others."

Leaving the Overlook, two vehicles came up the access road and we quickly ducked behind a billboard that advertised the Corn Palace. My mind tumbled back to a trip I made long ago with my parents to Mitchell, South Dakota. Mom thought the Corn Palace was an incredible work of art. Dad said it was a giant bird feeder. I remembered it was on that trip that we detoured to Mom's birthplace somewhere south of Mitchell. I couldn't remember the name of the town. I did know that Mom was of this land. She was a solid, hard-working, good-hearted woman who loved her family. She bore witness to the Great Depression and, as a result, never wasted anything. All purchases were carefully thought out and meant to last. Remembering Mom comforted and saddened me.

At the first gravel road we ventured south and rode past huge metal buildings, farm equipment, vehicles, metal granaries and enormous haystacks. Along the way we saw people walking among buildings and equipment, but we kept our heads down, didn't speak or wave and practiced being invisible. Frequent waterholes along the road kept everyone's thirst satisfied. Clouds played hide and seek with the morning sun and the wind hitting our backs seemed to be pushing us home.

I pulled Justice's reins back and stopped when I spotted an ancient Burma Shave sign poking out of the side ditch. "Anyone remember these?"

Lydia raised an eyebrow. "Some kind of rural advertising?" Her blank stare told me she was stating the obvious; she had no idea what I was talking about.

"When I was young," I explained, "roadsides were lined with sequential signs spaced about thirty yards apart. Each series had clever sayings. The last sign always said, 'Burma Shave,' which was a brand of shaving cream. One of my family's favorites went something like this. First sign said, 'Does your husband,' then further up the road, 'Misbehave,' then the next, 'Grunt and Grumble,' and next, 'Rant and Rave,' then, 'Shoot the Brute some', and finally, 'Burma Shave.' I remember Mom's favorite, 'Round the Corner, Lickety split, Beautiful car, Wasn't it?' then, 'Burma Shave.'"

"Ahh," joked Lydia. "Life before the internet."

Gradually the sky was being overtaken by a wall of dark gray clouds. Distant thunder rumbled and we searched for a safe spot to hold up. Thunder rumbled, hushed and low, then gradually grew stronger until it boomed. Lightning flashed and stabbed the earth like a knife. We wasted no time setting up a picket line, put up our tents and stashed our gear inside. We ducked inside just as the wind gushed and brought the first pitter-patter of rain. Within minutes, the wind picked up and the rain pounded hard. Hunkering down, we repeatedly had to lift the center of the tent to empty its growing belly.

Lydia kept her hands locked in prayer. "Please, Dear Lord, make this stop."

In time, the rain did stop and the earth smelled like laundry fresh off the line. We waited to dry out before we were able to move on. I'd fallen in love with the continuous changes in the night sky. "Lakota called stars, *Woniya of Wakan Tanka*," I said, in awe. "It means the Holy Breath of the Great Spirit." I stared at the Big Dipper, "We'd do well if we put our trust in the Great Spirit."

Lydia smiled, "I can do that, Maia."

It was early the next morning when we saw a black and white sign telling us the Hutterite colony was down a side road. Rosy gave me one of her looks. "You serious about begging these folks for food?"

"They are good people," I lobbied. "Rosy, at some point we have to trust others. I'm willing to ride down that road and take a chance."

Rosy looked from one horse and rider to the next, then dropped her head like a wet cloth. Slowly lifting her head, she said, "Well, okay then. Maia, it's me and you, we'll do it together." Our horses nickered, and Romeo brayed as we parted, informing anyone at the end of this road that visitors might be heading their way. The long gravel road was lined on both sides with twelve-foot corn. At the fields end stood three very long white buildings. A dozen bearded men dressed in black and wearing wide-brimmed straw hats emerged from the closest building and stood stoically on an enormous porch.

The colony was comprised of several large barns and enormous sheds, a huge feedlot full of cattle, a herd of dairy cows fenced near a milking parlor and hundreds of pigs and chickens. Several very large tractors and a bulldozer were housed under an open shed. Solar panels covered a south-facing hill near three wind turbines.

The battalion of bearded men made the short hair on the back of my neck stand up as I sensed a gun behind every window. The Hutterite men remained perfectly still as we dismounted. I humbly explained our situation, concluding with, "We are just trying to make it back home and we've got a lot of miles to ride before winter sets in."

One man stepped forward, stopping about a foot away from us. Instinctively, Rosy and I stepped backwards. "We do not welcome strangers. Outsiders bring trouble," he said, forcefully. "We have our ways."

I tried my best to assure him, "We do not bring trouble. Could you please sell us some food?"

He glared. "If we give you food, you must leave immediately."

Rosy and I nodded our heads, agreeing, then said, "Yes."

The man who spoke first conferred with two other bearded men. They nodded and dashed into nearby buildings. A few minutes later one man returned with two buckets of water and set them in front of our horses. Justice looked at the man before accepting his gift.

I risked a question. "Have you heard anything about what's happening?"

The lead man scowled. "The Bible says the world is not our concern."

Eyes down, Rosy strained to sound obsequious. "You know any place we could camp?"

That man lifted his arms and pointed. "Due east, about a mile straight down that gravel road, you'll see a brick silo and a big bur oak. Right behind is an abandoned farmhouse."

Another man returned carrying two brown grocery bags with carrot tops spilling out.

Rosy handed him two twenty-dollar bills and thanked him.

I lifted my eyes to make contact and placed the palms of my hands together in prayer. "May God bless."

"May God bless us all," the main man said with a hint of compassion.

Settled in our saddles, we each held a bagful of carrots, cabbage, onions and potatoes in our laps. Halfway back, we heard our horses whinny and then Romeo joined the chorus. Immediately, Catch and Justice answered their call.

Elle rode Bond to meet us and smiled seeing the bags of food. "What happened?"

"They sure didn't want us sticking around," I said, handing everyone a carrot. "They said there's an old farmhouse not far ahead."

"This carrot is the best thing I've ever eaten," said Sal. "Seriously."

"Wasn't that your first carrot?" Rosy snickered as she handed everyone vegetables to stuff into their saddlebags.

Sal leaned over, offering Thief her carrot's butt end. "From now on carrots are my favorite food."

Lydia smiled, "Mine, too." She then pointed at tall plants along the roadside ditch that had tops that looked similar to those of a carrot. "Are those wild carrots?"

"Nope," I said. "That's wild parsnip. It's a root like a carrot, but that plant is a terribly deceptive invasive. One time my father-in-law was out pulling weeds and wild parsnip was among them. With residue on his hands he unknowingly touched his face and neck. With his skin exposed to UV sunlight, that residue caused a mean, blistering rash and left his skin permanent darkened."

"Good information," said Lydia. "Good to know."

Ahead, a brick silo stood near a solitary oak that had huge gnarly, acorn-laden limbs. Getting closer, we saw a weed-choked, dilapidated barn that had one wall still standing. Rosy said that the old metal stanchion pipes on the rickety wall would work as a hitching post. Lydia led Romeo to the front of a once-white graying two-story farmhouse that had boarded-up windows and a door held in place by a single hinge. Inside, a rusty potbelly stove stood sentinel over the old homestead.

We fanned out. Immediately Lydia began to tidy up the old home and kept mumbling about how disorder drives her crazy. Kitty and Sal took our horses to graze in a side field. Elle found a water hole near the barn. Rosy got out our largest nesting pot, broke jerky into little pieces, added chopped fresh carrots, cabbage, onions and potatoes. I gathered firewood. This was the first time since we'd left our homes that we'd have a roof over our heads. Daylight poured in through holes in the rotten cedar shingles.

Elle was resting on the old porch and opened the book. "Look here," she said, pointing at the word Neodymium. "That's a substance usually powdered and mixed with iron and boron. Then it's compressed and formed into powerful electrical magnets that are used in motors and generators." The next page had a picture of a trapezoid. "It's one-tenth or one-twelfth of a disk magnet that spins and creates an electromagnetic field. You've got to be careful handling it because it can yank fillings out of teeth."

Kitty looked stunned. "How in the hell do you know that?"

"I worked in an MRI lab at Mayo," she replied. "Spoiler alert. Magnetic resonance imaging uses lots of magnets."

Sal peered over her shoulder. "I like geeky kind of stuff. Maybe I should take a look at that book."

"Way above my pay grade," said Kitty.

Lydia shook her head, "Me, too."

"Ditto," I said, handing Rosy an empty bowl to fill with vegetable jerky stew.

We patted our full bellies and rested on the front porch of the old homestead watching clouds boil and darken the sky. Rosy rubbed her fingers together, feeling the air. "I think we're in for another big one." The ceiling inside the old homestead looked like Swiss cheese, and we figured it would be best to set up our tents and position water containers and buckets under openings to collect the impending deluge. Thunder clapped and rolled. Lightning flashed. Wild squalls and violent cloudbursts brought sheets of rain. We huddled in our tents as the house moaned and the ground shook.

Rosy crawled out of her tent and peeked through a crack in a window board. "Could be snowing in the Black Hills." She pulled her collar up to cover her neck. "Leaving was the right decision."

Lightning speared the ground close by and the inside of the farmhouse lit up. We all jumped. Thunder cascaded across the soundscape. Chills coursed through my body. The storm was on top of us.

My body trembled. "I pray our horses are ok."

"Don't worry," Rosy said. "They should be somewhat sheltered from the worst of it."

I stood at the front door threshold, blinded by the downpour, staring at the hazy image of the one standing barn wall. Hidden from view were our animals and my Justice. My heart pounded. A palpable dread overtook me, a feeling something terrible had happened. I pushed the door open, but Rosy stepped in front of me and blocked my way. Grudgingly a captive, I retreated to my tent and waited.

Lydia prayed. "Thank you, God, for leading us to this safe place."

Rain hammered the roof and our water containers overflowed onto a floor already rife with puddles. It rained all night.

When first light penetrated our humble home, I dashed outside. Ground fog hung in the morning air. With each step, mud stuck to my boots, growing thicker and thicker. It felt like I was wearing snowshoes by the time I got to the wall and saw that Justice was gone. His lead rope hung limp, still attached to a metal stanchion. I whipped around and yelled, "We have to find Justice!"

Everyone began the search. Seconds seemed like hours as we each spread out. Suddenly, Kitty let out a blood curdling scream, "Oh, my God! No! Not Justice!"

I ran toward her shrieks.

Justice lay at the edge of the cornfield on the other side of the old oak. His neck was rigid. His stiff legs pointed straight away from his body. His brown eyes were wide open. His tongue touched the ground. A corn cob was in his mouth.

Panic consumed me. "No! No! Not Justice!" I screamed. "Justice is dead!" I sank to my knees and prostrated myself across his neck. My poor boy was cold and wet and covered with mud. I buried my head in that once-soft spot on his neck and sobbed convulsively and told him how much I loved him. A hole was torn open in my heart. I wailed, "How could this happen?"

Lydia knelt next to me and cradled my shoulders, pressing her body into mine, holding me dear.

Rosy touched the singed hair above his hooves. "Damnit," she said. "Lightning."

I tried to push Lydia away, but she would not let me. "Leave me alone," I cried, but I had no energy to fight her. We sobbed. Her body trembled and she moaned until Elle helped her to her feet and ushered her away.

Rosy squatted next to me and lovingly stroked Justice's cold shoulder. "He lived a great life, Maia. We all feel your pain."

Then, for what seemed like an eternity, everyone came and sat with me and tried their best to comfort me. They danced around the simple fact that Justice was the oldest and most fragile. They kept repeating how I was always good to him, like that somehow nullified the fact that I'd left him tethered outside in an awful, awful storm.

Kneeling in muck, I forced my shoulders back and thrust up my arms, despairing. My cheeks were streaked with mud. My eyes filled with a steady flow of tears. I stroked Justice, "Thank you for all the miles. For all the wonderful adventures. For everything you taught me."

Shivering uncontrollably, I leaned over and kissed his nose. Wet, cold and totally depleted, I let Rosy help me stand and go back to the house. Lydia wrapped my sleeping bag over my shoulders, lovingly massaging them until I pulled away and escaped into the tent, zipped it shut, yanked the sleeping bag over my head and wept.

Death was not new to me. I lost my parents, a brother, many friends, relatives, dogs, cats and guinea pigs. My parents got old and died. My brother was a smoker and cancer took him. Some friends self-destructed while others struggled and lost their fights with terrible diseases.

Rosy unzipped the tent and offered me a bowl of stew. "Please try to eat a little. It'll do you good."

"Leave me alone," I whimpered. Without another word Rosy zipped the tent flap shut. I listened as everyone searched to find words to comfort me. I heard them talk about moving on. Whispering how we'd solve the problem of being one horse short. Lost and numb and suddenly raging with anger and a surge of adrenaline, I burst from the tent. "One horse short?" I bellowed. "Maybe the answer is to cut this tribe down by one. I'll make it easy for you and stay right here."

"No way," Rosy said, coming closer.

I backed away and cried, "I want to know how this happened to my Justice!"

Rosy looked into my eyes "Maia, I took a look around the barn and I could see that all our horses were spooked by the thunder and lightning because the mud's all torn up. With the thrashing and kicking, somehow Justice snapped his lead and broke the rope on the barn wall and got free."

I slumped to the floor like a sack of potatoes. "I need to go to him." Rosy took one arm and Elle the other and we went back to Justice. I wove my fingers through his mane, and said, "I remember the first time you saw Liberty and you acted like a young stallion and tried to mount her." I choked, between wrenching sobs, "You big knucklehead."

Rosy tried to hold back tears. "He was a frisker that good ole Justice. Remember how you and Mark were so gall darned concerned about how he'd react to your purple trailer? I'd say Justice loved that Viking trailer."

Kitty leaned over his dead body, "How 'bout our riding through that buffalo herd?" She laid her hand on his cold shoulder. "You were one brave stud."

"That was a formidable experience," I said, smiling through tears. "There were so many really great times." We sat in silence as I tried to reconcile his death by a lightning strike during the colossal collapse of the power grid. I took the cob of corn out of his mouth. "Can we bury him?"

Rosy wrapped me in her arms. "Maia, there's no way we could dig a hole that big. You know we have to move on."

I searched her eyes. "Just leave him?"

She diverted her gaze. "It's the only way."

Lydia gave me a hand up and we went to the house to dry out. I listened as they discussed our next move.

The sun was about to set when I went to Justice to touch him one last time. Elle brought our scissors so I could cut a lock of hair from his tail. I snipped a handful, like a shaman performing a sacred ritual, then twisted it into a loose braid. I took a deep breath, pushed myself back up and struggled to stand straight. Then I left Justice for the flying, walking and crawling creatures that clean up the dead and return their bodies to the earth. I found comfort believing that after vultures consumed his flesh, he would fly. And when four-legged earthbound creatures took their share of my Justice, he'd run again.

"I found this when I was moving stuff around in the house," Lydia said, placing a small clam-like shell in my left hand. It was a stone, chipped thin with a sharp curved edge. The heavier back side had a small hole drilled in it. I pulled a few of Justice's hair from the loose braid and made a thin cord and pushed it through the hole.

"Whatcha got, Maia?" asked Elle.

I lifted the stone. "Could be a scraper for cleaning hides." The others gathered to have a look. "I'm keeping it," I replied and tied it to a strip of leather fringe on my saddle.

Rosy stashed my tack in the driest corner of the abandoned house and vowed we'd retrieve it when we returned for our rigs. I wrapped the braid I'd made from Justice's mane around the brim of my hat, and at sunset I turned to walk the road alone. The cold damp air matched my emptiness. Liberty continued to let out long, slow whines, calling for her Justice.

When the others caught up with me, Lydia dismounted, stood tall and insisted I ride Liberty. I kept walking and didn't respond. "You gonna be all right?" she asked.

"No," I said, trying not to scream as raw emotion jangled through my veins and in and out of my heart. "This is too fucking hard. No, I'm not gonna be all right." Everything about me hurt. I choked, "I had a profound relationship with that wonderful horse. He was my partner. My legs. I was his head. We had melded like a centaur."

Rosy rode up on my other side. "Justice died quickly. He didn't suffer and that was a gift."

I bit back. "There's no way in hell this is any kind of gift."

"Listen up, sister," Rosy said, forcefully. "We all feel your pain. You're not the only one who is miserable over what happened to Justice. He was a beloved member of this herd, like you are a beloved sister." She stepped off of Catch and forced his reins into my hand. "You will take turns riding our horses." At that moment, I gave up resisting and accepted her offer of giving me a leg up. When my butt hit the saddle, I burst into tears.

By sunrise, I'd ridden every horse. Bond was nervous, mirroring my emotional state. I felt Rio's snap. Catch and Thief were rock solid. Liberty felt like home. But none of them were Justice. Romeo, as if sensing my loss, walked alongside every horse I rode.

With the arrival of dawn, soft pastels spread across the horizon. We were surrounded by fields of sunflowers with their brown heads bowed over, facing down. I was alone. My head hung low. Morning brought no comet. Like Justice, it was gone.

A cargo container on an abandoned semi-trailer caught Rosy's attention. Finding it empty, everyone got busy taking care of their horses and unloading Romeo. I darted into the dark, dirty space. Exhausted and depressed, I curled in a fetal position, wanting only to be home. Throughout a fitful sleep, my sense of loss was overwhelming, the kind of uneasy that hangs over a funeral. A part of me had gone missing. Me and Justice had united and had become a well-tuned instrument.

Night descended and I watched as everyone saddle up. Rosy demanded I ride behind Lydia and she stuffed Lydia's saddlebags in Romeo's panniers. In the cold night air, I was warmed by Lydia's body and didn't feel so bitterly alone.

Single file we wove through eight-foot-tall bluestem in a vast ocean of yellowing grasses that swayed gracefully in the wind, like birds in murmurs. Our heads shot above the grassy sea and engulfed our horses. Romeo's panniers pushed the tall grass aside. Somehow the grasses responding to the whims of the wind reminded me of the sound of a peacock rattling its feathers. Grasshoppers, Western meadowlarks and bluebirds chimed in the morning serenade.

Time had become a fog. Even though Rosy's watch worked, time was always now. We'd stopped counting the days. Day became night and night turned into day. Robins' nightly chorus told us when it was time to saddle up. Our need for fire had changed. Nocturnal riding meant daytime utilitarian fires to boil and purify water and cook food.

Elle found a flat clearing for us to camp. After tending to Bond, she disappeared over a nearby hill to try her luck hunting.

As I drifted in and out of sorrow and anxiousness, I recognized that our animals were leading quite the life, building muscle, eating great grass and having easy access to an abundance of water.

We heard a couple of shots and watched Elle strut back with the shotgun slung over her shoulder, swinging a mottled-brown ring-necked female pheasant and a flashy rooster. She plopped the rooster on the grass, spread its wings out, stepped down on each wing, grabbed its legs, and slowly and steadily pulled straight up. We watched as the bird literally turned inside out. She handed the bare breasted fowl to Rosy.

"You think those were a couple?" Lydia asked.

Elle proceeded to undress the female pheasant. "For the record, this is not pheasant romance season, nor is there any such thing as pheasant monogamy. Last spring, that rooster mounted every hen in sight."

"Sounds like that old boy knew how to take care of himself," Kitty said, chopping the breast meat into small chunks and dropping them into a pot of rehydrating chili. As the sun dropped, so did the temperature, and we left our grassland oasis under a rising moon.

Making our way through once thriving prairie towns with boarded-up buildings felt like being in a mausoleum. Dwellings that still could be occupied by humans felt uncomfortable. Sometimes we saw lights. Once in a while dogs barked. Catch, our most trusted night horse, maintained a steady walking pace and, whenever possible, avoided stepping on noisy pavement. Numb, half-asleep, we were alert enough to react to whatever came out of the night.

In the early morning, the sun's rays lit expansive, unharvested fields of golden corn that looked dry as paper. In the Heartland, corn, the grain of the gods and bread of life, reigned supreme. Every August, Mark and I would harvest fresh corn and eat our fill of buttered corn on the cob. We harvested dozens of ears, froze the bulk of it and always dried a couple gallons.

With the arrival of light, we camped behind a series of billboards advertising Mitchell, South Dakota, and I fell asleep remembering my parents. For the first time since the deadly storm, I slept like a baby.

Chapter 16

Heart Land

Under a waning moon surrounded by a sea of stars, we ventured on. Early morning sunrays reflected on a metal cross atop a steeple nestled in a wooded area. The church was old and plain, with peeling white paint. Missing shingles testified how nature takes its toll, throwing elements at whatever stands in its way.

A deep-throated bark came from inside an old parsonage sheltered behind the church. Sheer white curtains billowed out an open window. Rosy dismounted and handed her reins to Elle, then walked along a wooden picket fence to the front door. She knocked. A dog growled. A female voice hollered, "Go away. I've got a gun and it's aimed at you."

In her best non-threatening voice, Rosy said, "We are not here to trouble you. We are six women riding back to our families in Minnesota."

The door cracked open. A black labrador pushed out its nose and a white-haired woman peeked around the door. "What do you want, then?"

"We need a place to rest," Rosy replied. "Be a blessing, ma'am, if we could rest up inside your church." The dog sniffed the air. She pressed on. "We're just trying to get through another day. We'll be gone by sunset. We'll do no harm."

The old woman opened the door a little wider, lifted her chin and made direct eye contact with Rosy. "You can stay. But keep to yourself." She paused, then before turning away, added, "Leave an offering in the church." Then slammed the door.

Rosy stood still for a moment and then thanked the door. "Much obliged, ma'am."

We hitched our horses to a post alongside the church. Lydia brought

Romeo over to the front steps to make it easier for us to schlep our gear inside.

Rosy lifted Catch's rear pastern up between her legs and with her knife carefully cleaned his hoof. "We've covered a lot of rough ground and his shoes are starting to wear out." She looked at Elle. "Best if we could get our horses shod in new steel."

After our horses were taken care of we entered the church. Several straight-backed oak pews were pushed along one wall. A simple wooden podium stood in front of an altar where a large, dark brown wooden cross hung. Just a cross. No Jesus. Lydia knelt at the altar, bent her head down put her palms together and lowered her head.

We'd finished unloading Romeo and were getting ready for a day's sleep, when the church door burst open. The white-haired woman stepped inside. "I'm Pearl," she said, reaching her hand out to Rosy. Pearl stood maybe five feet tall and moved like she was in her late 70s or early 80s.

Rosy took her hand and they sat together on a pew. "It was the strangest thing," Pearl said, her breathing labored. "Just minutes before you knocked on my door, I was studying my Bible and had just read, 'Do unto others as you would have them do unto you.'" Her words came in short spurts. "I felt the Lord pressing upon my heart to welcome you."

We all oozed our thanks for letting us hold up in her church.

Lydia sat on Pearl's other side. "Are you the minister?"

"No. Wade, my husband was." She patted her heart. "Wade was called home by the good lord three years ago."

Lydia patted the old woman's hand. "I'm so sorry."

After a respectful silence, Rosy asked, "Do you still hold church services?"

Pearl stared at the cross. "Once in a while this old church is used for weddings or meetings. Nowadays people like the bigger churches. This country church sits out here in the middle of nowhere. Ever since they put in that new road, hardly anybody ever comes down this road."

Rosy raised her eyebrows, registering the reality of being cloistered away in the middle of nowhere. "You sayin' you're off the beaten path?"

"That's an understatement," Pearl said, reaching down, using both hands to push herself up off the pew. "Go ahead and put your horses in the old fenced pasture by the barn. You'll need to check the fence to make sure it's secure. After you rest, come over to the house." She turned before leaving, "If you gals want, you can spend the night. It might do you good to get rested up before heading back out."

Rosy smiled. "It would be great to recharge before tackling our last stretch across Minnesota." She bowed her head, and said softly, "Thank you." Rosy took Pearl's arms and helped her down the church steps.

When Pearl was out of sight, Elle raised her hand for a high-five with Kitty. "Did we get lucky or what?"

Lydia smiled. "Huh, isn't that interesting? Another good person."

Rosy turned away. "I wonder if Pearl could help us find a farrier."

"First we check the fence," Elle said, taking the pliers out of our tool kit.

After we repaired the barbed wire, we turned our horses loose. Rio pranced around the perimeter in search of the most perfect spot. He pawed the ground and was first to take a dust bath. In my mind's eye, I watched Justice roll first on one side, then stand, roll on the other, get up and shake wildly.

"You okay?" Rosy asked.

I held back tears. "I am so sad. I really thought we'd make it home together."

Rosy leaned against a fence post. "What a strange twist of fate to lose him to lightning."

"It's fucking crazy," I choked. "Here we are in this pathetic situation. The world got zapped. There's no electricity and my Justice got put down by a vicious jolt."

"That old boy had a fabulous life," Rosy said. "He didn't have to succumb to the sting of a vet's needle, or watch a man walk toward him attempting to conceal a gun, ready to put him down. He didn't linger through old age in a pasture listening to people talk about how decrepit he'd become." She sighed. "I know it's not easy, Maia. You know I've witnessed my share of not-so-nice horse deaths, and I've heard some pretty gruesome stories, but as hard as it is, in a strange way, lightning was a good way to go."

"Yah, I know. I gotta say, I find comfort knowing his body will feed other animals," I wiped my eyes. "His soul will soar, and I believe he will run again."

Returning to the church, Rosy carried on about how Justice had a wonderful life. About how too many horses live their whole lives in stalls and never know freedom. "I know it's a sad story, but it's not a bad story. Justice was treated well, ate good, lived a long life and, luckily for him, death came quick."

"I know all that, Rosy," I said trying not breaking down. "It's still damn difficult."

Morning light warmed the musty smelling sanctuary, and we opened several plain glass windows. We laughed when we found two—now useless—electric fans. The storage room contained folding tables, boxes of white plates, cups and silverware. A pastor's robe hung in the cloak closet. A small oak table held a metal collection plate covered with dust next to two large candle holders, sans candles. There were enough pews to seat maybe fifty churchgoers. I thought about sitting on pews just like these at baptisms, confirmations, weddings, funerals and countless other gatherings. I remembered when I was young attending a summer wedding in a church much like this one. It was a hot day. The outside temperature was at least 90 and well over 100 inside. Several people fainted in the stifling hot heat and high humidity as the pastor rambled on about how women must serve men.

Late afternoon our group returned to Pearl's place and knocked on her front door. Pearl greeted us with a smile and graciously invited us inside. Stuff was piled everywhere. Her kitchen had pots and pans stacked high on an olive-green electric stove. Yellowing wallpaper peeled down in large scabs. Her checkered linoleum floor had once been black and white, and now was in dire need of a good scrubbing.

Pearl picked up a forked metal lever and slipped it into an opening on her wood-burning stove and lifted the firebox lid. She used a poker to stir the coals, then placed two chunks of oak in the firebox. She opened the oven door and slid in an iron griddle that held six individual corn breads shaped like corn cobs. She filled a kettle with hot water from her stove reservoir and set it on her stove top. Then she ushered us into her living room where an oil painting of Jesus, praying, hung next to an embroidered *Last Supper* over an ancient, dark purple crushed velvet sofa. A wooden hutch held fancy old plates and dainty little cups. Her ornate shelf box had a mirrored back that displayed whimsical little elves, each frozen in a different pose. A red elf perched on a stool with its fingers in his ears, radiated a devilish grin. My eyes strained to snoop at her shelves filled with books on physics, philosophy, poetry, various religions and nature.

Pearl saw me perusing her book collection. "Wade was quite the reader," she said. "He was a great researcher and big into genealogy. He spent years making detailed maps of where our people came from."

Elle rubbed her chin, "Could that include maps of Minnesota?"

Pearl pointed at a corner shelf. "Wade's collection includes plat maps of several states."

Elle asked, "Can I look at them?"

"Feel free." Pearl said, turning away, then pointing to her hutch. "We'll need those cups and saucers."

Lydia jumped up, eager to do her bidding. "I'm on it."

Elle and Rosy sat on the sofa, paging through Wade's maps. Pearl returned to her kitchen, opened the oven door and used a toothpick to poke each corn bread, evaluating each toothpick to make sure it came out clean. Placing a cob on each plate, she motioned to Sal. "Open that jar of syrup."

"Real maple syrup," Sal said, practically drooling.

Pearl opened her cupboard and handed Sal a green glass syrup boat. "My neighbor taps the trees. We trade. I get syrup. He gets goat milk."

"You've got goats?" Lydia asked.

Pearl smiled, "I have one great gal."

"Sweet," Sal said, placing the syrup boat on the table. We gathered around Pearl's kitchen table, and when Sal took a bite, she closed her eyes and purred, "Have I died and gone to heaven?"

"Seriously," Lydia smiled. "It just can't get any better than this. It's like. . .no, it's better than being home."

"Lydia, dear," said Pearl, "would you please pour everyone a cup of tea?"

Kitty held her pinkie straight up as she took a sip from her dainty cup. "Mmm, if this a dream, don't wake me."

After helping with the dishes, Pearl pushed back in her threadbare brown recliner. A fringed red, white and blue afghan fell on the floor and Lydia jumped up and lovingly laid it back across Pearl's lap.

Pearl smiled, "Thank you, dear."

Rosy studied Pearl before asking, "How are you holding up without electricity?"

Pearl rubbed her fingertip around her teacup rim. "Getting a bit tiresome, but I suppose I can't complain." She turned to look out a south window. "My family has lived on this land for generations with a whole lot less than what I've got." She sipped her tea and sighed. "Power outages are pretty common around here. But I gotta say this one is lasting a little too long. Oh, it's not that I'm worried. I'm pretty well set with food. Got my chickens and a great goat."

Lydia's mouth dropped open. "You have all that and you live alone? With no help?"

"It's all I know," Pearl replied. "Lived here my whole life. My grandparents lived in a sod house right out that window. Grandpa's oxen plowed the sod strips that he cut into bricks and made its four walls. Grandma wove the willow branches for the roof."

"Hard to imagine what their life was like," I said.

"True," replied Pearl, "but the longer the power stays off, the easier it's becoming to picture folks returning to live simpler lives."

Darkness was taking over when Pearl lit an old metal kerosene lantern that lent a golden glow to her home. "Not so bad, really," she said, "so long as I have lamp oil. Just like the old days."

I looked at my companions. "We'd like to thank you for letting us stay overnight."

"Aw, least I can do. Hard for me to imagine what you gals' lives are like, having to ride all that way. How long you been on horseback?"

"Weeks," I said, sucking in a deep breath. "It's been a long ride. A few days ago, I lost my horse to a lightning strike."

Pearl bowed her head, "I'm sorry to hear that."

Everyone stayed quiet until Rosy asked, "Pearl, do you know where we could find a farrier? Our horses' shoes have taken quite a beating."

"Lots of horses around here. Where there's horses, there's farriers." Pearl pointed to an old wooden telephone stand. "Get me the directory so we can find the closest one."

Elle slumped over, practically landing on Kitty's lap, then snapped up like she'd been zapped. "Phone! My God, I haven't thought about my phone. Back before this all started, I checked my cell every few minutes." She chuckled, "It's amazing how fast that habit became history."

Pearl paged through a thin country telephone book. "Closest farrier is a couple miles southeast of here." We got Wade's plat map and found the exact location.

"So how do we do this?" asked Elle.

"I sure would feel a lot better if we got new shoes for our horses," said Rosy.

Pearl yawned, "How about we figure this out over breakfast?"

Rosy agreed, "Let's see how tomorrow plays out."

"Time to hit the hay," I said, standing to leave.

"Can't wait for a real breakfast," Sal said, pulling the door closed.

It was exciting to sleep inside a building with a roof that wouldn't leak and windows that let in the night sky. Lying on the old oak sanctuary floor, waking from a sound sleep I heard yipping and yapping coming from a pack of howling coyotes.

"Hear that?" Lydia whispered. "How many do you think there are?"

"Lots," I said. I thought about when the coyotes would find Justice and how they'd feast and how he'd run again. Rosy was right. Justice did not suffer the indignities of old age. Even in death he'd serve a purpose.

Soon after sun-up the church door flew open and Pearl's Labrador, Pal, bounded in and delivered a round of sloppy licks. Pearl stood in the doorway, saying, "Rise and shine and give God the glory."

Sal yanked her sleeping bag over her head.

"How 'bout some breakfast?" said Pearl.

Sal jumped at the opportunity. The crisp morning air smelled clean. Vibrant summer green was being replaced with the sages and browns signaling the arrival of fall and the coming of winter.

Pearl led us through her front door and into her kitchen where everyone pitched in frying eggs, making pancakes and brewing mint tea.

We wolfed down every scrap of food. Sal lifted her plate and pretended to lick it clean, "Oh, my God. I never knew how much I love good food."

After we got everything cleaned up, I asked Pearl if we could walk over to see the sod house. "We can do that," she replied.

An impressive stack of firewood was piled outside her back door. "Last spring a big oak came down and my brother George came over from Sioux Falls, cut and split it for me." She pushed her shoulders back, bent her arm at the elbow, and flexed her muscle. "Stacked it all myself. Took a while, but I got the job done."

Chickens cackled and darted about their fenced-in coop. "I've got layers and fryers." She wiggled a finger. "My rooster just died." A white goat came bouncing out of a cobbled-together metal shack. Pearl scratched its head as the goat licked her apron. "This is Isis, my milking goat. She's had ten babies and gives the best milk."

Elle grinned. "Looks like this is a woman's world."

Pearl smiled. "My girls give me meat, eggs and milk and I take real good care of them."

Walking through an old orchard, Pearl encouraged us to feel free to pick apples and plums from trees still holding fruit. "Grandma and my husband planted all these trees. 'Course Wade was just a boy at the time."

The walls of the sod house were surprisingly intact. There had been two windows perpendicular to the door opening. Long ago the roof had disappeared. We ducked through the doorframe and Elle picked up two rusted metal bands and a bowed barrel stave. "Water barrel?"

"Mighta been," said Pearl. "Everything was about survival."

Six of us were crammed into the sod house when Lydia said, "Can you imagine? Well, I cannot imagine a family with this many people living in such a small space!"

"It's about the same amount space as we've got inside our two tents," Elle said, ducking to exit.

Pearl led us to a small cemetery and pushed open an old wrought iron gate. "Wade and Sadie, our only child, are buried here." She touched Wade's headstone. Pal pushed his body into her and she patted his head, "Thank God for this old boy." She kissed her finger and planted it squarely on Wade's tombstone "He was such a good man. One of those who practiced what he preached." She rested her hand on Sadie's gravestone. "Sadie was such a sweet girl. It broke our hearts when she passed. Our lives were never the same. Over the years Wade and I spent a lot of time right here, talking to her, telling her how much we loved and missed her." Abruptly she turned away and asked, "Who wants to pick some raspberries?"

Even though it was still early in the morning and the bees were not yet active, Lydia kept her distance while the rest of us picked and devoured heavenly bright orange, luscious berries. After filling a pail, we strolled back to Pearl's home. Along the way we commented on Pearl's garden, coops and corrals. It seemed to be an arrangement dictated not as much by design as by need.

Rosy held the backdoor open. Once inside, Pearl relaxed in her comfortable chair, and Rosy asked, "What do you know about what's happened since the aurora?"

Pearl's breathing was labored. She drew a slow, deep breath. "Not sure I know anything for certain except my electricity's gone. I can tell you what my brother George thinks." She lifted her cup, careful that a slight tremor in her left hand didn't cause a spill. She took a sip. "Not long after the aurora, George rode over on his motorcycle to check on me. For the most part, he and my sister-in-law live off the grid. Their roof and backyard's full of solar panels. George is a ham radio operator with lots of fancy antennas. All his life he's had a passion for communicating with people all around the world using Morse code. George told me the Midwest was hit the hardest. Cities in particular. Fires. National Guard supposedly taking care of things. He hasn't seen any soldiers. Practically speaking, other than a few neighbors stopping by, I haven't seen anybody until you gals showed up. George says some cities are in bad shape on account of their high population.

According to George, nobody's figured out how to switch the power back on because of an electromagnetic something-or-other coming from the sun that's still causing power surges. He did say that once they figured out some weird magnetic thing that we might be able to get the grid back rather quickly. He didn't know how long."

"That's interesting," Elle said, turning to Sal. "We need to take another look at that engineer's book."

"George said once that problem got figured out it could be anytime." Pearl smiled at Lydia and held out her teacup. "Dear, do you mind?" I too held my cup up. "Please refresh Kitty," she said. Lydia was quick to replenish everyone's tea.

Pearl continued. "George says if we can't get the electricity fixed, things could get a lot worse. People will run out of food. Hospitals will need medicines. George wanted me to go with him to Sioux Falls, but I said I'm holding tight right here. This is my home. My sanctuary. I keep my gun loaded and within reach." She glanced at the double-barreled shotgun leaning close to her front door.

Rosy chuckled, with an uncharacteristic nervousness. "I've already met your equalizer."

"I apologize if I scared you."

"No apology necessary, Pearl. I understand. We all do. These are dangerous times. During this whole ride we've done our best to avoid people for the same reason you pointed your shotgun at me."

Lydia interjected, "Have to admit, we've mostly run into good people along the way," Even Rosy nodded her agreement.

"Pearl, folks like you prepare for situations like what's happening," I said. "You've got a good water supply. Fuel, be it lamp oil or wood. You've got a serious supply of food with all those layers, fryers and even a mama goat."

Lydia set a kitchen chair down next to Pearl. "You're lucky to have George looking out for you."

Pearl patted her chest. "Praise God. That I am."

Lydia tapped her heart. "I wish I had a brother."

Pearl chuckled, "Oh, my! George he's a different kind of thinker. He's got all kinds of theories. He knows there's a lot of suffering going on, but believes that instead of everyone going crazy and killing each other, that losing electricity has had another powerful effect." She tapped her fingers on the armchair. "He believes it's possible that the electromagnetic shift brought about some sort of enlightenment. That without electricity,

161

people aren't bombarded with a constant electromagnetic charge and that has had a positive affected on people's psyches."

Rosy narrowed her eyes. "That's crazy."

Lydia's eyes popped open wide. "Wow!" she exclaimed. "That makes so much sense. Through all of this, I've been blown away with how people have been kind and helpful." She looked around at us. "And we've been good to each other. We've all been kind."

"Like the drunk guy who shot at us from the green car?" Sal added sarcastically.

Rosy pinched her lips tight. "I'm sorry, Pearl, but your brother George's theory of magnetic change of behavior sounds crazy."

Pearl leaned forward. "You don't have to believe his theory. But I for one hope and pray it comes true."

Lydia bowed her head, "Amen."

Pearl went on. "George said that over the years, the fear of losing electricity led many people to plan ahead and take responsibility for their needs should some terrible tragedy come their way. I know, I know," she said, setting her cup on the side table. "City people are a lot more vulnerable than us rural folk. It must be horrible being trapped in the very place and lifestyle people thought best for their families." She took a breath. "George believes that a lot of people in the Heartland invested in sustainable lifestyles, installed solar panels and wind turbines and grew and put up their own food. He's hoping that the local movement provided more than enough resources for people to take care of their own needs and be able to share with others."

"Like the Amish," I said. "They live sustainably."

She smiled, "Well, they sure do."

Lydia leaned forward, "I love hearing this."

"My brother believes people could return to the old ways and live just fine without computers and electricity. He figures that by folks spending more time together, that they'll figure out how to support one another and work together toward a common good that'll get us through this. In times of great hardship and catastrophe, people have had no choice but to pull together. I pray this time is no different."

Rosy shook her head side to side. "New-Age baloney. We're talking big cities and big problems. Age of Aquarius this is not."

"Pretty kumbaya, Pearl," Sal added.

"It's weird," said Kitty.

"Oh, I suppose it is far-fetched." Pearl closed her eyes. "But not impossible."

Rosy stood up. "Enough," and turned toward Elle. "If we're gonna get our herd shod, we best get a move on." In no time they saddled Catch and Bond and wrapped the other horses' leads around their saddle horns.

"Be careful," Pearl said as they took off, leaving a giant ball of dust behind. She smiled, "Good thing farriers work without electricity."

I sat on the porch stoop and thought about George's concept of a nicer world. We'd been out of touch longer than any of us could have ever imagined and been so fixated on staying clear of people, our fears might be worse than the reality. What if people weren't as bad as Rosy believed? George's theory did sound a bit too optimistic. Surely, there had to be mass suffering. The poorest people often pay the highest price when culture is threatened. I knew that people could be hideously selfish and, when desperate enough, they'd panic and could kill. Still, we'd seen for ourselves the resourcefulness and generosity of others. With the exception of that poor drunk idiot, people had been more than reasonable, given the circumstance. In fact, they'd been kind to strangers on horseback. I also knew that Rosy was right to keep vigilant and wary of strangers. Yet if it weren't for the charity of strangers, we'd never have made it this far.

Lydia and Sal were inside lounging on the sofa. Kitty sat in an old wooden rocker paging through a magazine. Pearl rested in her chair. I asked her what she thought of her brother's theory. "No matter what happens we've got to play the hand we're dealt." She smiled, "What choice do we have?" She lifted her eyes up to the picture of Jesus. "One of Wade's favorite sayings was that not all gifts are easy to receive but ultimately everything, especially something negative, has to be turned into a gift." She paused, "I know, I know. It's easier said than done. Wade said it was one of humankind's greatest challenges." Her eyes went to the window. "Be like the agile, swift hummingbird that can pivot and tilt and express great tenacity as it hovers over beautiful flowers and takes in the sweetness of life." She paused, "We are wired to adapt."

"I pray that's true," Lydia said, wiping her eyes with the back of her hand.

Pearl lifted her head and pushed her shoulders back. "You have to remember we have good people leading our country. So much of what happens is out of our control and lies within the power of those who we've given the responsibility to represent us. We have to trust our leaders."

"Sad to say," Kitty said. "I've met some of those men and all they're interested in is staying in power." She looked like she was holding her breath, "Dare I say?"

"Go ahead," I urged.

Kitty wrinkled her nose and shook her head. "Greed got hold of their balls."

"Men," Lydia said. "They do like holding onto their power."

Pearl strengthened and raised her voice. "The history of our country proves people look out for one another. Did your people ever talk about the Great Depression? Along with the sacrifices men made there were women who'd never worked outside of their homes and joined the war effort and worked in factories and some even served as pilots! Remember the World Trade Tower in New York and how cops and firemen and people on the street ignored their own vulnerabilities and ran to help? People do heroic things when they see others in need. People who have nothing find ways to support others. We are a resourceful lot. We make do. Something deep inside of us is drawn to serving others."

"People are herd animals like horses," Lydia said brightly.

Pearl smiled at her. "People always pull together. We find ways to strengthen our families and our communities. Who knows? This could be a great opportunity for humanity to evolve. It could be an awakening. This could be the time to go inside and ask ourselves what's really important. Is the answer another gadget? Or a new something-or-other? What if we decide to live in harmony? To live in balance? What if we choose to make living a sustainable lifestyle a priority? How about we connect with the land? Grow our own food." She looked spent and took a deep breath. "Sharing is grace in motion."

I thought about the possible positive impacts of this shut down. The skies seemed bluer. The air was cleaner. With people staying put, there could be less pollution. What if George was right and the loss of electricity would became the event that helped usher in a planetary morality? Could this situation ultimately strengthen us?

Kitty shook my shoulder. "Hey, pardner, penny for your thoughts."

I blinked. "I'd have to give you change."

Kitty reached out to give me a hand up. "Whadda ya say we go back to the church and figure out what food we've got left?"

Stepping outside, I asked, "What about Lydia and Sal?"

"Oh, they're following Pearl around like puppies."

Going through our food we found we'd done okay with our supplies with Ace's jerky, Kelly and Stella's apples and plums, Chip's steaks, vegetables from the Hutterites, and our foraging and Elle's hunting. Our fresh food was long gone, but we still had a couple of dehydrated meals, half a bag of jerky and some dried fruit. From here to home, no longer would water be a problem like it was in the Badlands. Elle would hunt and we'd glean corn and soybeans from the vast unharvested fields.

"I'll bet Pearl will let us pick some of her fruit," I said, lying on a pew. Next to me was the book Elle had found when we crossed the Missouri. I held it up and thought about all that happened since we left the Overlook. The night rides. The storm and that godawful house full of holes. The jabs of lightning. My Justice. The miles and miles of walking and riding. And now rejuvenating at Pearl's. Kitty sat down on the floor near me as I flipped through the pages. I showed her some of the drawings. "Any of this mean anything to you?"

"Above my paygrade, Maia. Whoever this belonged to must've been a genius mathematician or a wizard scientist."

"Check this out," I said. "It's about an electromagnetic something-or-other that causes power surges. Wasn't that what Pearl's brother was talking about?"

Kitty got up, "We've got to show it to Elle."

"Good thinking," I said, closing the book. "We should get back and help Pearl."

Pearl's house was alive with energy. Lydia grinned like a Cheshire cat as she washed the wall behind the kitchen stove. With every wipe, Pearl's kitchen got brighter. She dipped a cloth into a pail of dirty water, lifted her head, and said, "Mom wanted me to be the kind of lady that gave fancy parties and wore fashionable clothes." She squeezed the cloth and wrung out dark, dirty water. "Wonder what she'd think of me now."

I smiled. "She'd be blown away by the awesome woman you've become."

"Thanks," she said, taking another swipe at years of accumulated wood smoke and cooking splatter.

Already the kitchen crew had pumped water and lugged it in, washed the dishes, cleaned the kitchen cabinets, straightened bookshelves and were making headway rearranging some of the clutter.

"Maia," Pearl asked, "would you mind going into my bedroom? I'd like you to find a copy of *Prevention Magazine* somewhere on my bed stand. It's got an elephant on the cover. If I remember correctly, it had a cobbler recipe I'd like to make."

Pearl's unmade bed had blankets mounded off to one side. Piles of clothes, fabric, stacks of cardboard boxes, books and magazines almost reached the ceiling. I stopped cold when I caught my reflection in her full-length mirror. My skin was dark. My wrinkles were deeper. My boy cut revealed the gray hair I'd been denying for years. I flexed my bicep. "Not bad," I said out loud. I found the magazine and brought it to Pearl. Her hand trembled as she flipped through the pages searching for the recipe, tore it out and then directed Sal to go to the orchard for plums and apples.

"Come," she said. "Let's go to the cellar for lard and potatoes," and opened the door. The old wooden stairs creaked as I stepped down and had to duck to avoid hitting my head. Shelves lining one cold stone basement wall were loaded with jars of tomatoes, peaches, pickles, sauerkraut, meat, beets, beans, jams and jellies. Several large blue plastic containers were in a dark corner next to the potato bin.

"What's in those large containers?" I asked.

"Rice, steel cut oats, lentils, corn and beans," she replied with a satisfied grin. "Storing enough food to get from season to season isn't hard if you think ahead. When I get into town, I stock up on things I can't grow myself. Course you got to keep up with the harvest." She leaned against an empty freezer. "First thing I did when the power went was to use my frozen food. I ate, canned and dried everything I could." She shuffled over to the shelves of canned food. "Do you realize that not so many years ago our ancestors knew the importance of thinking ahead and keeping at least a two-year supply of food? Food was an insurance policy, just in case one year our crops would fail. I've held true to those old ways. Wade always said, 'plan for the worst and hope for the best.'"

I remembered a line from a Greg Brown song, "Gramma put it all in jars; love, rain, and the taste of summer." She lifted a jar of pickles. "Me and Wade put up these pickles the year before he passed." She stroked the jar and tenderly placed it back on the shelf. "This is our last jar." She smiled. "And I want it buried with me."

Kitty was sitting on the top step. "Pickles," she giggled. "Talking about Mae West's pickle in her pocket?"

I touched a finger to my lips. "Not now, Kitty."

"Sorry. Am I interrupting?"

"No, no," said Pearl, handing me a jar of lard. "We were just gabbing about canned goods and expiration dates."

I took the jar. "I'm hoping you're not plannin' on leavin' anytime soon?"

"Oh, heavens no. No," she said, heading back up the stairs. "But then again, like with your horse, you never know when the Lord calls and your time is up. I am prepared to take that call whenever my time comes. Until then, I'm well-stocked and have peace in my heart."

At the top of the steps, I handed the jar to Kitty. In the kitchen, Lydia was chopping and slicing. Everyone joined in to help mix and pour and add their energy to create a memorable feast.

Sal swooned as she stirred the thickening, scratch-made potato potage. "It's gonna be delicious."

"And nutritious," Lydia said, proudly.

Pal barked, alerting us that our pals, Rosy and Elle, were returning. Kitty bolted out the front door. Pearl wiped her hands on her apron and Lydia escorted her to the hitching post.

"We got the job done," Rosy said hopping down, handing Lydia Bond's lead.

"That farrier was a real decent guy," Rosy said reaching down and loosening Catch's front cinch. "He did a good job and his price was fair." She set both stirrups on her saddle, then pulled off the saddle and cradled it in her arms. "He was a volunteer fireman who spent the first week after we lost electricity helping nearby small-town departments figure out how to best respond to those suffering the deepest needs." She placed her saddle on the ground. "He knew the outside world had some big problems, but decided he'd be best off taking care of his family and other people's horses. He said his shoeing business was booming and never been better. Said a lot more folks are riding horseback and getting around in buggies."

"As long as he can keep a fire in the forge and don't run out of steel shoes, it'll boom," Elle added, setting her saddle on the church steps.

"What else did you learn?" I asked.

"When we arrived, another guy was getting his horse shod. We asked him what he thought about this situation and he said he didn't give a hoot about what's happening outside his barn. That he was staying put until this mess got resolved."

Elle sat on the church steps. "The farrier said he'd heard talk about truck traffic gradually increasing along I-90. There were rumors about long lines of tankers, but not many cars."

Rosy and Elle stopped at the outside pump to wash up and slap dust off their clothes before coming through the back door and entering the kitchen. "Holy Moley," Rosy exclaimed, taking a step backwards. "You've been busy."

Sal beamed as she stirred the soup. Lydia practically giggled as she strained fresh goat milk through cheese cloth.

Pearl opened a drawer and handed me a linen tablecloth and matching napkins, then directed me to get her silver and fancy china and set the table. It felt like I was back in my grandparent's home preparing a family meal. Sal and Lydia ordered us into the living room while they put the finishing touches on our feast.

"Come an' get it," Sal bellered and we came a-runnin'. We ate the best potato soup ever made, corn biscuits, green beans picked by Kitty out of Pearl's garden and an apple-plum cobbler for dessert.

"Wow!" Elle said folding her napkin. "That was heavenly," She pushed her chair back and took a long, deep breath. "Back to planet earth, ladies. We need to talk about leaving this paradise."

Sal piped up loudly, "Sis, I'm done riding." Then abruptly turned to face Pearl. Her voice softened, "Pearl if you'd let me, I'd like to stay here until this mess is resolved. I promise to help in every way if you just let me wait it out here."

Before Pearl or anyone else had time to react, Lydia stood and pressed her hands over her heart. "Me, too, Pearl. Honest. This is where I want to be. If you'll have me, Pearl, I would like to stay." She turned to Sal, "We can sleep in the church." She looked back at Pearl, "I won't use too much toilet paper and I promise to keep an eye on Sal." She knelt in front of Pearl. "There's so much I can learn from you."

Pearl stammered, "I surely would appreciate your help. It's getting harder and harder for me to keep it all together." She lowered her head. "I just can't do everything anymore. Can't stand on a stool and scrub grease off my walls." She winked at Sal. "Can't carry a load like I used to, either. These old hips and knees don't work like they once did."

Lydia bowed her head. "I'd be so grateful if you would let me learn from you and I'd be honored to help you."

Rosy fired back. "You what? Wait a damn minute. We need to think this through."

Eyes defiant, Sal focused squarely on Rosy. "You can't make me go one mile farther. I'm tired. Period. I want to stay here and be with Pearl. I'm not riding any more. My ass and my back have had it."

Rosy stomped her foot and the dishes rattled. She gave Sal a mother to teenage daughter glare. "We agreed we'd all stick together. We can't break up now. We're a tribe!"

Sal reciprocated with a teenager to mother look. "Sis, I'm staying. You tell Earl you'll pick me up whenever you come back for our rigs. I'm better off here and you're better off without me complaining about every little thing."

Elle leaned back in the wooden kitchen chair and rubbed her chin in
contemplation. "That would solve the problem of our being one horse
short. With only four of us riding, and being this much closer to home,
we wouldn't need to take as much stuff." She paused, looking around the
room and stopped at Lydia. "If we left Romeo here, we could travel a lot
faster and might make it home in a week. We've got two hundred plus miles
left. Our horses are in tip-top shape. They have new shoes. Thief would be
an extra horse and could carry our gear. We've got food and in this part of
the country water is abundant."

Lydia jumped up. "Yes! Yes! Please, please leave Romeo here with me!
I'll take good care of both him and Sal."

Elle hightailed it back to the church, got our map and spread it out
over the kitchen table. "Pearl, where are we?"

"A little north east of Canistota."

Kitty hovered over Elle's shoulder. "Sioux Falls doesn't look that far."

"We're not going anywhere near Sioux Falls," Rosy said with finality.
"We'll steer northeast, skirt the metro area and completely avoid people."

Pearl studied the map. "So, this is what I'd do. Head east by northeast,
cross the interstate near Humboldt, keep going cross-country on a
diagonal, go past Dell Rapids and into the Pipestone area. If you get to the
Palisades State Park before sunup, it would be a decent place to camp."

Rosy nodded. "After the Palisades, we'll stay north of I-90 and cross
into Minnesota."

Elle scanned the map for more detail. "After we'd cross the Interstate,
it looks like the railroad corridor goes straight to the Palisades."

"Sounds good to me," Rosy said. "Maia, whadda ya think?"

"Fine with me," I said.

Kitty nodded, "Me too."

"I think we've got a plan," said Elle, folding the map.

Pearl shuffled back into her living room and took a book off the
shelf. "Wade had family buried in southwest Minnesota." She opened
to a marked page. "Some of the Millers are buried in Rock county and
a few more are in Nobles." She choked up. "Right after we got married,
we visited the Palisades. After that, every couple of years we'd make a
pilgrimage to recharge our souls. Truth is that whole area's a geological
oasis right in the middle of an otherwise flat world. Wade believed it to be
the most spiritual place in the Plains." She bowed her head. "Center of
earth, Wade called it." Pearl placed the book on the table. "Geology alone

leads us to believe it is so. There's a layer of soft catlinite that's sandwiched between hard, erosion-resistant layers of Sioux Quartzite. I've heard say that it's the softest rock surrounded by rock second only to diamond. Soft catlinite is what Native Americans carve into their ceremonial pipes they call chanunpas. That's why the area is called Pipestone."

I asked, "Why is it called the Palisades?"

Pearl smiled and waited a moment. "There are two theories about this. Some believe water cut through solid bedrock and deposited the catlinite. Others believe two spirits got into a fight over something and wacked their tomahawks into the earth so hard that they sliced open the quartzite, making room for catlinite, thus creating the Palisades' spires." She shook her head as if tossing that memory back into place. "Take any maps you think might be helpful, but please bring them when you come back for Lydia and Sal."

"I promise we won't forget to return your maps." Rosy said, standing up, stretching and rubbing her eyes. "Pearl, we were planning on leaving tonight, but we'd really appreciate it if we could stay a little while longer, catch up on our rest and leave tomorrow night instead."

"Of course," Pearl said. "Give yourself a break. If you leave after sundown, you should make it to the Palisades by sunup." She struggled to lift herself out of her chair. "This plan will give us time to get some food together for you to take along."

"That would be much appreciated," Rosy yawned. "We all need to get some serious sleep."

Lydia held the church door open. "So that means tonight's the last time we'll all be together?"

Rosy crawled into her sleeping bag and said to Sal, "I'll miss you."

Sal chuckled, "I won't." Then paused, "Of course I'll miss everyone, but I'm so done with riding."

Rosy, Elle, Kitty and I slept till late morning. Arriving at Pearl's, we found that Lydia and Sal had aprons on and were hustling to make food for our journey. Six loaves of bread were rising on the warming shelf above the wood stove. Sal busily stirred the oatmeal cookie batter. Pearl sat at the table sipping morning tea. Breakfast was oatmeal smothered in fresh-picked raspberries. Pearl suggested we use the woodstove in her little summer kitchen to heat water and take sponge baths. Then she offered the use of her old winger washer and suggested we dry our clothes on her line. Thrilled, we jumped at the chance of scrubbing our bodies clean and wearing line-dried clothes.

While Elle got a stove fire going, we hauled water. Waiting for the water to get hot, Lydia turned to me. "I remember the first time I saw you. You were in the barn. Rosy was chastising you about the loose skin hanging off of Justice's penis. She said that kind of crusty crap can make a trusty stead cranky. You protested and said it was Mark's job and not yours. I remember Rosy standing, arms crossed, fingers tapping her forearms and pointing to a pail. She told you to fill it with soapy water and find a soft cloth. Then the waiting began for Justice to drop down. Kitty had a smart-ass smile plastered across her face. 'Sweet talk him, Maia. Massage his butt. Guys like that.'"

Rosy was feeding the first batch of our wet clothes through the wringer and chuckled, "If anyone knows about that, it's you, Miss Kitty."

Lydia let out a pig-snort laugh. "So then Maia rubbed his butt. Justice's flattened ears looked like airplane wings. Dropping his penis was not on his to-do list! Finally, his resistance proved futile, and he dropped an inch. Maia you grabbed hold as he struggled to pull back up, until he gave up the fight."

I laughed and cried at the same time. "I rubbed that old boy's pecker until it was smooth and pink." I looked at my friends, "Justice was a great horse," feeling more gratitude than sadness.

Rosy smiled. "We do share so many, many wonderful memories."

"'This ride has been the most difficult thing I've ever done," Sal said, struggling to keep it together. "On top of the whole electrical grid and the drunken sniper cluster-fuck, I had to give up booze." She sniffled, then blew her nose. "It is hard as hell not to drink when I'm around Earl. When I get home, I'll try to be strong. I hope I can stay on the wagon."

"You did face your dragons," Rosy said, patting Sal's back. She surveyed our tribe. "My whole life I've felt that I needed to take responsibility for others. For Mom. For Dad. For Ray. For horses and all those people wanting to get close to them." She gave Sal a squeeze, "Sorry if I been too hard on you, Sis."

Sal leaned into Rosy, "Sis, we wouldn't be here if you hadn't taken your trail boss job seriously."

"Don't get me wrong," Rosy said. "I'm still taking full responsibility for our safety. It's my job to worry about what we do until we get home." Demanding and sometimes autocratic, Rosy had our respect. "Although I now realize how real strength comes from interdependence and respecting others' intuition."

Kitty sat cross-legged on an old wooden bench. "For so much of my life, all I ever thought about was seducing the next guy and then the next guy after that. Married men presented the perfect scenario. I couldn't want them because they were already taken and I couldn't fail at trying to maintain a relationship. I think my "got-to-have-me-a-man" addiction started way back when Dad forced me to sit on his lap. He got his kicks rubbing on me. God, I hated him. I told Mom, but she never believed me. She said I was making it up to get attention. Looking back now, Dad was my first married man. It's so twisted. I can see now how I've spent too much time getting back at men by sellin' myself short." She paused. "Isn't that crazy? Now for the first time in my life, I believe I'm capable of a sustained, loving relationship."

Elle focused on the barn wood ceiling. "My pattern had been to seek thrills through travel and adventure and bury myself in work and gadgets. Now everything is different." She shook her head. "Who would have guessed it?" She smiled. "The amazing thing is that so much of what I thought was essential before this disaster was just an illusion. Strangely, living with less feels more like a beginning than an end. With all we've been through, our sisterhood leaves me hungry for more connection, for being in a more fulfilling relationship." She turned to look at Kitty. "Does that make sense?"

Kitty nodded, "Does to me."

"Justice helped me be braver," I said, looking toward the corral. "This whole awful, terrible time has helped me get out of myself and face my insecurities."

With our bodies clean and our clothes dry, we went to the church to organize our stuff and take a nap before leaving. Lydia and Sal returned to the kitchen to be with Pearl.

For a while we sat together in silence. I lay on the sanctuary floor and heard Elle ask Rosy, "What do you think about the idea that if people are no longer being constantly bombarded with an electromagnetic charge that it could have had a positive affected on human's psyches?"

"Maybe George is right," said Rosy. "Maybe the gall dang aurora helped everybody get nicer."

"What do you think about George and an electromagnetic shift bringing about enlightenment?"

"I don't know what to think about that."

Elle jumped up and got the "Prairie Power" book and plopped down next to Rosy. "Remember how George thought the grid could come back on if someone figured out an electromagnetic something-or-other that came from the sun causing power surges?" She paged through the book. "Look at this. It looks like magnets are put together in a ring, then several rings are somehow put together." She stopped at a large diagram. "Could the magnets be aimed at the sun?" She struggled to understand. "Look at all these circles surrounded by other circles." She squinted. "Maybe circles aren't circles and could be twelve-pointed stars."

Rosy shook her head pointing at a small rectangle. "So what are these little square pegs and all those lines?"

"Could be buildings. These lines could be roads."

Elle set the book down. "I don't know what to think. It's too much. Too abstract."

After a long nap, we went to Pearl's. Entering the kitchen, we were overcome with the smell of fresh-baked bread. The kitchen crew had been busy. The counter was covered with still soft oatmeal cookies, dozens of hardboiled eggs and plastic containers of freshly made applesauce. A tomato lentil soup with peppers and carrots simmered on her cook stove.

Gathered together around Pearl's table, we passed around a platter of pickled beets.

"I will miss you," Lydia said, handing me a thin plastic bag. "Will you make sure this letter gets to my husband?"

"Of course. Somehow I'll find a way to deliver it."

"Take my car and tell him I'm okay. More than ok."

"Consider it done," I said. She placed her jasper touchstone in my palm. "No, no, no, no," I said, handing it back. "You keep it." I smiled, "Just send positive thoughts."

"Telepathically," she said, squeezing my hand. "Can you believe I'm turning into an earth mother?"

"Our princess no longer needs glitter," I said. "You've traded your crown for an apron."

Chapter 17

Night Came Alive

Elle swung the church door open. "Brr! Bit brisk." She warned, "Tonight could get damn cold. Wear warm clothes."

The early October night felt more like November. Lydia brought Romeo over to the hitching post for us to say goodbye. While we saddled up, Sal presented us with two saddlebags packed full of freshly baked bread, oatmeal cookies, hardboiled eggs, several containers of jelly and applesauce, a big bag of steel cut oats, and lots of apples and plums.

Rosy secured one of Romeo's panniers on top of Thief's saddle, making sure it couldn't flop. Thief would haul our food, tents, sleeping bags, blanket, tarps, buckets, fishing pole, horse stuff, cooking gear, water purifiers and as many water containers as possible.

Pearl sat on the church steps wearing her red housecoat with an orange crocheted shawl draped over her shoulders. "I sure hope the food will keep your bellies full for a little while." She reached to touch Sal and Lydia's hands. "Thank you, thank you, Lord, for bringing me these two angels."

"That's a first," Sal cackled. "I don't think I've ever been called an angel."

Rosy chuckled, "I think you're right about that."

I went back into the church to leave an offering in the collection plate and make sure we hadn't forgotten anything and spotted our whiskey container pushed under a pew.

Back outside I handed Rosy the bottle. "It appears someone left a special offering."

Momentarily puzzled, Rosy slid the bottle into Thief's pack. "We'll keep this, just in case." She adjusted her wide-brimmed Stetson hat and buttoned her long brown coat. "Come on, cowgirls, it's time to say goodbye and head out."

Lydia wrapped her arms around Liberty's neck and oozed gratitude for the experience of a lifetime.

Sal kissed Thief's forehead, then turned to Rosy, "Please tell Earl I'm good."

Rosy hugged Sal. "I'll give him an earful, honey. I'll let him know you are in a good place."

Sal pulled away, looking like she was about to break down and bawl. Instead, she punched her sister lightly on the shoulder. "Parting is such sweet sorrow."

"Been an incredible time, Sister of mine. I'm damn proud of you." Rosy looked at everybody, "Love all of you, your strength and tenacity."

After a round of hugs and more promises of returning, the time to separate had arrived and the four of us mounted our trusty steeds.

"Everyone ready?" Rosy said, wrapping Thief's lead around her saddle horn.

The instant my butt hit the saddle, I felt energy course through my body. Liberty was not Justice, yet she felt great.

We were nearly out of sight, when we turned and waved. Sal and Lydia stood beside a wonderfully kind old gal. Liberty's whinnies had always been soft, but this time she cried the loudest. She, too, had fallen for Romeo. We heard Romeo continue to bray long after Liberty fell silent.

Clouds drifted across a waning moon, casting horizontal curtain-like streams of light. Catch, our night warrior, comfortable in darkness, led us away. Within minutes, Rosy let Thief's lead rope go loose, untethered, trusting the brothers would stay together.

Rio and Bond pranced with their heads arched and tails up. Liberty responded to my every move like we'd always been paired. I felt her welcome my touch when I threaded my fingers through her multi-colored mane. The four-beat rhythm of her hooves hitting the ground like a drum eased my anxiousness.

Just like the Cartwright brothers in Dad's favorite television show, *Bonanza*, we rode abreast on a remote country road. All Dad's life, he loved to talk horse. One time he went on about how ancient people considered horses sacred, like angels, whose job it is to transport souls to and from their earthly existence. Dad believed horses help us stay connected by an invisible thread that binds our souls from one incarnation to the next. I smiled, thinking about the very first time our granddaughter sat on a horse.

She sat tall, a mirror image of Dad. It looked like she, too, had inherited 'horseitis.' I remembered her telling me how she taught herself to parallel park a car. "It was easy, Grandma," Aly said. "It's just like getting a horse to move over. First you move the hip and then you put the shoulder in the right place." I ached to hug her.

"Look!" Kitty yelled. "A shooting star. Make a wish!"

"I want to be home," I said. "Please, please, let my family be safe."

Liberty nervously tossed her head back and forth as we trotted over the I-90 overpass. Immediately, we made a sharp turn onto a service road. Bond shied when a deer sprang out from behind a large stack of hay bales. The deer bounded away, and in the moon's light, we saw it stop at a safe distance, turn and wait for us to go away.

New railroad tracks and ties forced us to ride single file along the embankment to avoid the rough surfaces. Rosy reached down and patted Catch's shoulder. "Thank God we got them shod."

When we stopped to relieve our bladders, Rosy broke off a hunk of bread, then passed the loaf around. We ate Pearl's hardboiled eggs and sucked the juice out of apples then fed the cores to our horses.

"At first I didn't like the idea of Sal and Lydia staying with Pearl," Rosy confessed. "But I think they made the right decision. They're in a good place and we'll make much better time."

Dawn brought robin song, crowing pheasants and the gobbling of wild turkeys. As the eastern sky burst into a glorious, tropical fruit orange, we peered down a breathtaking deep river gorge with red, pink and purple quartzite free-standing towers amid fifty-foot steep cliffs. Rosy gasped, "Oh my God! It looks like a cathedral."

"An amphitheater for the gods," I said.

Kitty marveled, "If this is the Palisades, then Palisades are a slice of heaven."

"It's sacred," Elle said. "A jewel."

Dumbfounded, we stared. Before that very moment, none of us had a clue that a mini-Grand Canyon was in an otherwise bland eastern South Dakota.

Elle lifted her nose and slowly turned her head, attempting to locate the source of wood smoke. We all fell silent, then heard the cry of a baby, a sound we had not heard for a very long time.

"What should we do?" I asked.

"Baby means people," Rosy whispered. "People equal danger."

Elle, ever the compassionate nurse said, "Perhaps they need help."

"We can't go there," Rosy said. "The best thing we can do is not threaten anyone in any way." She made the clucking sound and Catch responded. We trotted down a narrow trail and crossed an old wooden bridge into an oak savanna forest that was away from the river gorge.

Rosy looked around nervously. "Best we take turns standing watch."

Deafening ghostly wind howled through the old oaks, rustling the leaves. With an abundance of acorns, this was paradise for turkeys, squirrels, deer and much more. This place felt like spirits of thousands of years still lurked and haunted.

After a refreshing nap, we decided to escape the raw, persistent wind and found a more secluded spot along Split Rock Creek. Elle went upstream to try her luck fishing. Rosy and I got a fire going. Kitty took off her boots, rolled up her pant legs and was walking in the river with Rio when she lurched backward and dropped out of sight. Rio went down, then exploded up, his front legs reaching up and out of the water. Kitty was caught in a swim-off with the current. Elle dropped her two gutted bass, sprinted to Kitty and dragged her out of the fast-moving current.

Rosy and I ran to help. Kitty was on the ground, choking and coughing. Fearing hypothermia, we quickly got Kitty and Elle out of their dripping wet clothes. They trembled and shivered uncontrollably as the cool wind robbed their body heat. We wrapped the space blanket around them and ushered them closer to our humble fire.

Leaning into the fire's warmth, Kitty turned to Elle and said, "Thanks, pal."

"That happened fast," Elle said.

Kitty trembled. "One minute I was in the shallows; then I was drawn down into what felt like a bottomless abyss."

"Even beautiful places like this can be mighty dangerous," Rosy said, laying Elle's fish on the grill.

Kitty rubbed her hands over the fire. Her adrenaline soared and she seemed eager to talk, as if the brush with drowning shook something loose inside of her. "Anybody ever hear about the horse that committed suicide?" she said, pulling her knees into her chest. "It's a true story. Honest."

"Tell us more," I said, feeding our fire more sticks.

"Here's how that story goes. There was this horse walking along the Lake Superior shore. Suddenly it turned, entered the water and swam out into the bay toward open water. A man in a boat circled the horse, trying his best to turn it back toward land, but the horse just kept swimming farther out into the open. The guy in the boat watched as the horse repeatedly poked its head underwater. Then it didn't surface."

"That's crazy," I said.

Kitty raised her hands, palms up, "Read it somewhere."

I said, "You know you can't trust everything you read."

"I know that," said Kitty, looking down. "As a kid I'd read in a magazine that a horse would absolutely, positively never step on a person." She drew a deep breath. "To test what I'd read, I rode my pony, Sugar, over my sister. I was certain what I'd read was the truth, so I talked my little sister into lying flat on the ground, her arms above her head, legs together, stiff like a board. I rode Sugar to the far end of our yard and urged him into a canter. When his right front hoof landed smack on my sister's belly, I knew the magazine lied. My sister howled, rolled over and screamed for Mom. She wasn't seriously hurt, but I was afraid Mom would whip me silly. I tried to explain what I'd read, but Mom didn't buy it. I spent the next two weeks grounded in my room. No riding Sugar. That was when I learned not to believe everything I read."

Elle asked, "What'd your Dad say?"

"By that time Dad was long gone. He bought me Sugar when I was eight. Right after that, he up and skedaddled. When I got older Mom told me he ran off with another woman. In all these years, never once has he contacted me." She sighed, "Oh, how I loved that pony."

"I'm sorry," Elle said, patting Kitty's knee. "That's sad."

Kitty pulled the space blanket up over her shoulders. "I've had more than my share of that kind of shit."

While eating our grilled fish sandwiches, we heard the roar of a motorcycle to our north, sounding like it was traveling a hundred miles an hour. I thought, bikes are a good way to get around and scratched my head, recalling a five-hundred-mile, week-long bike ride Mark and I did up and down Wisconsin's steep hills. Then I imagined sitting on my red fat-tire Schwinn bike, like the one I had as a kid, with its thick leather seat and wide fenders. I'd grasp the wide handlebars, squeeze the handbrakes, release, then lift the kickstand with my toe and push off. With splayed knees, sometimes I'd struggle to balance and probably looked like a circus clown. With renewed confidence, I'd stand and pump the pedals. I blurted out, "If my memory is correct, when we stopped for our first tank of gas at that Trading Post near here, didn't Lydia mention she saw bicycles?" I looked at Rosy, "What if?" I paused. "What if, let's say two of us got bikes and rode them home. We could open our coats, make a sail, each take hold and let the wind blow. Maybe it could take us a day or two, then we'd bring a truck and trailer and come back for the other two."

Rosy gave me a sour look. Kitty and Elle looked like deer caught in headlights. Elle stuttered, "You serious? No way. I'm staying with Bond."

"I'm with Elle," Kitty said. "No way I'd leave my Rio." She glared at me, and gradually her face softened. "I understand that you have more pulling you home than I do. So, if you want to go, I'll pony Liberty."

Instantly reality set in. Why would I want to exchange a living, breathing partner and the rhythm of hooves for the hum of tires? Biking demands staying focused on pavement; whereas riding horseback is a shared experience.

"Ok, ok," I said. "Just saying."

Checking Wade's maps, we determined which backroads would offer a straight shot to Albert Lea and I-35. "If we do forty miles a night for four nights, we'll be within spitting distance of home." Rosy paused, "Our horses are as fit as they'll ever be. Anybody think that's asking too much?"

"No, I don't think so," I replied. "The Amish family that sells vegetables at our farmer's market lives eleven miles outside of town. Every Saturday one horse pulls their buggy full of supplies with two people aboard, both ways up and down the hills." I paused. "So you asking if that's too much for us?"

Rosy replied, "I'm not worried about us. We are in good shape. Thanks to Pearl and her angels, we've got plenty of food, and we're traveling pretty light."

Dusk arrived earlier each night. Leaving Split Rock, Rosy buttoned the upper mast of her long coat and pulled her hat down over her ears, like a rough and tumble TV trail boss. The sun blended its orange, red and purple with blue swirls that brightened the western sky. Cloaked safely in darkness, we began our marathon. Night felt comfortable, like being with family. With Thief's load tightly secured, sometimes we'd fast trot and break into a gallop and sprint at top speed across flat wide-open land, sans fences. We took breaks, ate, walked and talked as La Luna, our faithful companion, made her nightly east to west journey. The Big Dipper appeared in the northwest and, on a clear night, the Milky Way came in from the southeast like a mystical creature with a spine, a core, rising up, filling the sky, floating and drifting southwest. Satellites still circled.

When a vehicle approached, we darted into fields or dropped down into a drainage ditch, some as deep as twenty feet.

Night was about to give way to light, when—in the distance—tiny red lights flashed. "Is that a turbine?" I asked as hope surged through me. Wind turbines meant Minnesota. My voice cracked. "Rosy, see those lights?"

"Sure do."

"Yahoo!" Kitty yelled. "We have arrived!"

I stammered, "Is there any possibility that could mean electricity is working?"

"Don't think so," said Rosy. "If electricity was back, we'd see more lights, hear more traffic, there would be more plane contrails and we'd run into more people." She then burst any bubble of hope. "Turbines have solar panels for power to make them independent from the grid, and those warning lights are for planes."

Elle looked at Wade's map and reported that the cemetery he'd highlighted was straight ahead. The cemetery was concealed behind a Norway spruce windbreak towering at least sixty feet high. We hobbled the horses and they feasted on the rich grass. Rusted sections of wrought iron fences with spear tops aimed toward heaven still protected some of the graves. It was difficult to decipher the engravings on most of the weathered tombstones. Granite headstones best kept their resident's identity intact. Many headstones simply said, mother, father or baby. One large red granite headstone was engraved with, 'Suffer no more little children that come unto me,' then listed the names of seven children buried side by side. "Typhoid or diphtheria," Elle said. We saw Baby Girl Nash, 1822 to 1825. Blanche, wife of Charles, 1842 to 1862. One section of the cemetery had the common date of 1918. "The Spanish flu," Elle said. "That pandemic was brutal."

"Over here," Rosy pointed at a headstone. "Miller. I'll bet this is Wade's family."

I got on my hands and knees and thanked Pearl and her Wade whom I could only imagine.

Kitty nervously kept turning around. "This place is haunted. I'm so glad we're not camping here tonight."

"We're here all day, so do your best to make friends with the ghosts," Rosy said, staking her tent in the shade.

With clusters of houses within sight, we were afraid to draw anyone's attention by hunting or making a fire and instead enjoyed Pearl's delicious food. The sun penetrated our tent and warmed our weary bones as we slept, until Kitty screamed, "No! No!"

"What?" Elle yelled. "What?"

Kitty was curled in a fetal position. "It was awful." Slowly she sat up. "It was a nightmare. I was caught somewhere between sleep and awake. Like a middle place. A zone. It was so real. I was in a barn and a man screamed, 'You fucking low-life.' Looking outside, I saw a dark-skinned man get thrown out of a truck bed. His arms were tied behind his back. His face was bloody and a rag covered his mouth. 'Stop!' I shouted. 'Stop or I'll shoot.' The big guy laughed and picked up a board about the size of a baseball bat out of his truck bed. He growled, 'So you wanna be next.' I backed up. 'Stop or I'll shoot,' I warned, but he kept coming, swinging his weapon at me. I pulled the trigger and kept pulling and then everything shifted into slow motion. The monster fell backwards. His blue eyes were wide open. Elle was there and knelt down and tore his shirt open. Blood oozed out. My bullets hit an artery and punctured his lung. Elle lowered his eye lids."

"That's pretty heavy," Rosy said. "Thank God, it was only a dream."

Kitty jumped up, "It felt like a premonition. Like somehow I knew that guy."

I put my hand on Kitty, "Don't let fear grab hold. We all have dragons that can pull our energy down. Consider this: sometimes when we are closest to success is when our darkest fears kick in and we focus on the bad things that could happen. Remember that this far we've done an amazing job. Now we have to trust we have the strength to meet life's challenges. Be positive."

"I never dream," Kitty said. "That scared the shit out of me. I want to get the hell out of this spooky place right now."

Days and night blurred as we pushed on through great stretches of agricultural land with huge feedlots housing cattle, hogs and turkeys. The land felt used up. Drained of spirit and energy. Only a fraction of the homesteads that were marked on Wade's maps still stood along the twentieth century corridor. Agriculture's continuous and insatiable consolidation opened up the land with wall-to-wall cropping. At times it seemed as though every square inch of land had been plowed under for cash. Steady depopulation was the result. People were gone.

The nutrient rich black soil once belonged to indigenous people, before pioneers made claim to it. Good water, land and grasses attracted settlers who knew the value of hard work and religious conviction. Teams of horses turned over virgin prairies. Newcomers constructed buildings, planted gardens and crops and raised families, all without gasoline or electricity. Settlers had high hopes and experienced grave disappointments. They suffered through loneliness, hardships like blinding dust storms, devastating hail, smallpox and measles, tornadoes, prairie fires and the locusts that ate everything but their mortgages.

Windbreaks surrounded most of the remaining homesteads, many ramshackle, still protecting and further isolating their inhabitants. Metal buildings caught the moon's light. Old cement silos, long unused, Quonset huts and grain elevators, obsolete and abandoned, poked through walls of trees. An occasional cellphone tower seemed obsolete with its feeble marker light. Hearing the hum of a generator we saw a light shining through a window of a home that had rooftop solar panels in a compound surrounded by razor-wire fencing.

Night was when the natural world came alive. Night-time awakened the senses. Stillness amplified the yipping coyotes, raccoons fighting over corn, night hawks calling, raptors diving as wind swooshed over their feathers, making a sound like water cascading over rocks. The honking of migrating ducks and geese penetrated the darkness as did the barred owl's calling, "Who, who cooks for you? Who, who cooks for you?" Trumpeter swans in flight sounded like trucks' honking nasal horns. Snow geese circled before dropping out of sight. Horses whinnied their greetings as they heard us approach. Complaining cattle waddled over to check us out, even though we tried to walk quietly and get out of sight before anyone or anything spotted us.

Morning brought a host of starlings that rose like waves and swarmed, forming long black ropes. With grand synchronicity the birds turned and, in a split second, matched each other's speed and direction. Their spontaneous magical dance was a graceful symphony in motion, a mysterious choreography of constantly changing shapes. Momentarily invisible, the starlings turned, fanned out into a beautiful helix, then retracted into a rope of birds, landing on power lines that sagged under their weight.

Transfixed, I whispered, "Murmur."

"Perfect word," Rosy replied. "Like us. We've come together. We move in harmony. In unison. We anticipate each other's next moves, like those black birds, we stick together. We, too, have become one."

Sandhill cranes rattled their bugle calls as they lifted from their night roosts in pursuit of breakfasting in open fields. Daylight brought robins, starlings, swallows and scads of purple grackles. Coots darted around ponds. A box turtle seemed intent on its way to somewhere else. Snowy egrets held court on the backs of cattle. Throughout the days, we saw lots of doves and Western meadowlarks with black V's on their chests. One day we were gifted with a golden eagle soaring high above us.

Expansive marshlands were home to huge flocks of migrating birds and numerous critters that provided a chorus of croaking sounds. A great blue heron, making harsh squawks, flapped its fingered wings, lifted and took off. Little black coots darted around brown cattails and tall arrowroot. Armies of grasshoppers flitted through tall grass, sounding like tiny buzz saws. Leafless sumac with burnt-red seed pods signaled fall. We rode past field after field of dry corn and soybeans. In the prism of crisp light, the golden shafts and turkey-foot seed heads of tall blue stem grasses shimmered, creating rainbows. Fields of uncut hay and dry grasses were so brown they looked plowed. Purple New England asters, goldenrod and dogwood provided enough seeds for birds to get their fill.

Rosy caught a scent and stood tiptoe in her stirrups. "I think I smell a grass fire, but I don't see any glow." She sat back down. "A prairie fire can move faster than a horse can run." She stroked Catch's mane. "Can you imagine those families trapped in their root cellars, listening to the roar of wind pushing an inferno? The crackling, popping, hissing of flames greedily consuming absolutely everything? Folks lucky enough to spot a fire coming could start a backfire to avert total destruction. Too often, when the smoke blew away, all that was left was burnt crops and barren earth."

"And we think we've had it tough," I said.

Suddenly Rio side-passed clear across the road, registering the smell of death. Elle flashed her light into the ditch, gasped and covered her nose with her hand. "Oh geez. It's a golden retriever." She craned over Bond's head. "That poor dog. His eyes are gone." She lifted her reins and turned Bond away. "That was no accident. Dog's got a big hole right between its eyes."

Rosy quickened our pace and no one spoke until the pungent odor was well behind us. "Told you, these are dangerous times."

"Who'd kill such a wonderful animal?" I said.

Kitty being Kitty, said, "Wasn't that our first roadkill?"

"You are demented," I groaned.

"Think about it," she said. "With less traffic, fewer animals could have been killed."

"Probably all hunted by now," Elle said. "We'll know more when we get home."

Like a horse headed to the barn, I constantly thought about arriving home. The loop played over and over. We were on the road to home as it dipped down into a haze of morning fog. Light filtered through leafless walnut trees. A welcoming call would come from a bald eagle perched on a snag in a limestone bluff surrounded by green cedar and pine not yet rusted. Our hardwood forest would be ablaze with reds, oranges, gold, yellows, burgundies and browns. Leaves would twirl down. Where the road split, the others would turn and head to Ray and Rosy's. For the first time in what seemed like forever, I'd be totally alone. My heart would race. Would Black Jack or Liberty be first to whinny? Would Black Jack be waiting at the gate, nickering and snorting? Liberty would lunge to her old buddy, eager to touch noses and share breath. Our dog, Will, would bark and announce my arrival. Mark would see me and for a moment he'd be dumbstruck. He'd run and our knees would buckle and together we'd tumble to the ground.

"Oh, my God!" he'd stammer. "Maia. How? What?" Then he'd hug me like he'd never let me go.

I'd cry. "We made it. I'm home." He'd help me into our home. I'd collapse on the sofa and he'd cover me with a flannel quilt, spoon-feed me soup, and assure me our kids were safe. I could almost taste our garden-fresh tomatoes topped with homegrown basil. He'd heat water for a bath. The very idea of bathing in hot water took my breath away. I'd turn on a faucet and splash hot water on my face and brush my teeth. I'd look in a mirror and try to fix my hair. I'd go into my closet and stand in front of an abundance of clean clothes. I'd look at our family's pictures. Then we'd crawl between soft flannel sheets, I'd snuggle into his warm body and we'd spoon."

Lightning chains wove through threatening thunderheads along the western horizon. "We're in for a good one," Rosy said, signaling Catch into overdrive.

"We're getting close to the I-35 overpass," said Elle. "Perhaps we could stash our gear under the overpass and prevent everything from getting soaked."

Rain spit in our faces by the time we secured our horses in a nearby hedgerow and covered Thief's pannier with a black plastic bag. We lugged our saddles and grabbed our sleeping bags, then dashed under the bridge. We climbed onto the wide concrete apron beam under the bridge deck. The shelf was littered with garbage and smelled like oil but provided enough space for us to tuck up and avoid wind gusts delivering horizontal sheets of rain. Lined on the shelf like books, we watched waterfalls cascade off the overpass, splash down and form puddles that ran like a river. Rain thrummed the pavement in a steady tempo. Lightning streaked, and again I saw Justice lying lifeless in mud. Bats hung from the gray concrete ceiling and serenaded us with their chatter. Wrapped in my filthy sleeping bag, I struggled to stay warm. My muscles screamed. My stomach growled. I was thirsty and hungry.

When the storm subsided, Rosy shoved her sleeping bag under her arm and went to our horses. "I'm with you," Elle said, following her.

Speeding semis made sleep difficult. A pickup stopped on the shoulder of the road below us. Kitty shushed me by putting a finger on her lips a she took her pistol out of her fanny pack. A man hopped out, took a pee, zipped up, got back in his truck and headed east. Kitty put her weapon away.

"What were you going to do? Shoot him?"

"I could have," said Kitty, "If I had to protect us."

I shuddered, "Not me. I'd freeze."

Mid-afternoon, while we waited for night, we entertained ourselves by watching clouds transform into dogs, cats, turtles and faces. Gradually the cobalt blue sky became covered with clouds layered one over another and looked like a fancy birthday cake. "Cake," Kitty said, smacking her lips. "I'm so hungry for cake. Remember Lydia's horse cake?" She shook her head, "That woman made the most dramatic switch I've ever seen."

"Lydia's in a good place," said Rosy. "So is Sal. I hope Sal can stay sober when she gets back with Earl. I hope she's mastered self-control."

Pearl's cookies and hardboiled eggs were long gone, but, luckily, we still had half a loaf of bread, a couple sticks of jerky, some apples, a dried food meal and a couple servings of steel cut oats. We picked black walnuts up off the ground, stomped them to remove their husks, pounded the nuts with rocks and devoured the rich nutmeat along with sun-dried wild grapes.

Elle knelt over the map to figure out our final route. "I'll bet we could take advantage of the inter-connected access roads running through the middle of the wind turbines." She bent closer to see the fine detail. "At I-90 the wind farm goes at least twenty miles straight east." Then she raised her arms above her head, leaned back and chuckled. "Ladies, may I please have your full attention?" She smiled. "Do we live in the Root River Watershed?"

We all nodded.

"Well, because we are horse women, we might be a bit limited in our thinking." She paused. "Tell me, is it true that one thing our area is known for is The Root River Bike Trail?" She waited for us to put two and two together. "Ladies, we can pick up the bike trail at Grand Meadow and that will take us within a few miles of home."

Rosy waved her arms. "That's brilliant!"

Elle continued, "I've biked many sections of that trail. The old railroad goes down into the prairie and all the way to the Mississippi. It's a flat, straight shot along the Root River with a reasonable downward grade, bridges, picnic tables, shelters and," she rubbed her hands together, "hand-cranked water pumps."

A military convoy rumbled across the I-35 bridge as we were ready to leave. "Military scares the hell out of me. Men, guns, rules. Way too much testosterone," said Elle.

"I'm so done with men," Kitty said, as we waited for their sounds to evaporate.

Elle cocked her head, "You sure about that?"

"This adventure helped me clear my head," Kitty said pensively. "So much of what I've lived my life was about my dad. When this situation is resolved I'm going to try to find him."

"I think that's a good idea," Rosy said, "Now let's move before anyone sees us."

Night arrived with a billion stars and the bedazzling Milky Way. Our plan was to cross I-90 before sunup. "One more night and we'll be sleeping in our own beds," I said.

"Can't wait," Rosy said. "When we ride in, Ray will be so proud of us." She paused, "He's not a crier, but I'll bet money I'll see my old boy shed elephant tears."

"I am looking forward to getting home, seeing my dogs, finding out about my family, seeing Mom." Elle paused, "I've said this before: this time together was beyond spectacular. I will so miss being with all of you."

"Right on," Kitty said, stroking Rio's mane. "I can't imagine not riding him every day." She smiled, "But maybe we'll need our horses to get around."

"We're not home yet," Rosy said, throwing a cold cloth our way. "But we're damn close."

"Pizza," said Kitty. "That's what I want."

Cheese was at the top of all of our lists. "We all need fat," Rosy said.

"I've dropped at least twenty pounds."

Throughout the night we continued to proclaim our desires. "Ice cream."

"A great bottle of wine."

"Potato chips."

"Guacamole."

"Root beer float."

"Hot coffee with real cream."

"Fresh baked rhubarb pie."

Chapter 18

The Last Leg

Like so many other times since I said my final goodbye to Justice, I held my white clam-like touchstone like a security blanket as we fast-trotted across the I-90 intersection, flew past a boarded-up gas station and The Old Dutch Mill restaurant. My touchstone gave me courage to face the unknown and helped me remember all we'd been through. How we, six women and our trusty steeds, met this formidable challenge. Strange, how only weeks earlier my hands gripped the steering wheel as we headed west on I-90. I was afraid to trailer our horses alone, without Mark. Afraid I'd get hurt. Afraid of the unknown. I felt deeply grateful realizing that fear and insecurities no longer controlled me, and I learned to trust not only my sense of knowing, but to trust others.

Pearl's brother could have been right about this disaster and maybe people didn't go bat-shit crazy, but instead pulled together. Could it really be true that living without electricity constantly bombarding everyone's energy gave people an opportunity to become more dependent, more creative and return to the basics of living?

At the access road, Rosy signaled Catch to slow walk. "I'm glad we're done with that hurdle." Liberty kept reaching out with her nose, sensing something. Did she sense we were close to home?

All around us red turbine lights flickered. We'd gone a couple of miles when headlights came towards us off the ridgetop. We walked down a steep hill through crunching oak and maple leaves and ducked behind a long metal storage shed until the vehicle sped past. It was the crepuscular time, the time hovering between dark and night. Going back up the hill, Catch lunged, and immediately tripped. His head dropped between his front legs and momentarily it looked like he'd topple down the hill. He was unable to set his front right leg down and struggled to balance on three legs. Rosy jumped off, switched on her headlamp and gently lifted his right front leg. "Holy shit! It looks like he overreached his back right leg." She looked up, "I thought I heard his shoe hit his front leg." She choked. "I'm afraid he's torn his suspensory ligament." She knelt down and placed his leg on her thigh. "This is bad. Really bad." She looked at Elle, "Get the Bute." Elle opened the tube of liquid analgesic and then stuck her thumb behind Catch's back teeth and administered a 10cc squirt of the pain-easing anti-inflammatory. Then she held his mouth shut to prevent any from dribbling out.

Rosy kicked the ground, looking like she could scream and cry at the same time. "Dangit to hell. Now we are stuck. We'd almost made it." She sucked in a deep breath, "We were so. . .so. . .close." She leaned on Catch's shoulder, let loose and wept.

We surrounded her and Catch and searched for what to say. This woman kept it together as we went through a buffalo herd and almost got through this whole journey without breaking down.

"It's not the end of the world," Kitty said. "You can ride Thief."

"It's a disaster," Rosy cried. "At best a torn ligament can take a year to heal. We've got less than forty miles left, and in a few hours Catch won't be able to walk more than a few feet. For him to heal he'll have to be confined and cannot be exercised or turned out." She bit her lip. "Too often injuries like this end a horse's career."

"I don't understand," I said. "What happened?"

Elle touched Catch's leg. Slowly and tenderly, she moved her hand down to his hoof. "His digital flexor tendon runs down this muscle and it contracts when he flexes his leg. The tendon is dense elastic connective tissue, kind of like a rubber band. It can instantly be torn if a leg is put under huge pressure, gets overloaded, or in this case, maybe Catch just reached way too far."

"Is he in pain?" I asked.

"Mild at first. That's why we gave him Bute. It should help him feel more comfortable until we're able to find a place to confine him. Now the most important thing we can do is to try to keep any swelling down. Elle handed her a shirt, then opened her canteen, drenched it with water, then wrapped it around his leg. "It will help for him to stand in cold water to draw out the heat and prevent swelling."

Catch's eyes glazed over, his head hung low and his ears looked like airplane wings. With Rosy's gear loaded on Thief, we slowly walked, searching for a place to hold up. Kitty spotted a grassy meadow behind a stand of trees with a small creek still swollen with runoff.

Rosy led Catch into the cold water. "This is the best treatment," she said. "If we minimize any swelling, he might recover faster." After a long silence, Rosy said, "We have to split up. I'll stay with Catch. You all hightail it home and get Ray and have him bring our trailer." She took a deep breath. "I sure hope he's saved enough gas."

"I'll bet Ray and Mark stockpiled enough gas so when the time was right, they'd come for us," I said, then took a deep breath. "I cannot imagine what they've gone through."

"Geez," Rosy said, "I pray they stayed put."

"Check this out," Elle said, handing me her binoculars. "That might be a good place for Catch."

Tucked away in a rise overlooking an industrial-scale windfarm construction site, surrounded by tall grasses, stood an old faded red barn with a classic gambrel roof. Abandoned cranes were next to towers. Bulldozers sat idle. An armada of semi-trailers held fifty-foot-long turbine blades and giant turbine housings. White tower sections looked like drumheads with their ends wrapped in blaze orange plastic. There were dozens of enormous rolls of thick high-tension powerlines, some transformers on poles, fiber optic cables poking up into junction boxes and large empty concrete tower pads.

Rosy evaluated the scene. "That barn could work," she said. "The milking parlor could have a water hydrant."

Walking along an old fence line, cottonwood leaves twinkled and rattled. Red-winged blackbirds and yellow-headed blackbirds made raspy chirpy sounds, flitting from bush to bush. We cut through the meadow of bluestem grass. Their golden shafts and turkey-footed seed heads held the stored energy of summer. Approaching the barn, Elle pointed to vegetation recently flattened and matted down. She stopped. "Someone's here," she whispered, slipping the shotgun out of her scabbard. Kitty unpacked her pistol. With eyes alert, searching for any movement, we crept toward the barn door. A yellow swallowtail with distinctive black spots was entangled in a spider web spanning a boarded window. Using the tip of her gun, Elle knocked on the once-bright red, now grayish door.

No reply.

Elle locked eyes with Kitty as she slid the door open. She yelled, "We're armed. Come out now. Show yourself."

We waited.

Above, from the loft, a man answered, his voice quivering, "We don't have any weapons. We're just trying to survive."

Elle repeated, "Show yourself."

A dark-skinned man, wearing a tee-shirt and blue jeans appeared in the southern corner and stepped on an old wooden ladder. Reaching the barn floor, he raised his arms up toward the timber roof. A woman wearing a yellow sweatsuit followed him down the ladder. She had a child, a girl, maybe five or six, wrapped in her arms. The child clung to the woman, and as she turned toward us I saw fear in her black eyes.

Kitty and Elle turned their weapons to face the ground.

Elle asked, "This your wife?"

He nodded, "Yes."

"Your names?"

"I'm Sidney." He turned his head, "This is Crystal, my wife. That's Lyla, our daughter." Lyla pushed deeper into her mother who stroked her jet-black hair and smiled at her reassuringly. Sidney kept his arms up. "From our upstairs window we watched you come through the meadow."

"Put your hands down," Elle instructed, then asked, "Why are you here?"

"We were on our way home from working in the fields, when all of a sudden everything went dark. We stopped in Rochester for gas, but nobody would sell us any. They said we were in a state of emergency and everyone was ordered to stay put. We were so afraid. We took backroads and kept our headlights off. Our car was running on fumes when we spotted this barn. We needed a safe place stay." He shook his head. "This is pretty white country, and we didn't have anyone to turn to."

He pointed south, "I stashed our car out there in the woods."

Rosy looked around. "Just you three?"

"Yes," he replied quickly.

"Anyone else around?"

His eyes darted to our horses standing outside the barn door. "I'll explain, but first I think it's best you get your horses out of sight." Once inside, the horses lunged for bales of Minnesota alfalfa hay. Rosy wrapped Catch's lead around a post and tied him short so he could hardly move, then gave him a slice of hay.

Rosy asked, "Has the farmer come by?"

"No. Nobody's come near the barn," he said.

"Is there water in the milk parlor?" Rosy asked.

Sidney nodded yes and we followed him though an inside door to the milking parlor to fill our bucket. Rosy lifted Catch's leg and placed his hoof in the cold water.

Back in the barn Sidney looked up at the loft. "Crystal and I made a living space behind those bales. We've kept watch out of a south and another north-facing window. Early one morning right after the full moon, a truck drove in, stopped at one of the newer turbines and we saw two men carry what looked like pretty heavy boxes into that tower."

"What?" Elle gasped, looking like a deer caught in headlights. "Two guys carrying heavy boxes?" She turned to Rosy, "Could they be the ones we saw?"

"What?" said Rosy, shaking her head.

Sidney said, "We watched them drive out and their truck logo said, 'Prairie Power.'"

Elle smacked her forehead with her hand, "Are you kidding me?" Wildly, we looked back and forth as she told Sidney about seeing two guys at the Missouri loading boxes into a black truck with that logo."

"You sure?" he said.

"How could this be?" We puzzled.

"Go on," Rosy urged.

"Late that night, after the men left, I crept over. The tower door was locked but empty flattened heavy-duty cardboard boxes were stacked by the door. The writing on the boxes looked Chinese. The insides had super thick linings with 4-inch holes that could have kept something from moving around. After that, it looked like those same two men showed up early several mornings and brought more stuff and left before dusk. Every time I went over and checked their garbage. One time I found the access door unlocked and went inside. I turned my flashlight on and saw an impressive control room with all kinds of tech stuff like consoles and computers and meters. A ladder about the length of a football field plus both endzones went up to the generator. I crawled up and saw a series of magnets that looked sort of like a strange gun."

Elle sprinted to her saddlebag and returned carrying the book. Our horses moved closer to us, as if interested in our conversation.

"Look at this. Maybe this could help us figure out what those guys are up to." Sidney peered over her shoulder as she paged through the book and stopped at a diagram of uniformly packed circles with neat rows of small dots staggered equal distance apart. In the upper right-hand corner, a curve came down along one edge to a small rectangle. "This looks like where we are." He pointed at a line, "Circles could represent this windfarm and the line could be the road to that turbine."

"Wait a minute," Rosy replied. "There are lots of turbines and substations all around this part of Minnesota."

Elle turned the page to what looked like a strange sort of gun. "That's what I saw!" Sidney said, "That's it!" He continued, "One morning three trucks rolled in and that night they left one truck here." He lowered his eyes. "I know it's wrong, but I syphoned some of their gas."

Crystal patted Sidney's shoulder, "We're hoping to get enough gas to get home."

"We get that," Rosy said. "We all do what we have to."

Crystal urged, "Tell them about the light."

"The next morning, the men came back and stayed throughout that night. We kept watch all night and we heard a woosh-woosh come from their turbine." He pointed at a bare lightbulb suspended by a wire hanging from the timber frame. "That bulb flickered. We could hardly breathe, we were so terrified they'd see the light and come in the barn."

Crystal laid her hands over her heart, "Thank God it only flashed on and off a couple of times, then, luckily, it stayed dark.

In unison, we all uttered, "Holy shit!"

Rosy stared at the bulb. "Very interesting."

"I don't know about this stuff," Sidney said. "But what if those guys have figured out a way to use magnets to generate electricity."

"Could be," Rosy said, raising an eyebrow. "Maybe this book could be valuable to them."

"Could be a bargaining chip if they find us," said Sidney.

Crystal asked if we wanted to see where they were living. Box elder bugs and Japanese ladybugs clung to the warm walls. Cooing pigeons were perched on the timber roof beams. Kitty and I followed her up the wooden ladder, through a narrow opening in the bales and into an austere space. Clothing was tossed on top of suitcases. Blankets were spread over hay bales. A few children's books and toys were on the floor near a window that overlooked the windfarm. Pepper, squash and pumpkin strips hung from thin ropes next to bundles of drying herbs. "Days get pretty hot up here and food dries fast," Crystal said. "During the day we go to the milk house to cook and get water. At night, Sidney leaves to find food. He's been pretty lucking snaring and trapping and I've gotten pretty creative cooking corn and soybeans. Some people around here had enormous gardens." She smiled. "Sidney's dug potatoes in the light of the moon and brought back pumpkins and squash and saved lots of tomatoes from rotting."

Climbing down, we heard Rosy and Sidney talking. "I'd like to ask you for a favor." Sidney nodded. Rosy asked, "Could we leave Catch and our stuff here? We'd like to ride home, get our trailer and, depending on what we find, come back in two, maybe three nights. If our husbands Ray and Mark have any extra gas, we'll bring you some."

"Of course we will," he said.

She asked Elle, "Is it okay if he keeps the shotgun till we get back?"

"Fine," Elle said.

She turned to Kitty, "You keep the pistol."

"Got it, boss," she replied.

"I say we stay here tonight, take a break, get some good rest and leave early in the morning. We're in our homeland and I'm no longer afraid of us being seen. We'll ride the ridge through turbine territory and then drop down to the bike trail. It should be empty and that's a straight shot home. Does that work for everyone?"

"That's a much better plan," Kitty said. "Ray'd go crazy if we showed up without you."

Rosy softened, "I can't wait to see him."

Elle lit our stove and added our last dried food meal to a pot of water. Crystal handed Rosy a bag of dried corn. "Sidney found a field of sweet corn and I dried as much as I could in case we got stuck here over winter."

A pigeon cooed and we all looked up. "That pigeon and those two red squirrels are my pets," Lyla said. "They make me laugh." She wrinkled her nose. "Dad said we might need to eat them if we run out of food." She smiled at Kitty. "Since we've been here, I've eaten squirrel, wild turkey and pheasants." She moved closer to Kitty and asked, "Are you a real cowgirl?"

"I guess I am," Kitty said.

"Your horse is so pretty," she said, leaning into her.

"Thank you. His name is Rio."

"Rio means river," she said. "I've never ridden a horse."

Kitty picked her up and set her on Rio's bare back. Her giggles were music that filled the barn. "He's so warm."

Rosy explained to her. "We're leaving Catch here a little while. He can't carry any extra weight so you can't sit on him, but you can pet and brush him as much as you want." Lyla glowed.

Liberty welcomed my touch, closing her eyes as I brushed her. I spread one bale of hay over another to make myself a soft bed. While taking off my boots, I sensed something move above me. Perched on a support beam, a squirrel seemed to be enjoying the activity below.

Settled in my sleeping bags for what could be our last night together, I thought about my quest to know if Mom was a native American. Even though finding that out had become important to me, in the end, my bloodline wasn't as important as feeling that my roots ran deep. I now felt indigenous to the land. Living close to the elements helped me connect to Creator in a new and powerful way, giving me a new confidence in myself and my abilities. It was time to go home. Home. I went to sleep feeling almost giddy.

Daylight streamed in through barn wall cracks. Rosy dished up the last of Pearl's steel cut oats and topped our breakfast with Crystal's dried wild grapes. Lyla asked Kitty if she could sit on Rio one more time.

Kitty took Lyla's hand, "Of course."

Lyla reached up her arms and Kitty got her settled in Rio's saddle. Lyla grinned from ear to ear as Kitty showed her how to use the reins to turn his head.

Rosy examined Catch and showed Sidney and Crystal how to wrap his leg and to get him to put his hoof in a bucket of water.

"We'll take good care of him," Crystal said, stroking Catch's mane.

Kitty turned to Rosy and said, "I'm worried about those men coming and hurting this family."

"We'll leave the book here with them. It won't do us any good and might be helpful if those men come to the barn. That way he'll have something to give them."

Kitty smiled, "Good thinking."

Sidney wrapped his arm around Crystal. Lyla, wiggled in between them. When we were ready to ride, he slid the barn door open a crack and looked to make sure nobody was around. Then we said our goodbyes and took off in a full gallop.

Reaching the eastern side of the turbine, Kitty looked back and reported that a black truck just drove past the barn. "I sure hope Catch doesn't whinny and draw them into the barn," I said.

"That Lyla will keep Catch distracted," Rosy said, rubbing Thief's mane.

For what seemed like hours, our conversation focused on figuring any return trip would depend on our supply of gas. "Here's what I think," Rosy said. "Ray and I will take our truck and stock trailer and make a beeline for Pearl's. We'll get Sal, Lydia and Romeo and on the way back stop for Catch and hopefully leave Sidney any extra gasoline. That's about a

500-mile trip and would take at least two tanks of gas."

"You know the back roads," Elle said. "If you're extra lucky you'd be able to do that in one, maybe two nights."

"If we only have enough gas to get a hundred miles or so miles, Ray and I will go for Catch and turn around and come right back."

We agreed we'd need four to five tanks of gasoline to get Lydia and Sal before the snow flew. Until we knew what was happening, we'd play it safe and most likely wait till spring to get our rigs, return Chip's shotgun and stop for my saddle at the house of holes where Justice's bones lay.

Feeling like Pegasus, we flew through the infrastructure of modern society, past several solar fields, an ethanol plant, transmission lines and cell towers. We trotted past silos, old windmills, chicken coops, corn cribs, pig houses, hay sheds, savannah remnants and grazing cattle. We passed old farmsteads replaced with big, modern houses, multi-car garages and acre after acre of un-mowed lawns.

"Well, isn't that a sight," said Elle as we rode by a John Deere mower stopped cold in the middle of a huge lawn.

"Don't laugh," Kitty replied. "I bet he's not the only landowner bent of shape because he ran out of gas."

I chimed in, "I can't help but wonder why anybody wants a lawn that big. I mean, it must take 5-6 hours every week and a whole hell of a lot of gasoline to keep it up, and for what?"

Elle shook her head. "It would be so great if everybody could see how alive Pearl's place was without much of a lawn and all those wildflowers and prairie grasses. It was inspiring to witness how deeply she was connected to the land."

"Totally," Kitty said. "If I ever have my own place it's gonna look just like Pearl's."

Elle agreed, "I'm turning every possible piece of land I own into prairies. No more mowing for me."

"If you're serious, when we get home," I said, "Mark can give you the name of a good friend who helps with prairie restoration."

"When we get home," Kitty said. "I'm gonna be interested in making a lot of changes."

"Right," Rosy said. "It's easy to talk big now, but what about when we get home and turn on the heat and take a hot bath?"

"I know it'll be temptin' to slide back into my old life," Elle said. "But being out here with all of you has texting and live streaming beat. I'd bet there are people stuck in lives filled with all the latest gadgets who'd give anything to have experienced our adventure."

"I'm not sure about that," I said. "People like the easy life."

Elle laughed, "Somehow I thought if I got the newest phone or updated my tablet that my life would be better. I was hunting for the latest so-called gadgets when I should've been hunting in the woods." She paused, "Helping provide food for this trip home . . .well that was real. It sure made me feel alive."

"So, Elle, if you ever need to feel alive, I'd gladly eat more roasted pheasant." Kitty said, smiling broadly.

"You're on," Elle replied.

"I wish we always remember how we're feeling right now," I added. "This whole damn trip was hard, but it was worth it!"

By mid-morning we'd left the prairie, its vistas and karst geology dotted with hundreds of sinkholes and descended into hardwood forests and the unglaciated river valley. We picked dried apples off an old tree, fed wild plums to our horses and devoured dried blackcap raspberries and grapes growing along fences. Reaching the Root River was emotional, and we stopped to watch and feel the free-flowing water. A beaver slapped its tail, demanding our attention. It swam upstream, went ashore and disappeared. Minutes later, it returned dragging a willow branch the size of an arm, it slid into the river, and the branch became its sail. In half the time it took the beaver to swim upstream, it returned and disappeared into its bank home.

We took a break by a stack of glacial rocks that once served as a fence corner. I remembered going to my Uncle Charlie's farm each spring and picking rocks out of his fields before he plowed. Afterwards, my Uncle Charlie would saddle Trigger, his Shetland pony, and I'd pretend he was Roy Roger's trusty steed, Trigger. That was the first horse I loved.

"That dream is still bothering me," Kitty said, lying on her side, watching the river flow. She shook her head, "Something about that guy that got beaten keeps hammering my brain."

"Sometimes dreams can run really deep," I said. "Give it time." I shared the recurring dream I had as a kid. "Over and over again I'd dream that Santa Claus would come down the chimney, smile at me, grab my sister and take her up the chimney with him." I took a deep breath, "Think there was tension between us sisters?"

"Ever work it out?" Kitty asked.

"Sorta," I said, "We may have had the same parents, but we interpreted life very differently."

No one said much as we climbed up out of the river valley, knowing that soon our time together would be over.

It was both exciting and traumatic when we arrived at the intersection where we'd separate. "Wow! What a trip we pulled off!" I said.

"One hell-of-a-ride," Kitty said,

"The adventure of a lifetime," Elle said.

"We did it. We are women warriors," Rosy said, lifting Thief's reins, turning him away, trying to keep her cool.

Light filtered through the now leafless walnut trees in a forest awash with reds, oranges and purples. I waited to hear somewhere in a limestone outcropping, a bald eagle issue a welcoming call.

A rooster crowed as I passed our Amish neighbors and I remembered waving at them as we left so very long ago. Then I recalled the day I drove over to buy eggs. A black horse was tied to a hitching post, standing in a pool of fresh red blood. I asked Sarah, the youngest girl why the horse was bleeding.

Standing tall, arms crossed, reluctant to answer, she said, "The men know what they're doing."

I pushed. "I don't understand."

"The men know what they're doing!" She repeated, then confessed, "They castrated that stallion."

Her words kept circling over and over in my head, only now they had nothing to do with the stallion. "The men know what they're doing!" I wondered, is that true? Do men really know what they're doing? Do humans understand their journey? That our every decision creates ripples that impact others? Does our insatiable need for technology, for power, for money lead us away from experiencing what makes life truly amazing? I named my horse Justice because I believe in the power of common good, of fair treatment and respect for others and I hold onto the dream of Liberty and Justice for all. I rubbed my touchstone. Not long ago, I was a woman full of worry. Now I understand the value of working with others and the strength inside of me. I made it through a herd of buffalo, survived a crazed gunman, rattlesnakes and the loss of my pal, Justice. I remembered the argument with Rosy about my cot. I was angry I'd have to sleep on cold, hard ground. That, too, ultimately became a gift. I learned to embrace being nimble and not limit myself because of age. This adventure gave me many gifts. I received the gift of being grounded and falling more deeply in love with nature. I learned how to listen better and certainly did a deeper dive into my own heart.

Less than a mile from home, the road dipped down, and fog blanketed the ground. The pull of my heart was so strong it was as though I wasn't even breathing. Again, I debated if Liberty or Black Jack would be first to whinny. When Liberty stepped on the road leading to our home, she became animated and, even though she was spent, whinnied harder and longer than ever before. Black Jack galloped along the fence line, stopped short and nickered sweetly. Liberty raced to him, eager to share breath. Wood smoke hung in the air. I dismounted. Will barked, ran and almost knocked me over. Mark stood in our doorway, holding a gun. He froze, then set the gun down and ran. We embraced. My knees buckled and together we fell on the ground.

"Oh, my God!" he cried. "Maia. How? What?"

I cried, "We made it."

I collapsed and everything went black. I awoke on our sofa with Mark hovering over me. We hugged and I bawled like a baby. "Our kids are fine," he reassured. "Everyone made it home." I drank in his words, relieved our loved ones were safe. "They're helping farmers harvest crops." He grabbed a tissue, "I thought about you all the time. Every day, I waited for you and Justice. I believed and prayed that you'd show up. That kept me sane." He blew his nose.

"What about the world?"

"All of a sudden nothing worked. Everything went dark. Right after the electricity went out, I rode Black Jack into town. Everyone was talking about the state of emergency. People were afraid to go against Homeland Security. Our governor issued a stay-at-home order instructing everyone to shelter in place. We were afraid city people would get desperate, freak out and we'd have to defend ourselves. The first week was a living hell. People died. Looting. Fires. Riots. Right away the government stepped up and began distributing food and medicine.

On my way back home, I stopped by Ray's. With a state of emergency in effect, we were afraid to come looking for you. We didn't want to make this horror any worse. We wrestled about knowing where we'd find you." His voice cracked. "We figured we couldn't risk a wild goose chase." He kissed my cheek. "Sorry, honey, you're not a goose. . .wild, perhaps."

I almost laughed and then reassured him that staying put was the right thing to do.

He pulled me closer. "It was uncanny. Ray and I believed—somehow we knew—you were heading home. We decided to wait until things quieted down to make our move. Then Ray got tossed off a horse and broke his ankle."

Mark got up, opened the wood stove door and added more split red oak. "Our saving grace was being so isolated. With the state of emergency, people didn't have access to fuel, so that limited movement. After the initial shock, people started to combine resources and work together. The Amish stepped up and helped people figure out how to do many things without electricity. A week or so after the flare, we heard rumors that some urban areas had surge protectors that prevented them from getting fried. Since then, the main focus has been to get the grid back up and running." He took a deep breath. "Two days ago, Ray came by and said that he'd heard an electric company was getting closer to getting our power back on."

"Thank God," I said.

I told him about having enough gas to get to the west end of the Badlands and riding through the desert along an abandoned railroad corridor. Then I told him that Justice died right after we crossed the Missouri River. "Lightning," I said and showed him my small clam-like touchstone. Mark said he was sorry and went on about how Justice was a great horse. I told him about Pearl and how Sal and Lydia stayed with her. I smiled, "Wait till you see Lydia. She's no longer a princess. She's become an Earth Mother."

He raised one eyebrow. "That's quite the switch."

He kissed my neck and twirled my hair. "You have got to tell me about this new do."

"You noticed," I smiled. "In time, you'll hear the whole story."

Chapter 19

Second Time Around

Ray's farm pickup had a half tank of gas, making getting Catch priority number one. Ray hooked up his old one-horse trailer, while Rosy gathered blankets, grabbed some packaged food and put the rest of our pooled money in an envelope for Crystal and Sidney.

On their return trip back home, they stopped at our place and told us that Sidney reported that the two men showed up right after we left. Again, Sidney witnessed the lightbulb flicker. Sidney said he planned to put the book by the turbine door when they were ready to leave. That Lyla had brushed Catch so much they were afraid his hair would be gone. Rosy told us that Sidney and Crystal promised Lyla that she could take riding lessons once they got home.

Ray said he'd already made a deal with one of his neighbors to borrow the diesel truck he'd converted to recycled oil. Then when the time was right, they'd take off to get Sal, Lydia and Romeo. We unanimously agreed it was best to wait until things had settled down and we had enough fuel to retrieve our rigs from Reed and Kelly

Early one morning I took Lydia's car to deliver her letter to her husband. I knocked on her front door and he answered, wearing a silk and satin midnight blue robe. I handed him the letter and he grumbled, "I told her not to go." A younger woman, wearing a matching robe, came and stood by his side, rubbed against him, called him honey and asked why I was there. When I told Lydia about Dick, with grace she admitted, "I no longer want that life anyway."

203

Epilogue

The aurora changed our world. The cavalier use of electricity had become a thing of the past. Only a few homes were decorated with holiday lights as we made our way to Ray and Rosy's for our yearly gathering. Lit candles inside brown paper bags lined their sidewalk. Lydia's pinecone wreath hung on their front door. Romeo was tied to their hitching post. I smiled, "She takes him wherever she goes." Her divorce settlement included a new truck, horse trailer and a five-acre farm for her and Romeo.

Once inside, we carried on like we hadn't seen each other for years. Lydia fluffed her salt and pepper hair. "I'm letting it grow."

Kitty brushed her hand over her short black curls, "Mine's springier."

Sal rolled her eyes. "Like you need more bounce."

Ray pushed his hip into Rosy as he stirred the split pea soup. "Thank God we didn't lose anyone." Lydia's eyes sprang to me and I knew she thought of my Justice.

"I lost Mom," Elle said, placing silverware on the table. "She'd been out of it for a long time." She looked up, "Did I tell you what my brother said?" She paused. "One of the last things Mom complained about was that her foolish daughter left her for a horse."

"Well, at least she remembered you," Lydia said, placing a platter of individual corncob-shaped corn breads, fresh honey and home-churned butter on the table. Every one of us women smiled as we remembered Pearl, her food and her wisdom.

"I miss Pearl," said Sal. "That woman made the whole nightmare worthwhile." She exchanged glances with Lydia. "Are we goin' back to help her?"

Lydia smiled, "You bet your sweet ass we are."

"Speaking of nightmares, remember the dream I had about a guy getting beaten?" Kitty said. "That dream haunted me. I kept thinking about my dad and decided to try and track him down. I found my sister and she said some guy in a bar hit Dad with a bar stool. He got beat pretty bad. He's still alive but has no memory. Is that weird or what?"

"Terrible," said Elle.

Kitty went on, "My sister said Mom married a rich guy and moved out of the country." We all waited, wondering how Kitty was taking the news. She paused, then surprised me by saying, "I do feel good about re-connecting with my sister."

This led to talk about all of the connections we'd made on our journey. We wondered about Ace and Lucille and hoped they'd made it back to Georgia. We hadn't heard from Sidney and Crystal and prayed they, too, got home safely. "That Lyla was a cutie," Kitty said. "I sure hope she's able to take riding lessons."

Then, with childish delight, Lydia ordered us to close our eyes. She rushed into the kitchen and returned, puffed with pride, carrying a horse-shaped cake. "I made it from scratch." Her jasper touchstone was the horse's eye.

"What a trip we had!" Elle said, raising her water glass for a toast.

Earl kept his distance until the party was almost over, then assumed center stage. "What just happened was child's play. A temporary loss of electricity. A mere inconvenience. An experiment in survivability."

Sal glared at her husband. "Earl, we just got through this one! Give us some time to recover!"

Mark replied, "He's right. We can't just ignore it, Sal. At some point, something really big will happen. Our world has the potential to collapse. We are a wasteful, self-centered people. . ."

Sal cut him off. "You guys, not all of us believe we have to accept that destiny. Think of Pearl, of people like Ace and Lucille."

"Don't forget Stella and Chip," Elle added.

"And Sidney and Crystal," Kitty chimed in.

"All of us learned so much about being independent in such a short time," Lydia added. "Sal and I have been talking about ways we can teach people all the things we learned from Pearl."

Mark said, "That's great. I mean that! But what about climate change? You know storms are more frequent and intense. And the global population makes demands our planet cannot endure. . ."

I broke in, "We all know that we need to change our ways and that's what we're talkin' about. We just need to keep from backslidin.' Nobody here is gonna take electricity for granted."

"We gotta play the hand we're dealt the best we can," Rosy concluded. "The truth is, we all know we dodged a bullet. We need to change our ways.

Each one of us has to take more responsibility, think ahead and be there for others."

"Enough!" Ray commanded.

Kitty had been pacing around the room, stopped and looked at Rosy, grinned slyly and asked, "Anyone up for another ride?"

Mark launched out of his chair. "Oh, no! I am never going through that again. Never again do I want to feel that empty."

A Shot in the Dark

Mattie Lufkin, a southern Minnesota film maker, said, "Years ago, when my friend Mary True Bell told me *The Long Ride* story, my reaction was cellular. 'You are sitting with the Holy Grail,' I said, then suggested she write the story for film. I envisioned talented and strong actresses breathing life into each character. I saw incredible cinematic pans of the mighty Dakota Palisades, breathtaking views of the Badlands, brilliant and majestic sunsets. And . . . wait for it . . .six women on horseback riding through a giant herd of wild buffalo! The potential for incredible cinematic suspense was endless!

"Although *The Long Ride* film is in an embryonic phase, I believe it could help others feel a deep connection to our precious Mother Earth, experience the love of horses and show how six women survive in the wilderness during a time of global environmental upheaval."

I invite you to check out the book/movie trailer video. For digital and printed book readers, please visit the website on a digital device using the following URL: vimeo.com/176625465/e67735e7e0

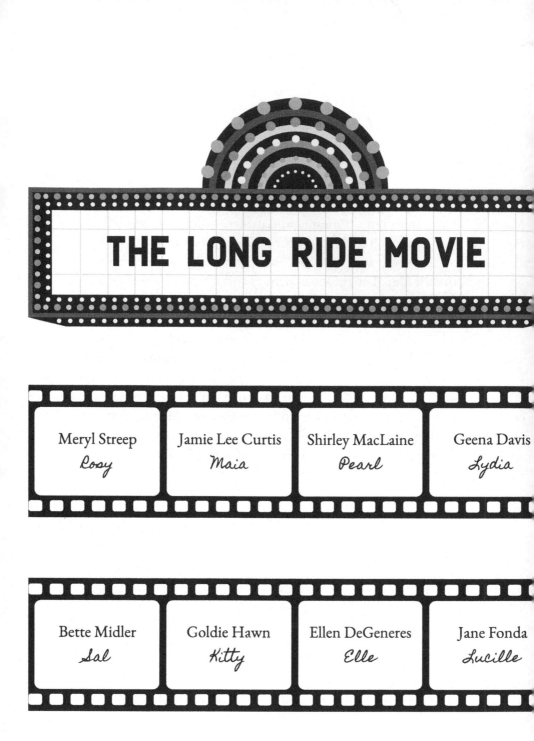

THE LONG RIDE MOVIE

Meryl Streep
Rosy

Jamie Lee Curtis
Maia

Shirley MacLaine
Pearl

Geena Davis
Lydia

Bette Midler
Sal

Goldie Hawn
Kitty

Ellen DeGeneres
Elle

Jane Fonda
Lucille

The story of *The Long Ride* came to me as a movie. My challenge was to write it. So, now, dear reader, I invite you to join me at the imaginary movie. Pop some corn, fill a glass or cup with your favorite beverage and let's dream together.

The screen fills with the gray before first light, and we watch vehicle lights stream down a gravel driveway. Black Jack races back and forth across his pasture.

Trail boss ROSY and sister SAL emerge out of one truck. Quiet ELLE and sexy KITTY stop next to their rig and hop out of their vehicle.

LYDIA is the last to arrive in her lipstick red Mercedes. The others help schlep her too-much stuff. Sal gawks at glitzy Lydia and grumbles, "I told you she's a friggin' Princess."

Ready to roll, MAIA and Lydia stash their cell phones in Maia's truck's glove compartment. These women had all agreed to leave the modern world behind.

AERIAL SHOT shows a cloudless blue sky as three horse rigs head West, tooling across I-90. At Dignity, the sculpture overlooking the Missouri River, Cantus voices gradually rise singing, "Shenandoah." As the trailers fade away we hear, "Away, I'm bound away, 'cross the wide Missouri." They cross the Missouri and the women leave the world they know behind.

PAN SHOT of the hills as the rigs climb out of the river valley. Then, the sky opens, and we hear "oohs" and "aahs" from the women as they breathe in the vastness of the landscape: the undulating rolling hills, stacks of round haybales, cattle on hillsides, rust-red sorghum fields and dancing prairie grasses and miles of yellow sunflowers dutifully following the sun. An antelope bolts across the interstate. We speed past jagged tower-like pinnacles and tapering spires.

AT CAMP, these horsewomen tend their horses. Enter ACE and LUCILLE. Kitty does another of her gotta-have-a-man routines when LANCE shows up. Rosy rounds up the women for their first trail ride.

After a full day riding trails, everyone gathers around a campfire. Smoke twirls and stretches into the darkness. Then, the magical lights of an aurora borealis flash. An omen? The aurora encompasses the screen, which gradually fades to black.

CAMERA SHOT shows a beautiful foggy morning as the women leave on a trail ride, get lost and have no other choice than to ride straight through a herd of buffalo. Upon returning to camp, they learn that the stunning aurora caused a solar flare that supposedly knocked out the electrical grid. Instantly, the world changed from the promise of a fun-filled ride to a test of courage. A close-up shot of their faces captures each woman's fear.

CUT TO PEARL'S as sunlight reflects off a metal cross atop a steepled plain white church riddled with peeling paint. Tired and nervous, Rosy knocks on PEARL'S door and gets permission to hold up in the sanctuary. Later, Pearl bursts into the church and the women ask what she knows about what's happening in the world. Then the riders begin to share their journey as a series of flashbacks that show their triumphs and heartaches.

FLASHBACK to being in camp. Rosy, in full trail boss mode, cements the decision to ride horses back home to Minnesota. We see how Kitty's seductive ways get Romeo. Then, Elle shows her hunting talents as she butchers a deer and they make jerky. The camera comes in close to show how Elle softens when Ace hands her a pistol.

WE RETURN TO PEARL'S and hear Greg Brown's song "Gramma put it all in jars, love, rain and the taste of summer." Sal sweeps as Lydia washes walls. Lydia gushes about experiencing the goodness of Ace and Lucille, and CHIP and STELLA.

FLASHBACK to Stella pushing cattle. Lydia shares the details with Pearl as we see Stella and Chip share their food and loan these women a shotgun.

BACK AT PEARL'S Sal chokes, "Remember the shooter in the green car?"

FLASHBACK to the green car incident. Horses scramble. Bodies fly and Kitty gets shot.

BACK TO PEARL's where Sal sits at the table complaining about the whole riding ordeal.

FLASHBACK through the Badlands, encounters with rattlesnakes, enduring the burning sun and the ever-present wind and the disappointment of the White River. With each incident, we feel how these women are changing.

The camera reveals the women's awful haircuts. Kitty recalls the cutting of each other's hair. FLASHBACK TO the strands of hair falling and witness how each woman is transforming, both inside and out.

BACK AT PEARL'S Maia peels apples with Pearl on the back porch and tells of Justice dying.

FLASHBACK and the screen turns black and white. The women are trapped inside an abandoned homestead by pouring rain. A storm rages. Lightning strikes and we witness the death of Justice. A gradual fade away as Maia looks back one last time at her Justice.

AT PEARL'S the women are gathered around the table when Sal stands her ground and refuses to continue on horseback. Lydia chooses to stay put and learn from Pearl. The camera rests on Rosy's face. She knows this is the right decision for Sal and Lydia. Four remaining riders continue on.

FLASHBACK to the Missouri where Elle picks up the notebook. We see the women climb up the steep slope. The sculpture Dignity greets them. The statue hadn't changed, but each woman had.

AT PEARL'S as the tribe splits, candlelight frames the faces of Sal, Lydia and Pearl as they wave good-bye from the warmth of Pearl's oasis. Embraced in the dark of night, Rosy, Elle, Kitty and Maia hightail it home. They experience the magic of night, the beauty and history of southwestern Minnesota and the impacts of human action.

Almost home, Catch gets hurt and they are holed up in a barn already occupied by SYDNEY, CRYSTAL and LYLA. Hope soars when Sydney tells of seeing the barn light bulb flash. The four riders leave Catch, confident he is in good hands.

The horses are eager to enter into the Root River Valley, as though they remember the smell of home. When the road divides, the women separate, but their bond is stronger than ever. They did not become victims; instead, they took control and worked together to meet the challenges of *The Long Ride.*

So, dear fellow movie goer, I leave you to dream about this story as a movie. I wonder, if you could cast the characters, who would you choose?

My Story

The Long Ride came in a dream and became my escape. I'd sit in front of my computer and within a few minutes I was on my horse, with my girlfriends, living in nature.

What kept me going, struggling to put my dream into words, was my desire to show strong, competent women responding and growing as a result of getting through a serious challenge. As a movie fan, too many times I paid money to watch women portrayed as victims. I vowed that my six women would not be victims. With stamina and creativity, my women pulled together, expressed emotion, showed great loyalty and evolved. I can't help but wonder how six men would have handled the challenge of the long ride.

One of my lifelong passions, other than my husband, family and the environment, has been drying food. As a food drying advocate, I've talked with people living in fear that if something bad happened in our world, that the men would pick up their guns and all hell would break loose. I feel that too often, fear and greed controls people. I believe money is a tool and how it is used is what is important.

For me, life is not about the stuff we own or how much power we wield, it's about being the best person we can be and that includes how we relate to animals.

My parents lived through the Great Depression, planted gardens and graciously shared what they had, lived with less and cared deeply for others. In times of disaster, a pandemic, political upheaval, living with the impacts of climate change, people have pulled together and repeatedly shown great humanity. I imagine a better way--the strengthening of the web of life and the healing of Mother Earth. My husband and I try our best to minimize the demands we make of this planet and live thoughtful, respectful and sustainable lives.

And Thank You

My heartfelt gratitude goes to everyone that lend a hand in shaping *The Long Ride*. I am grateful for Joe, my husband, side kick, and partner for also falling in love with horses and South Dakota.

Once again, my friend Ray Howe traveled the writing road with me. I tip my hat to my riding group and admit that some of my characters do resemble those gals. (Note - I did get permission to twist, turn and shape them.) I bow to the gals in my Tuesday Book Study Group, the Get-A-Grip ladies, and our Couples book group. I thank them for listening to my saga.

The frosting on this cake was when our granddaughter Alysse, a fine equestrian, agreed to read *The Long Ride* and made sure I treated the horses right. In the end, this book is for her.

Mary T. Bell

Character Reviews

City Sal said,
"This book is for tenderfoots who've always wanted to go on a trail ride but couldn't muster up the umph up to pull themselves out of their comfortable chair."

Sexy Kitty snickered,
"This book is both hot and hard."

Rosy, the mamma horse, uncrossed her arms,
"Even a boss can learn."

Elle smiled,
"Less is more."

Lydia said that Pearl said,
"Clothes count only when there's nothing else to say about the corpse in the coffin."

Maia looked straight ahead,
"Simply believing in something can make it possible."

A Blessing

Just off the highway to Rochester, Minnesota,
Twilight bounds softly on the grass.
And the eyes of those two Indian ponies
Dark with kindness.
They have come gladly out of the wildness
To welcome my friend and me.
We step over the barbed wire into the pasture
Where they have been grazing all day, alone.
They ripple tensely they can hardly contain their happiness
That we have come.
They bow shyly as wild swans. They love each other.
There is no loneliness like theirs.
At home once more,
They begin munching the young tufts of spring in the darkness.
I would like to hold the slender one in my arms,
For she has walked over to me
And nuzzled my left hand.
She is black and white,
Her mane falls wild on her forehead,
And the light breeze moves me to caress her long ear
That is delicate as the skin on a girl's wrist.
Suddenly I realize
That if I stepped out of my body
I would break
Into blossom.

James Wright

Made in United States
Orlando, FL
06 February 2022